Screams From Beyond The Veil

A Horror Anthology

Introduction by
Josh Malerman

Edited by
Heather Ann Larson

Table of Souls

List of the Dead

Introduction
Josh Malerman

Recurrently, leading the life I lead, a life of horror, a home office stuffed with book covers capable of icing blood, macabre props about the house (one friend's daughter won't enter our home for the lifelike child-doll Allison Laakko made), evil music from a thousand horror movie soundtracks on the turntable... recurrently I'm asked what the scariest thing to *me* could possibly be. It's an odd question because it implies the horror writer/reader is either fearless or seasoned enough to rise above traditional fears, scenes that might leave the questioner shook. This isn't the case, of course, and it's almost the opposite. The reason I'm eternally drawn to the genre is because of the very fact that I scare easy, in the same way a person who readily laughs would justifiably seek out comedy. Fear is a big experience. And when it's canonical, it's as memorable as any first kiss, first joint, first love.

So, what's my answer to the question?

Well, despite heretofore painting a portrait of an everyday marriage to horror, my answer *is* a particularly frightening one. And I think it says more about the hordes of us who lust for the grim than it does me as an individual. Here's my answer:

Losing complete control. But only for a specific duration of time. Losing my mind, committing an atrocity, then returning to myself, and therefore must live with what I did for the rest of my present, conscious, and sane days. To lose one's mind forever would be a death, of course, of the current self. But to lose it momentarily... and to live with any deeds carried out by whoever it was that took your stead...

Sounds a lot like possession, doesn't it? At least the ones in which an exorcism was successful. But, when the possessed regains control of their mind and body... what do they then have to live with?

Inherent here is a desire to maintain control, of course. Not in any sense of being a control-*freak*, but rather control of one's own actions *and* philosophy. Lament the poor pacifist who, while possessed (while *out of control*) becomes violent. Hell, shed a tear for the vegetarian who eats meat while taken over. Because these actions that some*thing* else might carry out on one's behalf go against the fabric of that person's being, stitch by stitch. And it's the loss of control of the essence, the soul, where fear lies.

But here's the wild part: fear is *fun.* Because fear is a form of ecstasy, a peak, an orgasm, in which all our senses are heightened, trained so from "early-man", so that we never feel quite as present as we do when we are afraid. And there's a suggestion there, too, isn't there? A suggestion of *more?* A hint of optimism buried within fear for, if ghosts and demons *do* exist, then they must come from *someplace* and that place must be different than our own. And what's more optimistic than an unidentified plane, the suggestion (or, perhaps for the lucky ones, *proof*) of there being more to this life than we know?

So, you see, fear can be desirable in many ways. Not the least of which is a form of conquering death.

For what is a ghost if not an entity that has exceeded life? Yet, what person could be faulted for freezing upon seeing one? We're told the human mind cannot fathom infinity, the experience would be too vast, too *big* for us. Yet, a ghost would represent this very thing. An entity about the house, any house, would expand our understanding of the material world, ballooning reality to a size we cannot comprehend. Who could be shamed for locking-up in the face of that?

So... you see. It's all terribly complex. When I'm asked what scares me most... the answer is not easily given. Because every ghost story eventually leads me to this same place: the incomprehensible. It's not solely a matter of potential bodily harm (what might this thing *do* to my body; will it make me hurt? Make me bleed?), but what it would likely do to my mind. And do these thoughts prepare me for an encounter?

Might I relish an encounter for having worked through it as we're working through it here, in the pages of this book?

That's what I would ask of any reader who is embarking upon the journey of these pages. Get scared. Get afraid. But find a way to *remember* the peaks. Make sure to memorize the colors, scents, sounds, *feelings* of fear that come from encounters with ghosts and demons. Because that sensory framework is something of a safe, a vault, in which lies key components of who we all are: if the possessor behaves in ways you would not... does this not tell us, inversely, who we *are?* And if one is haunted, is it not of the notion of infinity, afterlife, otherness, other planes, that we attempt to rid ourselves?

Concepts too big for us to handle? Ideas that might find us... losing control?

It's okay to run from the stories in this anthology. But if you do, and once you reach a place of (perceived) safety, take a moment to recall the peaks, the sensory summits, the very moment that made you run. Because in fearing ghosts and demons, we're attempting to hold on to who we are, body and mind. And maybe...

... maybe we should ask ourselves whether we should have run at all. For... what is fear if not the awareness of change?

Maybe we could all use a haunting. A good old-fashioned possession. If only for the sake of change.

If only to reaffirm the living, by way of all things unexplainable delivered by the dead.

–Josh Malerman
Michigan, late summer, 2024

Screams from Beyond the Veil

Heather Ann Larson

Mona's blazing bright-blue eyes held panic, and her raven-black hair was plastered to her head. She drew in hitching breaths that weren't satisfying her need for air. It was right behind her, and she didn't have it in her to keep running. She lay on the floor, giving up.

It had been chasing her through the house for what felt like hours, had haunted her for days leading up to then. She still hadn't seen it in anything but the form of a shadow, but she knew it was there. She heard it, heard its breath, its noises, its thoughts. She saw it bend the wall, bend the mirror, bend the air. It came to her in her dreams and her thoughts. Yet it remained a vaguely formed image, something only just beyond the veil of reality. But it was real.

Mona felt the floor beneath her envelop her, wrap around her like a warm blanket. She felt cold, bony fingers comb through her hair, heard the hushed whispers of the entity as it sang her an eerie lullaby. She was pulled into the nether, through the veil, her screams following her down.

Eyeing the house at 27 Brookstone Road had become a pastime. She was ready to own her own home, and it had to be *that* house. She watched that particular house for six months; she felt like she was holding her breath that entire time. Something drew her to it. If it sold before she put in her offer, she felt her life would simply stop. The house exuded an energy, like a magnet drawing lead shavings, pulling her. It was in her thoughts 24/7 from the first time she laid eyes on it.

She put in the offer on the last day of September and heard back immediately. Her offer had been accepted. The closing date was set for exactly one week before Halloween. She couldn't believe it—she was going to move in with time to adorn her very own home for her favorite holiday.

The second she got the keys, a huge weight was lifted. She instantly thought about how she would decorate and which room she would turn into what. She had already been scoping sales for home décor—her apartment was pint sized compared to the house. She was going to need to do some shopping. Mona had even already stockpiled some terrifying Halloween decorations she found at various discounts.

Her mom even surprised her with one of those famous twelve-foot skeletons, set up on the lawn when Mona arrived on move-in day.

"Is this it?" Sam asked, slamming the trunk of Mona's car. He hefted the box a little higher, distributing the weight more evenly.

Mona scrunched her face in thought. "I think so, but I feel like I'm forgetting something," she replied, deep in concentration.

"Well don't hurt yourself thinking too hard on it," he quipped back, laughing at his own joke. He always did think he was hilarious.

Sam didn't hesitate when Mona asked if he could help her move in to her new place—that was what best friends did for each other. He took the week off to help her pack up her apartment, then offered to drive the rental truck to her new place on the other side of town. He was so proud of her for buying her first house, and he wanted to do everything he could to help her settle in.

Mona and Sam had been friends since second grade. They sat next to each other on the first day of class and took to each other immediately. They quickly became best friends, spending as much time playing together as possible. Mona was always a bit of a tom boy, even though she loathed that term. Girls didn't have to play with Barbies and wear pink and braid their hair. She was more the rough-and-tumble type, which suited Sam just fine.

Neither was Sam the typical truck-and-mud boy. While he loved climbing trees and fishing, things he taught Mona to enjoy as well, he also liked to read and watch movies. Since those were two of Mona's favorite things to do, the two of them were like peas and carrots.

Twenty-five years later, nothing had changed except the obvious growing up.

It didn't take the two of them, with the help of Sam's brother, Allen, long to get the moving truck emptied. Allen also stayed to help set up the bigger furniture. Mona's mom had been given instructions on what was wanted where in the kitchen and bathrooms. She was so efficient at unpacking the boxes that everything was almost completely finished by the end of the day. All Mona had left was getting her bedrooms settled and putting up the décor she bought and the Halloween decorations. She figured they could wait until the next day.

Sam offered to stay that first night to make sure she settled in okay. He couldn't put his finger on it, but he felt she shouldn't be alone there. He got a strange vibe from the house; his arm hair bristled every time he crossed the threshold and his head felt a little foggy. He wanted to talk to Mona about it, to see if she was feeling the same things. But the huge grin stretching across her face told him she wanted to be on her own. He didn't want to piss in her Wheaties, so he hugged her and took off with Allen.

Sam slept fitfully that night. He dreamed of Mona's house and the uncomfortable feeling it gave him. Upon walking in the front door, it slammed behind him. He subconsciously knew it was locked—he didn't even try to open it. He moved forward through the foyer and into the living room, quietly calling Mona's name as he went. A chaotic array of lit candles suffused the room, the smell of cinnamon and death clawing its way up his nostrils.

He moved farther into the house, treading lightly lest he disturb something that didn't want to be bothered. He didn't know why he felt that way, but he knew it was so. He was perturbed by the silence. He couldn't even bring himself to whisper Mona's name at that point. He was afraid any sound would wake a monster.

He found himself lost inside, unable to find his way to Mona and out of the house. Every door he opened led to another door and another door, like a Russian nesting doll of doors except they didn't shrink. Panic seized Sam, and he was no longer walking from door to door but running, his breath coming in ragged gasps, his heart pounding within his rib cage. He needed to get out.

No, he needed to wake up. *This is a dream, wake up, Sam!* he yelled in his head. *Wake the fuck up!* Sam kept running, kept telling himself to wake up, kept opening door after door after door. Then he stopped. *What the hell am I doing? It's a dream, why am I still running?*

Sam closed his eyes and envisioned himself at the bottom of a pool and rising to the surface, a metaphor for his sleep state. When he opened his eyes, he was at the bottom of a tub full of water. It was the jacuzzi tub in Mona's master bathroom. *How the hell did I get here?* Sam wondered very briefly, just before he realized he truly wasn't surfacing. He was anchored to the bottom of the tub and couldn't get up. He was running out of air.

Just as Sam prepared himself to take the breath he knew would kill him, his eyes flew open. He stared at the ceiling fan above his bed for a long time, shivering with terror from the dream. He closed his eyes, did a breathing exercise Mona taught him (in for four, hold for four, out for eight), and opened his eyes again.

He realized he was shivering not just from terror, but also because he was soaking wet.

After his dream, Sam was reluctant to return to Mona's new house. *This is completely stupid,* he told himself. *It was a dream, that's all.* He was completely ignoring the fact he woke up drenched from the tub he hadn't actually been in. His mind wasn't able to wrap around the idea it could have really happened.

Regardless of the unsettling feeling growing within, he had taken the whole week off to help her with the small things as well as the actual moving, so he gave himself a pep talk and got ready. He returned the rental truck and grabbed a couple coffees and pastries from a local bakery before he headed to Mona's. He was running late, and he knew she would work that to her advantage somehow. He was using the coffee and baked goods as a peace offering.

She smiled in relief as he walked in with the coffees in hand. "I haven't been to the store to stock the pantry, and I'm all out of coffee," she said as she inhaled the aroma of the cuppa. "I suppose I'll overlook your tardiness." She winked at him as she loudly slurped her first sip, knowing it drove him crazy.

She looks exhausted, Sam thought. *Moving takes a lot out of a person, but she looks like she didn't sleep a wink.* "Did you decide to burn the midnight oil and keep unpacking?" Sam wanted to tread cautiously; he was still unsettled by the dream and the feeling the house gave him. He wanted to test the waters to see if Mona was feeling the same thing.

Her shoulders slumped, and he could see the tears threatening to spill. "I tried to sleep, but new house, new noises. I tossed and turned all night. I kept hearing the strangest sounds. I know it'll take time to get used to it, but after all the moving in yesterday, I'm running on fumes here." She set her coffee on the living room table and flopped dramatically onto the couch. "I don't know that I feel up to getting much of anything done today."

Mind made up, Sam flipped on the TV. "Thank god you got the internet hooked up right away." He picked their favorite horror movie, *Alien*, and snuggled up with her. She laid her head on his shoulder, and he put his arm around her. She was out in minutes.

The two decided to get started on projects mid-afternoon. The nap Mona took was enough to revitalize her, for the interim at least. She already had a list for Sam to start on, including installing new smoke and CO2 detectors and changing all the lightbulbs throughout—most of them were burnt out, anyway—while she tackled painting the two bathrooms. The main floor was only a half bath, and she knew it wouldn't take her long.

The two loved to buddy read, so Mona threw on the audiobook of Stephen King's *Fairy Tale* while they worked. She took one ear bud, and Sam took the other. She had agreed to Sam staying over that night—for some reason she felt more relaxed with him there, less on alert—so it would give them something to talk about later that night. The two worked straight through the afternoon.

The strange noises Mona heard during the night continued into the day, and she felt the painting would let her mind zone out, focus on the book, and just rest her weary brain. But partway into the first coat on the main floor bathroom wall, the hair stood on her arms. The humming that had been present during the twilight hours got louder, and the air around her seemed distorted. She blinked a few times, thinking the lack of sleep was really starting to get to her. She glanced in the mirror and gasped at a dark figure that appeared to be right over her shoulder. When she spun around, there was nothing there. She took five, sipping on a cup of tea and closing her eyes. When she got back to work, she felt a renewed energy and was able to lose herself in the words of the narrator.

Evening arrived, and they realized they hadn't eaten since late breakfast. They decided to order Thai, throwing back a couple IPAs while waiting for the delivery to arrive. Sitting in a comfortable silence in the living room, they stared out the floor-to-ceiling windows, Mona staring at her gifted skeleton whom she named Randall, neither one feeling the need to fill the quiet with unnecessary conversation. Between moving boxes the day before and all the work they put in that day, they were bushed.

Eventually, mother nature called. Sam made his way to the bathroom, only to be confused on where to find it. He knew it was the first door on the left, had been there several times throughout the afternoon to confirm Mona's directions on certain projects, but when he opened that door, it was the office. Sam's gut fell, and his mind got a bit hazy.

"Mona, you decide to do some remodeling without telling me?" Sam joked, an edge to his voice Mona picked up on.

She felt bad for asking so much of him, but she would do the same if he requested it of her. But it also seemed odd he got mixed up on where the bathroom was. *He must be exhausted,* she thought.

"No, it's still the last door on the right," she replied. She shook her head. Men could be so dense sometimes. She even thought about the time Sam's then boyfriend told Mona that Sam had no clue they even had a linen closet, and they had lived in their rental for six months at the time. She shook her head and smiled. Then she stopped. "Wait, no, that's not right. It's the first door on the left," she said in a dense haze of memory, the edges of her world feeling fuzzy. She was glad she was sitting, because she was suddenly a bit dizzy. *I should have eaten before I drank a beer*, she scolded herself.

Sam felt disoriented. He only had a couple beers. They were on the stronger side, but this wasn't his first rodeo. He knew the bathroom had been on the left. So what the hell was happening? He wandered farther down the hall, stopping at the last door on the right. *This is totally fucked,* he told himself. *I've got a bad feeling about this.* His gut churned with a feeling of extreme unease. He reached out to grab the door handle, then hesitated. He really didn't want to open the door

The nightmare suddenly at the forefront of his mind, Sam swore he saw a bit of water come out from under the door. Concerned there was an actual catastrophic problem pushed through his apprehension, and he quickly entered the bathroom. Initially having a dimness to it, a ripple felt through the air and the mirror bending a bit, the room briefly had a *Matrix* vibe to it. When Sam closed his eyes, shook his head, and reopened his eyes, everything was normal, stable, nothing was shimmering. He chalked it up to the beers and the nightmare.

He relieved himself, washed his hands, and creeped back down the hallway to the living room, where Mona sat. Her position didn't look right; she had her head slightly cocked to the side like she was listening to something, but there was nothing there. Her eyes were vacant but wide like she had seen something. Suddenly the hairs on the back of his neck were standing at attention, and the temperature in the room felt like it dropped ten degrees.

"Mona?" Sam quietly asked as he came up behind her. He didn't want to frighten her if she had just zoned out, but he had a feeling something more than that was going on. That feeling of unease was back in the depths of his gut.

He slowly worked his way around the couch, moving cautiously, watching Mona intently as he rounded on her. "Mona, you okay there, buddy? Just dozing off a bit?" His breath caught when she slowly turned her head toward him.

Her eyes were vacant, black holes, and her mouth was open in a silent scream.

The lights flickered, and the power went out. A faint glow of candle light danced from a light breeze flowing through the area, carrying with it the scent of cinnamon and rot. There was a vibration humming through the room, like the house was shuddering in anticipation of something.

The light pressure of arms giving a hug wrapped around Sam, and he screamed. He called for Mona, tried to reach out his arms in the dark to find her, but they were pinned to his sides. The pressure around him became slightly stronger. "Mona, can you hear me? Help me out here, Mona-roni." Of all the things occurring, her lack of answer was the most disturbing.

Giving it a final go, Sam made a sudden lunge forward and fell into Mona's lap. The lights popped back on, and the doorbell rang. Mona blinked several times, coming to a little more with each one. She gave Sam a look of confusion, shaking her head like she was clearing the mental cobwebs.

The doorbell rang again, and Sam jumped to his feet and dashed to the door. The delivery guy was there with their Thai. "Bro, what took you so long? I've been ringing the bell for three minutes. I knew you were there; I could hear y'all talking. Doorbell broken?"

Sam stared at the guy in disbelief. "Three minutes? Sorry, man, yeah the bell must be broken. Just moved in yesterday and haven't tested it yet." Sam didn't know what else to tell the guy. *What conversation was he hearing?* Sam asked himself, terrified to know the answer. He moved to take the food from the driver, but as his hand crossed the frame of the doorway, he felt a painful jolt down his arm. He ripped it back, cradling it against his chest with his other hand. He looked at the driver with eyes wide.

Freaked out by Sam's behavior, the delivery dude set the food inside the door and walked away. He didn't get paid enough to deal with these tweakers and didn't feel like getting jumped.

They sat in silence, individually contemplating what happened. While the fog in Mona's head cleared, she couldn't remember what happened during that time period. All she remembered was Sam heading down the hall, then he was screaming her name in the dark and the lights suddenly came on and the doorbell was ringing.

Sam, on the other hand, remembered everything that happened and was in complete shock. He found some chai tea bags in the pantry and boiled some milk to brew it in, throwing in a ridiculous amount of sugar. He was slowly sipping it, trying to warm up from the inside. But the shaking wouldn't stop, and he wondered if it wasn't cold he was feeling but something more sinister.

He couldn't wrap his head around the events that played out. The incident in the bathroom terrified him the most; looking back, it wasn't just a trick of his imagination. He had also tried once more to put his arm out of the house, the result being the same. The jolt was more harsh that time. His arm still felt tingly from the attempt.

Although she couldn't remember what happened, Mona was having an easier time dealing with it. Sam filled her in on his version of the events, and she knew he was telling the truth. He wasn't just telling the truth as he believed it happened, either; she knew it was real and he wasn't making it up.

She always had a proclivity toward the things beyond, and she was piecing together why she was so drawn to the house from the get-go. There was a force present in the house, and it called to her like a siren to a sailor. She felt a hum in the background of everything, the hum of a presence, and it was calling to her. Looking back over the last twenty-four hours, the hum had been increasing in intensity and volume. She realized she heard it all through the night before, along with the creaking of the house. It was calling to her, slowly warming her to existence.

Having been friends for the large majority of their lives, Sam was aware of Mona's penchant toward the unknown and supernatural. He was open in talking with her about it, and they used the evening to talk through what was happening. He listened as she told him about her overwhelming desire to own the house (he hadn't known just how obsessed she had been about it), what she fully experienced her first night there, and what she thought could possibly be going on.

He also shared his dream with her, told her how vivid the images were and how real it felt. He told her he woke up soaking wet and that after everything that was happening, he was convinced it had truly happened.

They decided it would be important to stay together. They knew from all the horror movies they watched and books they read that the number one rule was this exact thing. The two decided to camp out in the living room. Mona had purchased an over-sized modular couch from Costco, and it was more than enough to comfortably fit the both of them. They decided to take turns sleeping, one of them always being awake in case something should happen, not that they knew what that could be. Sam took the first shift. They decided to sleep in three-hour increments in an attempt to mimic a couple sleep cycles. They figured that way it was a more natural time frame.

The house had different plans for them.

The humming grew louder by the minute. "Can't you hear that?" Mona asked Sam, feeling her tolerance wavering, ready to snap if the noise didn't stop soon. When Sam replied he didn't hear anything, Mona hit her tipping point. "I'm getting the fuck out of here. I can't take this anymore!" She leaped from the couch and headed toward the front door. Sam hollered for her to stop, but she couldn't hear him over the humming and her own whimpering.

She ripped the front door open and threw herself outside—or tried to. It was like an invisible barrier protected the doorway, and a dark mist appeared to grab her. She was thrown backward, landing hard about five feet from the door. The door slammed shut.

She lay there on her back, staring at the ceiling. Tears streamed down her face, pooling into her ears and hair. Sam came to her, and they lay there together, finally falling into fitful sleep.

They spent the next few days in and out of delirium, trying to plan their escape in between bouts of unrestful sleep. Although the streaming services were still working, they had no cell or internet service on their phones or Mona's laptop, meaning they couldn't call or email out. They tried banging on the front door and the windows when they saw people passing by, but it was to no avail. The people continued on their way as if they heard nothing. Even when Mona's mother stopped by, knocking on the door, Sam and Mona staring out at her through the window attached to the door, yelling and pounding on the glass, she gave no indication that she saw them. They couldn't even hear her knocking, although they could see her knuckles rap harder and harder against the door, could see her yelling for Mona to come out and let her know she was okay.

Sam and Mona felt unable to go on, defeated and broken.

During that time, the walls of the house seemed to expand and contract, like the house was breathing. Every mirror they passed rippled, like a still lake disturbed by a skipped rock, and had a dark shadow looming in the background. And every time they went to any of the various rooms of the house for whatever reason, it was in a different place. The bathroom shifted again, from the last door on the right to the middle door on the left, then to the first door on the left, then back to the last door on the right. The office shifted from the last door on the left to the top floor, first door on the right. Even Mona's bedroom jumped locations several times.

On the fourth day, Sam went into the kitchen to make them coffee and uttered a shrill cry. Mona cautiously but quickly made her way to him, slowing and peering in when she was close enough. What she saw dropped her to her knees.

The basement door, the one door they knew the entire time had to stay closed—because they watched enough horror movies, and everybody knew you didn't enter the basement—was open. They purposely hadn't gone down there since move-in day because they just knew.

A shadow had Sam in its grasp, pulling him into the dark depths. It didn't have a form; it was simply a shadow. The dark mist seemed to be behind a screen, not quite visible but not transparent, either. Sam's face was etched in terror, a scream trying to unleash.

Mona tried to help him, but something held her to her spot. She felt a firm pressure holding her back. She looked on, completely transfixed and horrified as the shadow pulled Sam through the doorway. The door violently crashed shut. The second the door was closed, Mona found herself free from whatever was holding her back. She rushed to the door, yanking on the handle. It wouldn't budge. The handle wouldn't turn even a millimeter.

Just like that, Sam was gone and Mona was utterly alone.

It took Mona several minutes to pull herself off the floor. She couldn't do this anymore. The warping, the changing rooms, the humming and vibrating, and now the shadow—it was too much. Her mind was cracked, and her body was a shell of its former self. She was done.

She went into the master bathroom, finding it to be in its original location, and started the shower. It had been days since her body had seen a bit of soap, and she was tired of smelling herself. Even through her fractured mind she knew she needed this one basic thing, this piece of normalcy.

She crawled herself into the shower and sat on the tiled floor, head between her knees, crying the tears of the wholly heartbroken and beaten. She made the attempt to wash herself while she remained on the floor, and the soap seemed to invigorate her just a bit, enough to get her to stand up and finish the job. She might be broken, but she still had a bit of herself in there somewhere, and the scent of her favorite soap was drawing that kernel up from the depths of her being and bringing it to the surface.

She finally turned off the water, stepping out of the stall and into the steam-filled bathroom. After she wrapped herself in her towel, she used a hand to wipe the mirror. As she did so, the mirror bowed, distorting her image. It turned dark and foggy before snapping back into place. In the space above her right shoulder was a dark mass, a hint of something that was there but couldn't be distinguished. She whipped around quickly, her hair flying behind her so fast and hard it made a *whap* noise as it hit the cabinet mirror. She drew in a sharp breath and screamed.

Standing in the corner opposite the shower stall was the shadow that pulled Sam into the basement. It still seemed like it was behind something, like a thin pane of iced-over glass, or on the other edge of something. It had taken more of a form, the form of an obscure human shape. It had an elongated, slender head and neck, arms that were too long for the body they were attached to, and thick trunks for legs. There were dull, glowing embers of pale-yellow light in the place eyes should be. What should have been a mouth was a jagged slit, much like a jack-o-lantern, with razor-sharp teeth sticking out.

The figure reached for Mona, and it seemed like the air reached with it, around it. She ran. She didn't know where to go; she only knew she couldn't go out and couldn't go to the basement. She decided on the living room as it was the most brightly lit room in the house. The sun was shining, and she felt safer when she was there. She stood near the window, praying the sun would give her sanctum from whatever it was that was haunting her. She stood panting, trying to catch her breath. She scanned the room, certain that if the entity appeared, it wouldn't simply be from following her down the hall. It seemed to be one with the house, an actual part of or manifestation of it.

She waited ten minutes, fifteen, then felt the being wasn't coming so sat on the lounge chair, shivering in the cold of the house. They had tried to turn the thermostat up when the temperature started dropping, but the house never seemed to warm up. At the thought of fussing over the thermostat with Sam, Mona let out a little hitch of a moaning cry. That moment seemed like a lifetime ago, and she hoped that whatever Sam went through in the basement happened quickly. She couldn't bear the thought of him in pain.

Exhaustion hit her like a bus, and she allowed her eyes to slip closed. *I just need a few minutes*, she thought. *Just a few minutes to rest, and then I'll get dressed.* Those few minutes turned into two hours, and Mona awoke with a start. Confusion overtook her sleep-deprived mind; she couldn't remember where she was.

As the heaviness of sleep left her, she remembered the bathroom and running into the living room, remembered sitting in the chair for just a few minutes. She looked down and realized she was still in her towel. She was freezing—her still-damp hair wasn't helping matters any—and she decided she didn't care anymore. She was going to her room to put on clothes. If she was going to die, she wasn't going to do it in a towel.

The house breathes with me, in and out, feels what I feel, becomes what I want it to become. It changes at my whim. It has been me, this house, since it was created. I have been here eons before that. I came from the earth, when it cracked in the time before. It released me into the world when it was empty, when the old gods ruled the land.

This is my place, my sanctuary, and I will not let these interlopers have it. I shall regain what is mine once again. I have done it many times; I will do it many times more. I have foreseen it to be so. Each battle to regain my stronghold makes me stronger. One day the land will return to its former self, and I will rule as the ancient gods once did.

But for now, Mona awaits me.

The hours blended together. Mona wandered the house, never finding the rooms to be in the same spot twice. There always seemed to be a thin veil around everything, and there was a dimness on the other side. Everything seemed warped and twisted. She hadn't had decent sleep in days, and the constant fear and lack of sleep had her mind in a tailspin. The entity was messing with her, trying to wear her down completely.

Its job was nearly done.

The doorbell rang, something she hadn't heard in days. She jumped up, rushing to see who was there and if she could finally get through. She quickly peeked out the window and was met with the image of small children dressed in fun costumes standing on her porch. Their buckets were ready, their faces smiling in the excitement of what they might get.

But it wasn't to be. No matter how hard she pounded and pulled on the door, the knob wouldn't turn and the kids didn't act like they were aware anybody was on the other side to give them the rich treats they were seeking.

Mona leaned her back against the door, allowing herself to slide down. She sat there, slumped, with her head against her knees. Sobs wracked her body.

Suddenly, the floor shifted, coming at her like the waves of an angry ocean, knocking her on her back.

She tried to get up, and the floor bucked again. She waited until it passed, then leaped to her feet and took off down the hall. Every mirror and picture frame she passed rippled, a darkness behind the image it displayed. Then the glass would distort, put itself back together, and show the being standing alongside her. She saw this all as she ran.

The hall seemed to go on forever—she could see it stretching out before her. It wavered, shimmered, like a mirage but not the kind you want to see. She felt like she was running as fast as she could but wasn't getting anywhere, gaining no traction in distancing herself from the thing. It was exactly like the dream Sam described to her.

The walls reached out for her with arms made from nothing, made from shadow, made from the thin veil between her world and its world. Fingers brushed her arms, her sides, her hair. The feather-light touches became pinches, pulled her raven hair. Her bright-blue eyes held nothing but terror.

She came to a door, opened it, and threw herself inside. The room swayed like a ship in a hurricane, but at least she was out of the goddamn hallway. She had to stop running; she didn't think she could make it another step. There was a grandfather clock in one corner, one which had never been there before, that bonged in that hollow, echoing horror-movie way. It chimed three a.m. It was Halloween, and it was the witching hour. It was time for her to die.

She was tired of running, tired of being scared, tired of knowing the end was coming but still fighting. She was ready to give up. She laid on the floor, watching the entity come toward her, its shroud moving with it. She let it come to her, let it get near her.

The floor beneath her moved, made the shape of a cocoon, wrapped itself around her. The wood of the floor didn't feel hard. It felt soft but dense, like a sensory-deprivation tank, something that was forming to her shape but had substance, something she could float on. Her body seemed to melt into the floor as it sucked her down.

She could hear screams from beyond the veil. She thought they were from the being, but as the thing from beyond reached for her and she succumbed, as she retreated farther into the nether realm, she realized the screams were her own.

Peeping Polly

Leigh Kenny

"Peeping Polly peeks a person
Lying in her bed
Peeping Polly peeks inside
And now she's in your head
Peeping Polly creeps upon you
'Til she finds a thread
Peeping Polly pulls your strings
And peeps until you're dead."

"**G**et to the gruesome bit!"

Sarah nudged Mike in the ribs, her cheeks flaming under the withering glare of the tour guide. "I'm going to kill you," she hissed.

Mike pulled a face and grasped her hand as the group moved along. "Let's face it, babe. It's what everyone wants to hear, but I'm the only one brave enough to ask. If she doesn't tell us soon, the whole tour is liable to die from boredom. Maybe that's how the place became so haunted in the first place!"

Sarah rolled her eyes but sniggered despite herself, earning another disapproving glance from the stuffy Ms. Landry.

A very distant, so-far-that-you-could-squint-and-still-not-see-the-connection relative of Lord Lucian, the original owner of Lucian Castle, Ms. Landry left the running of the old stronghold-turned-hotel to her very capable team. She still insisted, however, on running the guided tours herself. Perhaps a way to remain in the spotlight or an opportunity to remind people she was descended from royalty, she refused to hand the reins to anyone else.

Bedridden with a particularly nasty bout of flu a couple years prior, she had had no choice but to allow a temporary replacement. "The show must go on," she had crowed theatrically from the hand-carved four-poster bed in her private quarters.

A young kitchen porter with a penchant for local history had taken the role and savored it. The guests had loved Tommy and the flourish with which he recited the history of the castle. He was well aware of Lucian Castle's reputation as the one of the most haunted places in the world, and Tommy gave the people what they wanted. Once or twice, he even involved one of the waitresses, a slight-framed girl with a mane of sleek, black hair, who relished the gasps and screams she elicited from the guests as she skulked around the darkened hallways in her hastily-applied Peeping Polly costume.

The general manager had been pleased to report back to Ms. Landry about how successful her replacement was. The old woman made a miraculous recovery the following day, and Tommy had been resigned to the kitchen, where he belonged. He still loved both the history and the lore surrounding his workplace, though, and had been going steady with the pretty, dark-haired waitress ever since his stint as tour guide.

Ms. Landry appreciated how the rumours of hauntings drew a steady stream of guests to her castle, and she loved having a constant audience to listen to her preen. She did not, however, care for the ghost stories themselves. They were violent and crass, and she wished people took more interest in the building and its rich history. But the ghouls couldn't get enough of their ghosties.

Especially Peeping Polly.

With a heavy sigh, Ms. Landry stopped once more outside a wooden door halfway along the old, stone corridor.

"Polly was a maid…"

Cheers rose among the gathered guests, and murmurs of Peeping Polly moved through the crowd like leaves on a breeze.

A small smile crept upon her lips as Ms. Landry cleared her throat and raised her voice, beginning her monologue once more, satisfied with the hush that fell swiftly and suddenly over her rapt audience. She had their full attention, and despite herself, she delighted in it.

"Polly was a maid here at Lucian Castle for Lord Lucian himself. As a maid, she was very good at moving unseen around the castle and, as such, became privy to all the scandals and gossip. Much like modern times, people wanted to be in the know, and some would pay handsomely for particularly juicy pieces of gossip from within the castle walls. Polly was doing okay for herself, squirrelling away a little at a time towards a nice nest egg, with plans to eventually leave Lucian Castle and set herself up on a small homestead. And then she happened upon the biggest scandal of them all.

"Lord Lucian's son had been betrothed to a neighboring lord's daughter since the time of his birth, and the wedding was fast approaching. But the son loved another, a servant girl who worked in the castle. The two had grown close over the years and stole away together in secret at every given opportunity to whisper sweet nothings in each other's ears, as lovestruck youths are inclined to do."

Mike snorted, earning him another poisonous glare from Ms. Landry. The woman cleared her throat before continuing.

"Polly was one of the few within the castle who was aware of the young man's secret trysts with the servant girl. Perhaps greed took hold, or maybe she was just a nasty person, but Polly decided to alert the lord. She tried to use the information as leverage, perhaps spurred on by the prospect of an even earlier retirement, and threatened to inform the neighboring lord. Knowing it would ruin his family's reputation, the lord hatched a plan with his son.

"That very night, the son cornered Polly in her quarters and murdered her in the most brutal of fashions. In exchange for the deed, his father furnished him with two horses and enough coin to start a life with his beloved servant girl, and the two left the castle that very night. The lord sent false news to his neighbour that his son had died suddenly and the wedding would no longer take place. All was well, until it wasn't.

"Some said the burden of guilt became too much for the lord. Others said that he was being haunted. Indeed, one stormy night, his shocked servants found him deliriously pacing the floors of his long-dead-servant's quarters. Polly was tormenting him from beyond the grave as punishment for her death, he told them. The man divulged the secrets that had burdened him, before plucking out his own eyes, climbing onto the window ledge, and hurling himself to the ground far, far below.

"His son had beaten Polly. He had removed her eyes so that even in the afterlife she would not see things that were not for her to see. He removed her tongue so she could not speak of things that were none of her business. He killed her and hid her body, stowing her corpse within the stone walls of the castle, where she would remain entombed for eternity."

The gathered crowd was silent, until eventually a shaky voice said, "Did they ever find her?"

Ms. Landry's gaze traveled along the small sea of faces. "No," she said, "they did not. There is no proof that such a thing ever happened or that such a person ever existed. It's just a legend, and probably a false one at that."

The tour clearly at an end, the crowd groaned and began to disperse, the rich smells wafting along the hallway more enticing than a history lesson, especially a history lesson with no ghosts.

"What about Peeping Polly, then?"

Mike gazed impassively at the older woman, who glared at him with disapproval.

Beside him, Sarah wanted the floor to open up and swallow her.

"Peeping Polly is a silly urban legend that has been perpetuated by the so-called ghost hunters and paranormal experts who swarm these halls like vermin, hoping to cash in on an old fireside tale that was most likely invented to scare the children of the castle." Ms. Landry's use of air quotes when citing ghost hunters and paranormal experts left no doubt in anyone's minds about how she felt about these people. "Despite the rumors which burden Lucian Castle, nobody has ever actually claimed to have seen this Peeping Polly. Not one single person." She cast an eye toward Mike's t-shirt, then turned on her heel and stalked down the corridor, her low heels clicking against the stone floor as she disappeared into the gloom.

Glancing across at her fiancé's shirt, the words MYSTERY MIKE loomed large alongside the cartoon ghost logo, and Sarah felt her cheeks flame once more.

"There's no smoke without fire!" Mike called after the spectre of the retreating woman. He turned to Sarah and narrowed his eyes before croaking, "Peeping Polly peeps a person..."

"Jesus, Mike. Please, not the stupid rhyme again." She sighed as she turned in the opposite direction and followed the small crowd meandering back toward the dining room and those incredibly enticing smells.

"They say if you see her, you're as good as dead. She stalks you, or 'peeps' you, until she works her way inside your head. Then she drives you insane, and you end up cutting out your own tongue and eyes, just like the lord's son was rumored to have done to her."

The couple sitting across from them glanced at each other in amusement, and Sarah found herself sliding farther down into the plush velvet armchair. To her left, the fire crackled in the grate and cast looming shadows around the room. She stared longingly at the undulating gloom, wishing for it to swallow her whole.

"Who exactly is 'they?'" the young, attractive black man asked, a Cheshire-Cat grin threatening to split his face in two.

Mike, oblivious to the amusement of the two men before him, continued enthusiastically. "There have been plenty of people over the years who have died suspiciously after staying in this place. I bet if you checked the death records for most, it would mention self-mutilation. A buddy of mine, he knows some people, and he said there are definitely at least two confirmed cases just like that, both victims unconnected except for stays at *this* hotel not long before their deaths!"

The couple glanced at each other again, but this time they couldn't contain themselves. Both men howled with laughter.

Sarah continued to disappear into her chair.

"Look, man... Mike. It's been a riot, but we'd better get going. Eric is already tipsy, and we haven't even opened the complimentary champagne in our room yet." The man stood, stretching his muscular arms before reaching down and offering his hand to his other half. Eric brushed a stray blond hair from his flushed cheeks and stood. The two men sauntered away hand in hand, whispering and giggling, no doubt still tickled by Mike's ridiculous ghost story.

With a sigh, Sarah reached for her wine glass and drained it before standing. "We should really hit the hay too, Mike. It's been a day."

Oblivious to her displeasure, Mike put on his best hangdog expression. "Aww, babe, we haven't even gone exploring on our own yet. The night is still young!"

As though in answer, a raucous cheer erupted in the corner, where a group of men celebrating the impending nuptials of their friend began dropping the latest round of shots. The waitress shook her head but smiled good naturedly as she returned the empty glasses to the tray she had only just removed them from.

Sarah knew she was fighting a losing battle. Mike had been the life and soul of the party ever since the day she met him. Hell, it was his magnetic charisma that had first drawn her to him. Despite the headache blossoming in her temples, she offered him a half smile. "Compromise? Ride the elevator to our floor with me, then you're free to return and join the party."

"Deal." He grinned at her, drained his own glass, and stood, sweeping a hand in front of him in the direction of the bank of elevators. "M'lady, your carriage awaits."

Sarah jolted awake and was instantly perturbed by her alien surroundings. The room felt wrong. The furniture was wrong. Even the sheets pooled around her sweat-soaked skin felt different. By the light of a silvery moonbeam falling through the large arched window, things finally fell into place as Sarah remembered where she was.

Lucian Castle.

As the cobweb of sleep drifted from her, she smiled to herself, amused by her own reaction. Glancing toward the empty space beside her, Sarah sighed. Mike still hadn't come up. Had she been asleep long? Maybe he had gone to one of the stag party rooms for late drinks. If he went for late drinks, there wasn't a hope in hell she would be able to get him up early enough to catch breakfast before check-out time.

As if on cue, a chorus of loud voices drifted through the door, raising in volume slightly before fading away again.

That had to be them!

Sliding from beneath the covers, she grumbled softly to herself as she slipped her dress back over her head. The chill air pimpled her bare skin, and Sarah reached for her cardigan as she made her way toward the door by the light of the moon.

And then stopped.

The hair on the back of her neck bristled, and she felt the unmistakable weight of eyes boring into her. Slowly, her heart rabbiting in her chest, she turned toward the window.

There was nothing to see, though.

They were too high up for anyone to be there, and even the breathtaking vista she gazed at earlier was all but invisible in the dark of night.

Her breath shuddered from her chest, and she slapped the switch on the wall. The room flooded with bright light, and the uneasiness fell from her like a weight.

Cursing Mike for putting stupid ghost stories in her head, Sarah moved to the window and pulled the drapes across, blocking out most of the moonlight. And whatever had been watching her.

She wished the curtains were heavier. So much for it being a luxury hotel. The thought made her giggle as she headed for the door. Grabbing the keycard, the room was suddenly plunged into darkness.

Sarah thought her heart might explode. "It's the keycard," she whispered to herself, ignoring the tremor in her voice. "You pulled the keycard out, you moron."

Still, she wasted no time in yanking the door open and gratefully stepping into the bright hallway.

She stood, head tilted, and listened.

Beneath the normal hotel sounds of doors closing and toilets flushing, she detected the faintest chorus of jubilant male voices to her left. With a satisfied smirk, Sarah moved in that direction.

With each step she took, the voices she sought grew fainter and fainter. Reaching the first intersection along the hallway, she stopped and strained her ears for any sound.

The hotel was eerily quiet around her.

There were no more slamming doors or hushed chatter, no more toilets flushing or intermittent electronic buzzing.

Dead silence.

Uneasiness bloomed in her stomach, and Sarah retraced her steps. Footsteps, accompanied by a soft humming, sounded in the direction she had just come from. She turned, a grateful smile on her face as she waited for whomever approached the corner of the intersection to appear.

But nobody did.

The footsteps stopped, but the humming continued, and it was then Sarah noticed the face peering up at her from the corner. The figure was low to the ground, as though they were crouched on the floor as they looked upon her, and their fingers were splayed against the wood paneling of the lower wall.

"Hello? Can I help you?" she asked gently.

Their face split into an enormous grin at her acknowledgement. It was an awful grin, and the uneasiness in Sarah's stomach turned into something heavy and cold. She turned and ran.

Behind her, the footsteps started again, and to her horror, they sped up. Sarah raced along the empty corridor, her lungs bursting and her eyes wide with terror as the slapping footsteps behind her grew closer and closer.

She screamed for help, but all the doors she passed remained closed.

Except for one.

She passed it so quickly that she wasn't sure she saw what she thought she did, but the image seared in her brain said otherwise.

A woman stood in the shadows of the open doorway.

Her eye sockets were empty.

Her mouth was set in a horrifying grin that framed a bloodied stump where a tongue once was.

Fumbling with the keycard, Sarah could barely hear her own muffled sobs beyond the rush of blood in her ears, coupled with the frantic footsteps that followed her along the hallway.

Then her room was in sight!

She jammed the card into the door without looking back and collapsed through the opening. With her eyes squeezed shut, afraid of what she might see, Sarah kicked the door closed right before something thumped against the other side.

Terrified, she opened her eyes and watched the tiny strip of light beneath the door. Something or someone moved along the carpet outside.

Crawling toward the door, she rested her head against the wood. There was only silence from the other side, but her mind had already conjured up all kinds of disturbing images of the eyeless, tongueless woman staring right at her through the heavy door.

Slowly, her heart rate returned to normal, and she stood and slotted the keycard into place. The room remained in darkness, though. Only the silvery light of the moon allowed her to discern one shape from the next.

It dawned on her the curtains were open once more.

She glanced toward the bed, hoping to see the lumpy shape of her fiancé beneath the covers, but his side of the bed remained untouched. The bathroom door was shut tight, with no light visible around the cracks.

Annoyed with herself for being so easily frightened, Sarah marched across the room, berating herself. She probably hadn't even pulled the curtains properly in the first place. She was still half asleep and imagining all sorts.

The anger she felt at herself shifted toward Mike, and she promised herself that tomorrow she would sit him down and have a long overdue chat about their relationship. She loved him, but she was done being embarrassed by his childish behavior and being let down by his aversion to responsibility.

Sarah grasped both ends of the flimsy curtains and pulled them closed with a sharp tug.

All the breath left her body as she stared at the figure before her, nothing separating them but the thin material of the drapes.

The blood drained from her and was replaced with ice as she stared through wide eyes at the person on the other side of the curtains. The shape was mere inches from her, the moonlight framing them from behind. Although she couldn't clearly make out any defining features, her horrified gaze was drawn to where their mouth would be as she watched the material flutter gently, moved by the breath of this intruder in her room. Soft humming broke the silence.

Sarah stood face to face with the figure behind the curtains for what felt like an eternity. She knew she needed to move, needed to do something.

With a sudden ferocious scream, she pulled the curtains apart, hands instantly balled into fists and swinging. But they swung on thin air.

There was nobody there.

Confused and trembling, Sarah left the window uncovered and crawled into bed, discarding her clothes as she went. She pulled the sheets over her head and wept softly, alone in the hotel room.

Mike woke the next morning with a hammering in his skull and a thirst like never before. His mouth felt as though it had been stuffed with cotton, that post-alcohol fuzziness coating his teeth and tongue. He opened his eyes and winced at brightness. Panic washed over him.

What time is it? Why hasn't Sarah woken me?

His stomach dropped and he groaned. She had probably gone to breakfast without even bothering to wake him. That meant she was super pissed!

He knew he needed to get a handle on his behavior. He did love Sarah, and in the cold light of day, he wanted to be better for her. Under cover of darkness, though, especially when the drinks were flowing, he found it all too easy to push her to the back of his mind, just for a little while.

Those guys had been a ton of fun last night, though. Mike winced again as a steady drumbeat clanged in his head.

Dragging himself upright, Mike gasped.

The thin curtains that covered the window did little to keep the sun at bay, and even less to conceal the dark figure that stood behind them.

"What the fuck are you doing in my room?" he yelled as he slowly pulled himself from the soft confines of the bed. His eyes never left the shape behind the drapes.

The shape never answered him.

As he crept closer, he realized the person was humming.

It was an off-kilter tune reminiscent of some disjointed version of a child's playground rhyme. It had all the effect of an ice-cream van appearing on the street in the dead of night, or of sharp nails on a chalkboard.

Mike stopped when he was just inches from the figure. The humming was a little clearer, and he recognized the tune. It was unmistakable. He had spent enough time driving everyone crazy with the Peeping Polly rhyme. It was really only surprising he hadn't caught onto it instantly.

He watched the figure inhale and exhale, the material moving in sync with their slight frame.

"Who are you?" he whispered, then pulled the curtain aside in one swift motion.

Sarah, her eye sockets empty voids of scarlet gore, shrieked through a mouthful of blood before collapsing heavily to the floor.

With a bellow, Mike skittered away from her bloodied form and toward the door, but not before he watched her eyeballs fall from unclenched hands and roll across the carpet.

Under

Nick Botic

When I woke yesterday, it was with that ineffable feeling in the pit of my stomach that something was wrong. When I checked my phone, that feeling worsened as I was made aware of the seventeen missed calls from my brother. He had been trying to reach me for the better part of four hours and, of course, on the first night in months I had taken a sleeping aid. I called him back and hadn't gotten through even the first ring before he answered.

"He's back... and he sees me," was all he said before I listened to his phone tumble to the hardwood floor that runs throughout his house.

I knew at once what he was talking about and of the "he" to whom Brandon referred. I threw my sheets off and was in my car and barreling across town to Brandon's house in under a minute. As I waited impatiently at a red light, my heart a dull thud in my ears, my knuckles white around the steering wheel, I recalled a number of memories I thought long forgotten. I recalled the first night (of many) in which I heard my brother's screams coming from the next room, not the cries of a boy plagued by a nightmare but the howls and shrieks of a child truly and sincerely in fear for his life. I recalled the nights that followed and, each time, our parents hurrying in vain to comfort him. I recalled the strange organizational solution that was found to keep his night terrors at bay. And I recalled the therapists mom and dad took Brandon to and the subsequent diagnoses.

Through these remembrances, I was able to calm myself down some and remind myself Brandon's issue was one we had been dealing with for the past three decades. And while it had at times become rather obstructive to our lives, Brandon's most of all, we had figured out what kept my brother's particular plague at bay and adhered to it, even through three moves—from our parents' house to Brandon's first apartment, from the first apartment to the second, and from the second apartment to the house in which he has lived for the past six years. The furniture, and Brandon's insisted-upon amendments to each and every piece of it, has been the most important aspect of each move, making helping someone move, an already inconvenient task, even more loathsome.

I pondered what could have led to my younger brother calling me nearly twenty times in the dead of night, leveled guesses as to the inciting incident for this apparent breakdown when he had been doing as well as he had for so long. I knew what he was going to say was happening, and I knew the solution was historically attainable by way of cardboard and duct tape. But in the two words he spoke to me when I finally called him back, in the way only a brother could, I heard something different in his voice. Gone was the visceral but directionless hysteria he would expel before mom and dad rearranged the furniture in his bedroom, replaced by an affect of total resignation.

And that scared me.

I came to a screeching halt in Brandon's driveway and hurried out of my car and up to his front door, neglecting to knock out of the sense of urgency. I stepped into the foyer and turned to the right, seeing that the solution my parents had found to Brandon's night terrors, the one which for decades had been effective enough for his liking, was apparently no longer sufficient for him.

I was six and Brandon was eight that first night. I was awakened by his screams, a terrible blend of agony that was both high pitched and guttural. I sat up in bed, wanting to make sure my brother was okay but afraid of whatever it was that had elicited such a terrified response from the person I looked at as being the bravest I had ever known. The shadowy corners in my bedroom seemed darker, deeper, more predatory, as I listened to my parents' bedroom door swinging open and colliding with the wall behind it, to their footsteps shuffling from their room to Brandon's and to their own fearful crying out of their first born's name, and to them bursting into Brandon's room and their confusion at what had frightened him so severely. I listened as my brother screamed and cried with such force that he vomited. It took them nearly a half hour to calm him to the point of coherency, and once they did, I heard only fragments of their hushed conversation, during which mom and dad told him that whatever had happened had been a nightmare despite Brandon's insistence to the contrary.

When I asked him the following morning about what had happened, my big brother looked at me with the thousand-yard stare of a mentally-scarred, battle-worn soldier and simply shook his head, neglecting to divulge the particulars of his ordeal while telling me without words that whatever it was had changed the course of his life. And indeed, he was never the same after that first night.

Each of the next five nights went much the same way, including the fourth, in which he slept in the living room, and the fifth, when he spent the night on the floor in my room. Our dad was against allowing Brandon to sleep in his and mom's room, but his patience for spending the small hours tending to Brandon's hysteria was wearing thin. The next morning, a Saturday, dad went to a U-Haul rental facility and purchased a stack of large cardboard moving boxes. For the next several hours, our father cut those boxes into strips and panels of varying sizes and used them to obstruct any space between the bottom of every piece of furniture in Brandon's room.

His bedside table had cardboard affixed to the spaces between its four legs and duct taped to the floor at the bottom; his desk was much the same. His bed frame was removed and his mattress and box spring placed directly on the floor, negating the need for cardboard altogether. When our dad finished, anything with empty space between it and the floor had gotten a cardboard and duct tape makeover, leaving his room a patchwork of light brown and grayed silver amidst the movie posters and pinned-up covers of comic books.

This redesign of Brandon's furnishings brought about a period of relative peace for my brother who, while perhaps not sleeping the whole time, was able to make it through the night without any debilitating fits of screaming and horror.

During this time, I was still unaware of what exactly had caused his need to have the space under his things obstructed—he refused to tell me no matter how much I pestered him, and my parents insisted it was Brandon's burden. They said in no uncertain terms that if he wished for me to know, he would tell me, though they also made it clear to me that I had no cause to be concerned for myself, if not for my brother.

And though he made it through the night, it was plain to see something had broken inside my big brother. He was only as social as he was expected to be, spent little time with the kids who at one time he had been all but fused to, and was vehemently opposed to sleeping anywhere but his bedroom. I also saw his personality go from that of a lively, fun-loving, fearless boy to one who was jaded, reserved, and, more than anything, in a constant state of feeble trepidation.

The first time I was awarded any kind of insight into Brandon's peculiarities was the night of his twelfth birthday. He had gotten as a gift, to my inevitable and immeasurable envy, a television of his very own, which in turn prompted him to change the layout of his bedroom in order to accommodate it. At some point during that undertaking, the cardboard panel that blocked off the empty space underneath the dresser on top of which the TV was meant to be placed as seen from the side suffered a puncture wound at the bottom from our father's foot—a grave, inadvertent mistake that went unnoticed until that night—when Brandon screamed louder and for longer than ever before, repeating the words he repeated to me two mornings ago, only at the top of his lungs.

"HE'S BACK AND HE SEES ME! HE'S BACK AND HE SEES ME! HE'S BACK AND HE SEES ME!"

This prolonged fit of terror ended in a terrified catatonia and resulted in his first stay in a mental health facility.

I learned later that during his stay at Brayhill Memorial, he had slept in the nude and used his clothing and blanket and bedsheets to block off the empty space created by the bed and desk which furnished the small room.

Through the years, Brandon would manage his delusion with varying degrees of success. He would see periods of up to four years wherein there would be no episodes, but such lengths of time would ultimately come to an end.

I came to learn his issues were tied to wherever he slept. As such, his bedroom at any given home was where he slept, and he did not waver in that resolve but for the handful of times over the years in which he spent the night at my house for one reason or another. Only, before he would enter my house, he would need my solemn word that the space below all my furniture was completely blocked off, and though our parents, by way of his doctors, would insist that giving in to his demand was simply enabling him, I never had the heart to deceive him. That, and I knew how it would end.

Because his ailment seemed to be limited to where he slept, Brandon was able to hold a regular job, something he has maintained since he was fifteen years old.

Sometime around his twenty-sixth birthday, Brandon moved out of our parents' house to live alone for the first time, something none of us had ever been certain about the possibility of, and stayed in that apartment building—a decrepit place, but one he made his own—for four years. With my help, he moved to his second and much nicer apartment and lived there for three years, then finally to the house he currently inhabits.

And while I knew he had outfitted his home with all the necessary blockades to empty spaces beneath his furniture, it had become something of a non-issue, little more than Brandon's eccentricities which he—and I, his only guest—had accepted as a fact of life. Two weeks ago, however, I received a text from him.

I've been hearing him

It took me a day to get in touch with him, but when I did, my brother assured me his mind was simply playing tricks on him and, owing to two decades' worth of minimal relapses in his mental illness, I saw no reason not to take him at his word.

There was simply no way for me to know if it would have changed anything that followed, but I wish I hadn't.

Upon bursting through the front door, I saw at once the heartbreaking excess to which Brandon had fortified his house. Rather than the strips of cardboard of varying sizes that had served him since childhood, his furniture now had pieces of plywood fastened to it with large nails and screws. Beyond that, it was no longer only the furniture which haunted him.

I noticed first the area rug in the center of his living room, into which the front door opened. The entire outer edge was secured by numerous strips of duct tape, all cascading outward and onto the hardwood floor. Likewise, the picture frames and various art pieces adorning his walls were held down on all sides by similar layers of tape. To put it simply, if its surface could cast a shadow, no matter how minimal, Brandon had used one or more of any number of materials to make certain that it didn't. His home had transformed into a wooden and adhesive perversion of safety and comfort.

From my vantage point standing in the front doorway, I could see my brother straight ahead from me, sitting with his back against the wall in the hallway that separated the living room from the kitchen, his knees pulled up to his chest, his phone on the floor where he dropped it after uttering those regrettably familiar words to me not twenty minutes prior. Nevertheless, I let out a sigh of relief that the scene I walked in on was what it was rather than something more final as has always been a lingering concern I harbored since I first became aware of the concept of such a tragic end.

"Brandon!" I hurried over to him, noticing mid stride he hadn't yet acknowledged me with so much as a glance, his eyes instead darting to and from each piece of furniture in the living room and occasionally the kitchen. When I got to him, I kneeled down and held his tear-streaked face in line with my own, and finally his bloodshot eyes connected with me. "B, B, you're okay, I'm here, okay? I'm here."

My brother swallowed hard, and I saw his eyes avert for a moment before returning to me.

"I... I should have told you not to come," he said in a whisper.

"What do you mean? Stop, you know it's not a problem. I'm always here for you."

"I don't... I don't know what he will do."

I had wondered for thirty years who Brandon was talking about when he said "he." It was a detail Brandon refused to divulge and about which he had sworn our parents to secrecy; to their credit, and to my frustration, it was a secret they had each taken with them to their respective graves. In my mind, "he" was the formless representation of my brother's ill mind, a conjuration of fear and delusion, Brandon's nightmares given form on the stage of the theater of his imagination for which he would provide no description.

"Who? There's nobody here, B. It's just you and me."

Brandon's gaze looked past me again, and this time, it held. He was looking into the living room.

The feeling of eyes on me remained. I felt the hair on the back of my neck rise and gooseflesh prickled my arms. I felt Brandon's arm raise and hold, and I knew at once he was pointing at something. I was apprehensive to turn, concerned I might have not noticed something in the living room, some consequence of Brandon's delusions having finally come to a head, evidence of some horrific crime committed not out of malice but out of my brother's unique brand of unwellness. Nevertheless, I slowly turned around and followed an imaginary line from the tip of Brandon's outstretched finger to his coffee table, three sides of which had been properly closed off; but the fourth, that being the space between the legs on the short side of it which faced us, had a piece of plywood leaned against it at an angle, the pitch darkness within clashing with the natural light from without. I peered into that void cast by the plywood leaning against it, an oblong, vaguely-square lacuna of empty space perhaps twelve inches in length and width and unfathomable depth.

As I stared into that space, I felt the subdued tremors which spasmed out of Brandon as he began to sob. I wanted nothing more than to turn to comfort him, to tell him it was going to be okay, but the space underneath the coffee table was almost hypnotic, in its way.

And then something moved within that space.

An electric jolt reverberated through my body as I refocused my gaze, cocking my head slightly.

"He's under there," Brandon whispered. "And he sees you."

With my breath caught in a painful ball lodged in the recesses of my chest, I watched as something in that dark space underneath the coffee table moved again, the light from the living room lamp bouncing off it for a fraction of a fraction of a second, so brief that if not for the overwhelming distress coursing through my body, I might have been able to convince myself I hadn't seen it at all.

My gaze narrowed and I moved to separate myself from my brother, but he took a handful of my shirt in a vice-like grip and pulled me closer to him.

"Don't... I don't know what he'll do," he said.

What was I to think? In that moment, I thought that perhaps a rat or mouse had found its way under the table or that, in the throes of his delirium, Brandon had put something of the sort there intentionally.

"B, it's okay, alright?" I said in a calm tone that betrayed the tightness in my muscles and chest. "I'm just going to look—"

Brandon pulled me even closer and wrapped an arm around my neck in a forceful, begging hug and cried so hard I thought he might faint.

"Brandon, Brandon." I pushed away from him just enough to get my hands on his cheeks and make him look me in my eyes. I could see for the first time just how much older he looked, older than he rightfully should. His eyes were underlined by deep purple bags, his skin marred by stress lines, his hair grayed and thinning and unkempt. "Brandon... I'm just going to look, okay? I won't even get close, yeah? I'm just going to look, and then, if you're up for it, I'll show you that there's n--nothing... nothing there, nothing to be worried about."

If I sounded somewhat unsure to myself, I sounded entirely unsure to my brother. But he reluctantly loosened his grip on my neck and shirt. I stood and turned, my eyes trained on the side of the coffee table. I took a few cautious steps into the living room, not daring to tear my eyes away from the opening in the coffee table's plywood skirt. When I got to a good position from which I could see into it, I stopped. The light from the living room crawled into the space, reaching an inch or two underneath the table before being extinguished by the darkness. And as I looked inside, I could see that just past the point where the light died out, something was moving, slowly, the kind of minute, almost imperceptible movements a person would make when attempting to stand perfectly still. I could make out the vague suggestion of a form, something substantive, and it was made worse by the twin glints lingering just below the underside of the table.

I looked back over at Brandon, who was switching between looking at me and the space. I took my phone out of my pocket and turned on the flashlight, shining it toward the hole. It illuminated a fraction of an inch beyond that of the living room's light before being swallowed by the darkness. I looked at my brother and took a deep breath.

"I'm just gonna get a little closer, B, just so I can get this light in there and show you it's all good. It's probably just a... just... something..." I trailed off, not at all believing my own words while praying they were, nevertheless, true.

Brandon began whimpering again, unable, I suspected, to put forth the effort of trying to sway me from doing just that.

I moved closer to the hole with small, hesitant steps. When I felt I was close enough to see the whole of that empty space beneath the coffee table, I took in another deep, trembling lungful of air and shined the light inside. My heart plummeted to my stomach.

He was under the table, coming up out of some apparent absence in the hardwood flooring beneath, some cosmic void that had replaced that section of pine floor. I could see his face down to his mouth, and four fingers on either side of it as someone peeking over a fence. He was bald, whether by choice or necessity I couldn't say for certain, though I presumed it to be the latter as its skin was the texture of a burnt piece of driftwood, ashen and flaky and gray and black and white and wilted and tortured. Beneath the ash which covered him was a surface of pale yellow which peeked out in small rivers and spots. Its eyes were also yellow, slightly too large for his face, and squinted as it smiled. It wasn't the horrific rictus grin of so many tired horror stories but, rather, a smile made somewhat slightly larger by the overall size of the maw itself, lips curled in an otherwise natural smirk, as of a predator observing its prey as the imminent victim toils away, exactly where he wants it.

I was only stricken immobile by this creature for a few moments as my mind struggled to reconcile the impossible. With my breath still held, I turned and ran the few steps to my brother and exerted more strength than I ever had before as I lifted him to his feet, shouting to him we needed to go. Rather than risk moving back through the living room, we went the opposite way, through the kitchen and out the sliding glass door. But at the last moment before the living room disappeared from my view, I looked back and saw the whole of the gray and yellow face of that horrible thing which lurked in the empty space beneath my brother's furniture, saw the inhuman length of its flaking, peeling fingers slithering up onto the wood floor from the depths of whatever hell it came from.

As I drove Brandon and myself back to my house, I silently ruminated on the horror my brother had been living in for over thirty years. There had been only perhaps six incidents in which he encountered that grotesque thing, but I suddenly understood the years of fear and the frustration he must have felt by everyone telling him he was sick and confused rather than haunted and plagued.

He waited outside while I outfitted my home with the necessary blockades, unfortunately only with the cardboard I always kept readily available in the event of an impromptu visit. I insisted to Brandon that we go to the hardware store once it opened and get plywood, but he insisted on staying at my house, that the cardboard would suffice.

We spent the day with seldom a word spoken between us, instead letting the sound of movies and television fill the stale air. I was in something akin to a state of shock—I didn't know how to proceed. My entire worldview had been turned upside down; all I knew and believed had been perverted by the introduction of this horrific thing which lurked in the empty spaces beneath couches and tables and desks. When the sun set, the adrenaline from the day had long worn off and fatigue replaced it. My brother slept on the couch in my living room, me in the recliner (not reclined, to be sure) mere feet from him.

And despite our close proximity last night, I awoke in the living room alone.

I found a note on the coffee table next to the couch, which prompted me to scurry about my house, screaming my brother's name, hoping against hope, praying to a god I had never been and certainly at that time was not sure existed, that he hadn't done what I thought he did.

But there, in the guest room, a panel of cardboard had been deliberately moved from along the foot of the bed, splinters of Brandon's fingernails lodged in the wood floor. From within that empty space, a cackling laughter sounded a mile away, its echoes bouncing off the walls of a cavern the size of a universe. The thing wasn't there to greet me, because he was preoccupied. I replaced the cardboard.

I read the note Brandon left to me several hundred times, the paper streaked by splotches and lines of discoloration left behind by his fallen tears, and I knew that thing, that thing which haunted the shadowy space beneath furniture, I knew it would return.

I'm sorry

I can't do it anymore

All I can do is hope that it stops with me, but we both know that's not true

I really hope I never see you again

I love you

Several hours after I discovered the opening under the guest bed, the scratching started. I could hear it no matter where I went in my house. The thing went under whichever piece of furniture I was nearest to.

He's back.

He's back and he sees me.

Drowning Hope

John Durgin

"You sure you can make it that far?" Matt asked Johnny as they stared at the island fifty yards out.

"Doesn't look that far, right? I'm no Phelps, but I can swim a few hundred feet," Johnny said.

The boys were enjoying their last summer before heading off to college. The sun beamed over the lake, a light breeze sending ripples across the glistening surface. Johnny had never been a great swimmer, but over the last few years, he had gained more confidence, even if it was mostly swimming in pools. The closest thing he ever got to swimming lessons growing up was his grandmother tossing him in the river and eventually lifting him up when she realized he was on the verge of being carried downstream.

Matt, on the other hand, was an excellent swimmer. He also happened to be one of the most athletic kids in their graduating class. Johnny didn't grow up hanging out with him, but after school ended, and the importance of the popularity hierarchy was a thing of the past, they found themselves hanging out more and more. They were both set to attend the same college and had run into one another while touring the campus. After grabbing dinner following their tours, they realized they had quite a bit in common and started hanging out.

They were killing time before their double date with a couple girls from town later that night, where they planned to go see a movie and sneak in some booze.

"Okay then, let's do this. Once we reach the island, we can check that shit out, see if the rumors are true..." Matt said. He kicked his flip flops to the side and approached the water.

Johnny wouldn't admit it, but he hoped there was nothing *true* about the rumors at all. The previous summer, a girl named Nancy Frost went missing. She was a few grades below them, so neither had talked to her much. That didn't matter in a small town, where even the most reclusive types couldn't avoid the population knowing everything about them. Authorities found her body floating against the rocky embankment of the lake after weeks of searching for her. The rumor was she had been held captive on the small island, which was uninhabited. The term "island" was used loosely, as it was really just a few giant rocks that had trees and overgrown bushes occupying the limited amount of real estate it offered.

The thought of someone holding Nancy prisoner there then tossing her body in the lake and getting away with it sent goosebumps across Johnny's skin.

Matt didn't give him the chance to second guess his decision to swim out, as he carefully climbed down the rocky shore until he was low enough to jump in. He looked back up at Johnny, who hadn't started his descent yet.

"Come on, don't be a pussy!"

Johnny scoffed and climbed down to meet him. He scanned the perimeter of the lake, taking in all the amazing lake houses around the perimeter. For such a beautiful day, it was odd to see the place essentially a ghost town.

Matt walked into the water until it was up to his waist. "Well, my balls just inverted up into my stomach..."

"Wow, you really make this sound appealing," Johnny responded.

"Your balls can't shrink anymore on you, ya little bitch. Let's go!"

Johnny shook his head and laughed, then entered the water. Matt was right, it was fucking freezing. After a few unseasonably cold nights, it was as if the temperature of the water dropped back to early spring temps. After a moment, his lower half adjusted.

"Ready?" he asked.

"Hell yeah," Matt said.

They lunged forward in unison, leaving the land behind. The breeze relaxed Johnny as he stroked through the calm water.

Matt pulled ahead of him, showing off his oversized wingspan.

"Hey, asshole! Don't go too far ahead," Johnny yelled.

Matt paused between strokes and lifted his hand high in the air to give Johnny the finger, then picked back up his speed.

The water was clean, but a black hole existed beneath the surface. Johnny looked below as he swam, surprised he couldn't see more than a few feet below. He had a fleeting thought of Nancy's corpse rotting at the bottom of the lake before finally breaking free and rising above. He knew it was ridiculous—her body had been found and brought to the morgue. Still, he picked up his pace, anyway.

After a few minutes, he paused to look back to see how far he made it, guessing he was about halfway to the island. Matt was twenty yards ahead of him. His muscles ached, and he wasn't looking forward to the swim back. Once the adrenaline wore off, he knew his body would let him know it had no desire to go through this whole process again. He turned back toward the destination and began to swim once more when a sudden jolt of pain shot through his left hamstring.

"Fuck!"

Johnny realized his leg was cramping, locking up and becoming useless. His hamstring was rock solid, the muscle tightening so much he thought it might explode beneath the skin. He closed his eyes, fighting off the pain. It was something he had dealt with through his teen years, often waking up in the middle of the night to his calf feeling like it was being squeezed by an invisible set of claws or his hamstring pumping his leg full of agony. In those situations, he just jumped out of bed and stretched the impacted muscle until the pain subsided, then went back to bed and dealt with the dull sensation that remained the next few days. This time he had nowhere to jump, no place to stretch his muscles.

There was no way he could continue swimming until the cramp let up. He turned on his back and attempted to stretch the leg, reaching out to pull on his toes. He realized he was starting to sink due to the lack of swimming, and panic overtook him. His chest tightened. His heart hammered against his ribs.

Swim on your back. Use your arms and let your legs relax, he told himself.

"Matt! I need to go back! My fucking leg's cramping hard!"

He had no idea if Matt heard him or not; he couldn't see him from his vantage point. He realized there was no advantage swimming in either direction, so swimming back made the most sense. Johnny returned to his back and began to backstroke toward land, immediately feeling a sense of relief as the pain softened. After a few minutes of swimming on his back, his arms began to tire. He had no idea how much distance he had covered, but he was facing the island again and noticed Matt kept going toward it.

"I'm really struggling, man!"

Matt stopped swimming and turned back to face him, his head only a quarter-sized circle in the distance.

"What? Are you fucking with me?"

"No! I think I need help!"

Embarrassment took a backseat to pure terror at the thought of drowning. Matt said something, but Johnny couldn't hear him as water continued to smack against his face, his head bobbing up and down. He needed to try using his legs again, fight through the throbbing pain in his hamstring. After flipping back to his stomach, Johnny kicked his legs back and forth to jolt himself forward. The rocky shore was still a few hundred feet away, but he was making progress.

Just when a little hope found its way back to him, his hamstring twitched violently, locking his leg in place. This time, his toes joined in on the fun, curling into the bottom of his foot. The pain was excruciating, like something had burrowed beneath the surface of his foot and clamped onto the muscles and tendons.

Johnny pushed forward as tears streamed down his cheeks. His arms burned from exhaustion; his legs were giving up on him. There was no way he could make it back to land on his own. Out of desperation, he decided to see if he was close enough to the shore that he could walk back. He let himself sink, praying that when his feet hit bottom, his head would still be above the surface. His body lowered, descending below the water until his entire body was submerged. He kept falling until his feet finally touched the bottom. Johnny opened his eyes and looked up, realizing he had to be at least fifteen feet deep. As his leg continued to cramp, the fear intensified, overtaking the pain. He pushed off the lake's floor and reached for the surface, stretching his arms as far as they would go as if that would somehow save him. The water was a cloudy haze of dirt and algae spreading from the force of the current. He kept kicking, trying to put most of the strength on his right leg.

As he closed in on the surface, something moved behind a patch of mossy grass in the darkness. He screamed, sending a line of rapid-fire bubbles from his mouth. The shape of a human figure floated in the distance, disappearing into the void. He couldn't make out any of the features, but he was certain he saw it. For a brief second, it took Johnny's attention off drowning. He kept his eyes locked on the space while still laboring his way toward the top.

Johnny couldn't tell if his vision was fading due to lack of oxygen or if he had just stirred up the dirt on the ground below so much that it clouded the area around him. But he knew he saw something watching him. A large fish? No. It was much bigger than that. Maybe his brain was starving for air so bad that it was fucking with his other senses. He couldn't wait around to find out. Finally, he reached the surface, forcing his head out of the water like it was a womb releasing him into the world for the first time.

The air invaded his lungs, commingling with the water he had swallowed to force a violent coughing fit. He felt himself wanting to stop fighting for a second, to allow his limbs the chance to regain some semblance of strength. The depths below pulled at him, trying to take him back below.

"Help! I'm drowning!"

The empty docks surrounding the lake didn't respond. Just when he thought he was about to sink below and take his last breath, he felt an arm wrap around his shoulders.

"Turn to your back, man! I'll help you!"

Matt. Thank fucking god for Matt.

Johnny wanted to turn over—he just couldn't do it. His body went limp. Everything turned black and, with it, so did his thoughts, except for the image of the figure watching him underwater.

Johnny awoke to something slamming into his chest. His eyes remained closed, but he heard someone panting as they pressed firmly beneath his sternum, over and over. It wasn't until he felt his mouth forced open and air blowing into his lungs that he realized someone was giving him CPR. He tried to open his eyes, but his body wasn't ready to listen. Every fiber of his being was exhausted to the point that even the thought of moving made him want to go back to sleep. A pounding headache greeted him, but he pushed through it and blinked, initially met with a wall of blurry shapes. The sun blasted down, making it even more difficult to see. A silhouette stood over him, huffing. Johhny blinked again, seeing the figure more clearly. The rotting corpse of Nancy Frost leaned over him, her matted hair clinging to her algae-covered skin. Her eyes were milky-white, her teeth caked in green sludge.

Johnny screamed, but the cries were cut short as water escaped his lungs, forcing him to cough up the gallons of lake water he swallowed. He rolled to his side and threw up, sending another jolt of pain cracking through his temples. Once he finished vomiting, he turned back to look at the figure, only she was gone. In her place, Matt stood watching him with fear plastered across his face.

"It's okay, man. I got you. Holy shit, I thought you died. Can you breathe?"

Johnny couldn't talk. Had he just died and been revived by Matt? Was he seeing things? As foggy as his brain was, he was certain it was Nancy standing over him before, wheezing in and out as soggy air escaped her water-logged lungs. He tried to sit up, but his body felt like it had just been in a car wreck. Instead, he lay back down and let the warm sun calm his fragile nerves. After his body regained some strength, Johnny sat up—and thought he was going to throw up again. He forced the bile down and closed his eyes, taking deep breaths. His lungs burned, and his entire body felt like a deflated rubber ball.

"Thank you, man. You saved my fucking life..."

Matt let out a panicked laugh. "Yeah, well, you sure had a funny way of showing it. Elbowed me right in the goddamn head when I tried to turn you over. I thought you were gonna kill both of us."

"Shit. Sorry. I... I panicked. My hamstring locked up and I just couldn't make it. Tried to touch bottom and realized I was still way too far out."

"You were screaming when you came up, like you saw a damn shark or something. You good?"

Johnny waived off the concern. "I'll be fine. We can't tell my parents about this, though. They'd kill me for almost dying. Not sure what the hell I was thinking, trying to swim out there."

"I have no desire to tell my parents. I know I'll get yelled at, too, for going out there. Ever since Nancy, they don't want me near this place, even though I used to come here every summer. Let's get you back to the car and we can get the hell out of here."

Johnny wasn't arguing that. He got to his feet, momentarily feeling lightheaded. After blinking away the tiny white dots floating around his vision, he looked out at the water one more time. He could've sworn he saw a dark mass moving beneath the surface, heading back out toward the island. He pushed the thought aside and headed back toward the car.

Johnny sat in the back of the dark theater, unable to focus on the movie playing, but not because the movie was bad or because he was bored on his date. If only it could be that simple. The reason he couldn't focus on the movie was because the image of Nancy standing over him at the lake wouldn't leave his head. No matter what he was doing or where he went, her face was chiseled into his memory. Over the past few hours, it had become so bad that he started to wonder if maybe he was short of a few brain cells after his heart stopped momentarily. Or maybe his imagination was adding to the shape he saw, creating a more detailed image the longer he pondered it.

For example, he didn't initially see the pain in her eyes, the cries for help. No, instead he saw a monster, a freak, ready to haunt every waking moment of his life. Why did she show herself? It wasn't just at the lake, either. When they left, Johnny laid his head against the passenger window and tried to sleep away the exhaustion from fighting for his life. Only, when he looked in the rearview mirror, Nancy was staring back at him, green water pooling in her dead eyes and sliding down her torn cheeks. Matt asked him what was wrong after he jolted upright in his seat, but he lied and said it was because he felt more water in his throat and thought he was going to throw up.

Later, while on the double date, sitting in the back row while his friends passed the bottle of cheap vodka to one another, he was too busy watching the shadows. Every time someone got up to use the restroom or screamed at one of the jump scares, he thought it was Nancy coming for him. On more than one occasion, he almost jumped from his seat and ran out of the theater. Johnny knew he was acting strange around his friends and knew the chances of a second date were at the bottom of the lake with Nancy's ghost.

Was that a ghost? She looked so damn real, he thought.

After dropping the girls off, Matt pulled into Johnny's driveway and turned to face him.

"Dude, what the fuck's going on with you? I know that shit was scary today, but you're acting like a damn creep ever since."

Johnny debated telling Matt what he had been seeing and decided against it. The truth would only make him look even more crazy. Instead, he decided to get some sleep and hope he woke up in the morning feeling like a new man.

"I just can't believe I almost died today. I owe you, man. Don't think I'll ever forget what you did for me today..." He trailed off, unexpectedly choking up.

"Hey, hey. Stop being a bitch. You would've done the same thing for me, at least if you knew how to swim. Stop getting all mushy."

Johnny laughed and shook his head, then opened the passenger door.

"I'll give you a call tomorrow. Later," he said as he shut the door.

Matt gave him a wave and backed out of the driveway. Johnny watched the red Honda drive away and the taillights fade into tiny dots before he turned toward his house—and came face to face with Nancy Frost. She stood inches from his face with her mouth open wide, revealing her stained teeth. Her face was frozen in a muted scream, only a wheezy breath escaping her. Johnny froze, fear gripping his throat and squeezing it tightly. He wanted to run into his house and escape the nightmare in front of him, but she was blocking the door. Her milky eyes looked more like two dim orbs with the streetlight shining down on her. Johnny closed his eyes and took a deep breath, hoping his mind was just fucking with him. If he continued seeing these visions, he knew he would have to tell his parents about the lake. He had heard of hypoxia killing people hours after they almost drowned.

Panic gripped him at the thought of passing away in his sleep, but then the warm breath coming from Nancy's dead body tickled his skin and he realized it wasn't just in his head. He opened his eyes, hoping she was gone but knowing damn well she would still be there. He wanted to scream for help, but Nancy wasn't doing anything, just standing in front of him and continuing to breathe on him. Her breath was rancid, wafting into his nostrils and making his eyes burn like a poison gas leak.

"What do you want? Why are you following me?" he whispered.

She looked up at the night sky, and that's when Johnny noticed the laceration spreading across her throat, a trail of pus and infection corroding the once-smooth skin of her youth. He instinctively took a step back when her arm shot out and grabbed hold of his wrist. This time he did scream, but as he did, his vision blacked out, followed by a set of still images playing through his mind like an old film projector—Nancy swimming at the same place he almost drowned, Nancy looking back and smiling toward whoever stood behind Johnny's eyes. Then the images darkened, less visible yet somehow clearer. The sensation made Johnny stagger, but he held his ground. Nancy was running, looking over her shoulder with tears pouring down her face, hiding in the underbrush of the small island. The last shot he saw was hands wrapped around her throat, and while it was a still image, Johnny knew they were squeezing tightly.

He broke the connection with the Nancy-thing and realized he was crying. His throat hurt. Whatever she was doing to project those images, he felt every emotion that came with them. He blinked away the images in his head, ready to ask her why she was showing him, but when he opened his eyes, she was gone. Johnny stood alone in his driveway, his heart pounding against his chest. He stood in the driveway for a few minutes, numb to the world. It wasn't until the motion light went out on the garage that he snapped out of it. He walked into his house, going through the motions of saying goodnight to his parents, then entered his room and dropped to his bed. After all he had dealt with throughout the day, sleep consumed him. His body was exhausted, but his mind continued to put in overtime.

Nancy Frost was trying to tell him something...

"You're telling me you almost died out there yesterday, then you've been haunted by Nancy ever since, and you want to go *back*?" Matt asked, flustered by Johnny's demands.

"I'll wear a life jacket. I didn't tell you about her yesterday because I knew it sounded crazy. But she wouldn't leave me alone. She wants us to go back to that island, I know it."

"And do what exactly? The police searched that island after her death. It led to nothing. If what you're saying really happened to you, and you're not just batshit fucking crazy, what would she want us to do out there?"

"I don't know, man. Maybe there's something that will help solve her murder? Something the cops missed? At first, I thought she was just haunting me or that I was really dead and a ghost myself or something. But those flashes I saw... she went to that spot with someone she trusted. I think it was someone from town."

"Ok. I'll do it. But you're not only wearing a life jacket, you're wearing arm floaties and flippers too," Matt said with a shit-eating grin.

"Piss off."

They rode the rest of the way in silence, stopping by Matt's house on the way to grab life jackets. When they arrived at the lake, Johnny was blindsided with a burst of anxiety. Thinking about it was one thing, but seeing the water where he drowned and, more importantly, where Nancy was killed hit him a lot harder than he anticipated. He took deep breaths to try to ease the tightness in his chest, but that only helped slightly. Matt stared at him as he got out of the car.

"You sure about this? You look like you want to shit your pants. I'd prefer it if you don't do it in the water near me, like Chris Proper in the town pool."

They laughed.

"Remember how pissed the whole school was at him? Had to shut the pool down half the summer because they were worried about E. coli," Johnny said.

Matt opened his trunk and handed Johnny a life jacket, then grabbed one for himself. Johnny wasn't sure why Matt decided to wear one but assumed it was to make Johnny not feel like such a loser. Regardless of how much they ribbed one another, Matt was a good friend.

Once they had the jackets on, they climbed down the rocky embankment to the water's edge. Johnny couldn't help having second thoughts about the whole thing. Not only was the sight of the water bringing on a panic attack, he hadn't had a vision about Nancy all morning. Maybe the initial shock had worn off and things were back to normal.

As if on cue, something moved between the trees on the small island. It was too far away for Johnny to see what it was, but he knew. *Nancy.* The brief glimpse of her gave him the motivation he needed to get in the water. Matt followed, and before they knew it, the boys were on their way to the island again. The first few strokes were made with trembling arms for Johnny, but once he was deep enough for the life jacket to hold him above water, some of the fear subsided. *Some.*

Once they passed the spot of the near-drowning, Johnny picked up his pace, regaining some of his confidence in the water. Before he knew it, they reached the perimeter of the rocky shore.

"We made it! It only took a near death experience and a ghost haunting you to get us here," Matt joked.

Johnny, normally one to return the banter, was too focused on the section of trees to respond. His eyes were locked on the place he saw movement a moment ago.

Matt realized he was looking into the trees and brought his own focus there as well. "Do you see her right now?" he asked in a tone that was a mix of fear and doubt.

"No... But I can *feel* her. Let's go."

They climbed up the rocky edge and came to a flat space—a large granite rock covered in moss. Even on a bright and sunny day, and *even* with only a small area of trees, the boys were engulfed in darkness the moment they entered the mini forest. A chill crawled up Johnny's spine, and he could tell by the look in Matt's eyes that his friend felt the same. The island went deeper than Johnny expected as there was a sloped drop-off that couldn't be seen from where they parked. They climbed down carefully, taking in the rocky landscape.

"This is pretty wild. Can't believe this wasn't used as some epic drinking spot by seniors. Seems like the perfect place to hide from the cops and be as loud as you want, doesn't it?" Matt asked.

Johnny answered without realizing it, just mumbling a response as he scanned the area ahead of them. There was another batch of trees around the corner, and the granite path transitioned to dirt. Johnny stopped and focused on the path.

"What's wrong?" Matt asked.

"The ground. This trail looks pretty well-kempt for a place nobody uses. Shouldn't there be weeds and shit overgrown on the dirt?"

"How the hell should I know? I would've failed agriculture if it wasn't for Mr. Barrett being friends with Coach."

The temperature must have dropped by ten degrees beneath the canopy of leaves hanging overhead. Johnny didn't know what he was looking for, but the island was fascinating either way. They stopped and took a break after the strenuous terrain and swim. Johnny sat against one of the larger trees and closed his eyes.

"I don't know. Maybe I'm crazy. Besides the fact that this place is way bigger than we expected, seems like a waste of time. Maybe we should just go back..."

"Yeah, doesn't seem like there's anything here," Matt said.

Help me...

Johnny jerked up, turning in a circle to scan the tree line.

"Did you not just hear that?" he asked.

Matt furrowed his brow and said, "Hear what?"

Johnny froze.

Over Matt's shoulder, Nancy stood in a rigid posture, staring deeper into the island. She raised her arm with its saggy, drooping skin clinging to her withered bones and pointed. Johnny took off in a sprint in the direction she was facing.

"What the fuck, man? Why are you running? We should go!"

Johnny didn't respond, but he heard Matt following behind. As he rounded the corner, he came to a sudden stop. The land ended, dropping off to the water below.

What the fuck was she pointing at?

With nowhere else to go, Johnny turned around as Matt caught up. That was when he spotted a stone wall that, at first, looked like no more than another large granite rock. But a sliver of light seeped through a crack between two rocks.

"Look! At those rocks!" Johnny yelled.

Matt turned, confused by the excitement in Johnny's voice until he spotted the same light.

"Shit," Matt whispered.

They slowly approached the light and looked at each other. Without a word, they each grabbed one side of the large stone and pulled with all their strength. The rock only moved a few inches, but more light poked out as they shimmied it back some more. An earthy aroma escaped the small hole they created, but the scent wasn't alone. Death, rotten meat, and body odor came with it. Backing up, Matt put his mouth into the crook of his elbow and gagged.

"Nah, no way in hell am I about to see what's causing that smell, man. Sorry."

"We have to. She led us here…"

"She led *you* here. I was minding my own damn business," Matt snapped. He scoffed and stepped back up to the rock, shaking his head.

They pulled back again, this time sliding the granite mass back another foot, making a big enough opening that they could see an entrance into some type of small cave. The source of the light wasn't obvious from the outside. Johnny crouched and leaned into the opening.

"You're going in there? Are you out of your fucking mind?"

"You don't have to. Just make sure the rock doesn't fall back against the opening and make it completely dark in here." Johnny wasn't convinced the cave would hold any light if the rocks closed, and he didn't want to be encased in a pitch black space.

Johnny entered the black hole, crouching even lower as jagged rock forms poked into his back from above. The floor was dirt, but it looked manmade. The walls were granite on both sides, narrowing to a small crawl space the deeper he entered.

"Anything in there?" Matt yelled, his voice echoing off the rocks.

"I can't see much—"

A low whimpering came from somewhere in the darkness, cutting his sentence short.

Johnny stopped crawling, hoping the sound was in his head, that maybe it was Nancy's ghost trying to communicate some more. The crying continued, picking up intensity after hearing the commotion coming from the entrance. *Shit, shit, shit.*

"What's happening? Johnny!"

Johnny tried to talk, but fear seized his vocal cords. What could this mean? Was there another victim up ahead? The murderer's next kill?

"There's someone in here! Come help, man!" Johnny yelled.

Matt said something, but it was too quiet for Johnny to hear the response. Not that it mattered how loud Matt spoke, Johnny's full attention was on the path in front of him. The more he crawled, the louder the pleas for help got. The darkness began to dissipate, and finally, Johnny reached the end of the path. The crawl space opened into a deeper cave-like space with a light hanging from the ceiling of the rock enclosure. He got to his feet and immediately spotted a hunched figure cowering in the corner. A dancing shadow flickered over the body as the light hanging above slowly spun from the faint breeze coming in.

"He-hello?" Johnny whispered, afraid to get an answer.

The body moved, and Johnny jolted back with a start, smacking his head off a rock hanging overhead. He ignored the pain, keeping his attention on the person. After a few seconds of silence, the pained moans started again, muffled by something. He pictured whoever it was with a gag over their mouth. He inched closer, squinting to try to get his eyes adjusted to the darkness. The dull light did just enough to outline the contour of the victim, but all the features were a blotchy smudge.

"Are you ok? I'm not going to hurt you," Johnny whispered.

He crouched, slowly reaching for the limp body. When his hand touched the skin, he was shocked to find the victim ice cold. It was another girl but wasn't someone he recognized. She flinched when Johnny attempted to pull the gag from her mouth, but once she realized he was helping, she allowed it.

"It's ok. What's your name?"

"Sadie... Is he coming?"

"Who did this?"

"I don't know his name. He was a college kid, I think. Please... help me out of here before he's back!"

"Shhh, it's ok, there's nobody else coming. What did he look like?"

"Tall. Handsome. He offered me a ride after meeting me at the beach."

Johnny worked at the rope tied tightly around her wrists and ankles. The ankle rope loosened after working it for a minute, but the wrist rope was tightly knotted, digging into her skin.

"He offered a ride? What type of car did he have? Any info you have can help catch him."

"It was red. A Honda, I think. We have to get out of here, he told me he'd be back later. Please..."

Johnny heard her, but he wasn't listening. The moment she mentioned the make of the car, dread weighed down on him, blackening the edges of his vision.

Matt had a red Honda. It was Matt who wanted to show him the island. Johnny recalled once reading about how killers loved to return to the location of their murders, and at once, everything clicked. Johnny realized it wasn't dread making everything darker but something blocking the light. Sadie looked over Johnny's shoulder and screamed just in time for him to turn and see Matt swinging something toward him.

Johnny tried to dodge the strike, but the club still connected with his shoulder, sending a jolt of pain down his arm.

"What the fuck! What are you doing, Matt?"

"I wish you didn't push and push. Or maybe I should have let you drown. The problem is if you drowned here, it would bring more attention back to the island. They would question why I was here. I couldn't afford that. But now you leave me no choice, Johnny. I can't let you out of here."

The expression on his face told Johnny that Matt *actually* felt bad. He didn't intend for it to go this way. The guilt quickly vanished, and Matt swung the club again, this time cracking it against Johnny's ribs. White-hot pain flashed through his vision, dropping him to his knees.

Matt lifted the club again, but Sadie charged at him. Matt saw her coming and directed his swing at her, smacking the thick wood off the side of her face. Sadie dropped to the ground in a heap.

Johnny grabbed at his ribs, attempting to get to his feet. As he did, Matt lifted the club overhead, ready to bring the killing blow. Johnny didn't have the fight in him; instead, he cringed and waited for impact—only, it never happened. He opened his eyes to see Matt backing away, the white of his wide eyes showing stark against the darkness around him. Johnny looked over and saw Nancy inching closer to them, her eyes letting off a dull glow. Matt tripped over a jagged rock sticking out of the ground, landing hard on his ass. Nancy darted at him, swarming him like a horde of angry wasps.

Matt screamed as she tore at him, her claws digging into his skin, ripping the flesh. Her hand shot to his throat, forcing through bone and muscle, then ripped a handful of flesh free. Matt gargled on blood; his eyes were frozen in permanent shock. He was bleeding out, his skin draining of all color. He looked to Johnny and reached for him as if his friend was going to try to save him. Johnny was in shock, everything happening so fast that he didn't have time to register it. Matt's body went limp, his eyes staring at the ceiling in a dead gaze.

Johnny didn't move until he heard Sadie shuffling behind him. He turned and was relieved to see she appeared ok. Nancy was gone. It was then Johnny realized she wasn't just trying to get him to the island to help Sadie but to warn him of his friend's true identity. It all came crashing down on Johnny. When Nancy disappeared, Matt and Johnny weren't hanging out yet.

Sadie stared down at Matt's dead body with disgust, then turned her attention to Johnny and he saw the start of a smile. She helped him toward the crawl space, toward the exit.

When they made it back to land, Johnny would call the police and break the news. While a piece of him was now missing, never to return, he also knew Nancy's family would find closure. The town would grieve, but they wouldn't live in fear wondering if the killer was still out there.

Myrtle

Elizabeth J. Brown

"I'm scared." Poppy's lower lip trembled, tears glistening in her large brown eyes. Her small fingers worried at the woollen strands of her ragdoll's pigtails.

Wrapping her in a hug, Louise kissed her daughter's forehead. "There's nothing to be scared of, Pops. You'll have a little sleep, and when you wake up, your finger will be all better."

Poppy gripped her tighter, nuzzling into her chest. "Promise?"

"I promise." Louise forced the words past the lump in her throat and gently detangled herself from Poppy's arms. Fixing her smile in place, she brushed a lock of blonde hair from her daughter's damp cheek. "You'll be fine. Now, let's get this gown done up."

Louise cast a sidelong glance at her husband. Martin was sitting in the visitor's chair on the other side of the hospital bed, glued to his phone, no doubt texting his mother, as usual. Shaking her head with a tut, she secured the oversized gown in place. It looked ridiculous, gaping at the back despite the knots she just tied. Clearly, they didn't make gowns for six year olds.

Poppy lowered herself back down and prodded at the waterproof dressing on the back of her hand. The numbing cream shifted with each poke, a thin ribbon of white squeezing out of a tiny gap where it wrinkled in on itself.

"Don't do that," Martin scolded, shifting to the side to put his mobile back in his jeans pocket. He scowled at Louise. "Why are you letting her do that? I thought you were watching her."

"I'm not *letting* her do anything." The words were clipped. God forbid he give her a little support. She opened her mouth, ready to point out he was just as capable of keeping an eye on their child as she was, when she noticed Poppy watching them. Clearing her throat, she softened her tone. "Want to do some coloring?"

Poppy nodded.

Reaching into the glaring-pink backpack, Louise pulled out a pencil case and a coloring book and set them down on the overbed table in front of Poppy.

"I'm going to get a coffee." Martin pushed himself up off his seat and stretched. "Want anything?"

Louise shook her head. The truth was, she could do with the caffeine, she barely slept a wink last night, but the idea of eating or drinking anything while she was this nervous set her already-roiling stomach into overdrive.

Watching her husband disappear through the veil secure entry doors and out of the children's ward, she shuffled back in her chair. Try as she might, she couldn't relax. Intrusive thoughts nagged at the back of her mind, offering up every worst case scenario. Until Poppy was safely back home, she would be on edge. She hated hospitals. The last time she had been inside one, she had watched her mother die. The time before that was her father. Her fear had become so irrational as a result that she had opted for a homebirth with Poppy, convinced something would go horribly wrong otherwise. Martin had argued with her, called her paranoid, crazy, stupid. But she had won out in the end. Hospitals meant death.

As if in response to her thoughts, a chill fingered its way down the back of her neck. She shivered, goosebumps pricking at her skin, and turned to look over her shoulder.

Nothing.

It was just her imagination getting the better of her. Even so, she tugged at the privacy curtain surrounding Poppy's bed to check that nothing was behind it. One of the nurses smiled at her from the other side of the reception desk. Warmth blooming in her cheeks, Louise returned the gesture and quickly pulled the curtain back in place.

Blowing out a breath, she leaned back and closed her eyes. For a while, the only sounds were the gentle scratching of pencil against paper and the muted conversations of the nurses and the two other families sharing the ward.

A shadow fell across her. She snapped her eyes open, bolting upright.

"Sorry, Mrs. Williams, I didn't mean to startle you. We're ready for Poppy now," the woman in blue scrubs said kindly.

"Oh. Right. Sorry, I was a million miles away. Come on, Pops." Wheeling the table back so Poppy could swing her legs off the bed, Louise helped her daughter with her slippers then took her hand as she hopped to her feet. She glanced at the empty seat left by her husband, wondering whether she should send him a text. He knew Poppy's surgery was scheduled first thing that morning, plus it wasn't like it would make any difference; only one of them was allowed to accompany their daughter to the anesthesia room, and Poppy had chosen her.

"My doll!" Poppy grabbed the ragdoll from the bed, hugging it tightly. She looked up at the nurse, the unspoken question clear.

The woman smiled. "You can take your dolly. She can keep you company while you're asleep."

Bending to grab the bottom of the oversized gown so her daughter wouldn't trip, Louise gave the woman a nod. She was ready.

The nurses behind the reception desk waved at them as they passed, offering words of encouragement to Poppy and telling her how brave she was. That earned them a shy giggle in return.

As the doors swung shut behind them, the feeling of eyes on her back made Louise shudder. She glanced over her shoulder, looking back through the glass panels, and saw a dark shape hovering next to her daughter's bed. Surely Martin wasn't back with his coffee already? She blinked her bleary eyes in an attempt to focus, but the shape was gone. Swallowing, she looked away. It was just her mind playing tricks on her. She was exhausted, after all.

They walked on, making their way through the corridor, past an elderly couple who were studying a way-finding sign and bickering in hushed tones, toward the lift. As the doors slid open and they stepped inside, Louise gave Poppy's good hand a reassuring squeeze.

"How are you feeling, honey?"

"Good." Poppy's smile faltered.

"Everything will be fine, I promise." Whether she was trying to reassure herself or her daughter she couldn't say, but it made her feel a little better all the same.

The lift lurched to a stop, making Louise's stomach flip. She gripped her daughter's hand tighter, watching the doors slowly yawn apart before stepping out.

The walk to the anesthesia room seemed somehow simultaneously endless and all too short.

"Right, mum," the nurse said, handing her a pair of blue overshoe covers, "pop these on, and then we can go in."

She did as instructed.

The room seemed tiny. What with her, Poppy, the anesthesiologist, the surgeon, two other men she didn't recognize, and the nurse who brought them up, there was barely any room to breathe.

Under the instruction of the doctors, Poppy climbed tentatively onto the operating bed.

Blinking rapidly, Louise fought against the tears pricking at her eyes. She had to stay strong. Crying would only upset Poppy or, worse, scare her even more than she already was. Everything was going to be fine. It had to be. If anything happened to her baby... she pushed the thought away before it could fully form.

The anesthesiologist she spoke to earlier that morning removed the waterproof dressing from Poppy's right hand and wiped away the numbing cream. He met Louise's gaze. "We're going to put the cannula in this hand so that it doesn't get in the way while we're operating."

She nodded robotically, aware he had spoken but not registering the words.

Something flickered in her peripheral vision. Her chest tightened. She turned her head, but whatever... *whoever* it was had gone.

"Are you okay?" the nurse asked, catching her look of confusion.

"I thought I just saw someone walk past." Doing her best to ignore the growing feeling of unease, Louise smiled down at her little girl. "Not long now."

"You're doing great." The anesthesiologist angled himself in an attempt to shield the cannula's insertion from Poppy. "Does your mummy call you Poppy, or do you have a nickname?"

"Not really. Sometimes she calls me Pops."

"And who's this you've got here with you?" He nodded to the ragdoll resting against the crook of her elbow, using the distraction to secure the thin, plastic tube in place.

"Myrtle."

"Myrtle?" Louise's forehead wrinkled. "I thought her name was Daisy?"

"It was." Poppy paused, watching as the anesthesiologist injected a clear liquid into the cannula.

"Lie back now, Pops," he said, swapping out the syringe for one filled with a milky-white substance. He caught Louise's eye. "Ready, mum?"

Louise gave a single nod, her stomach knotting.

Poppy continued, "But the lady in black said that she liked Myrtle better."

The hairs on the back of Louise's neck stood on end. "What lady in black?"

But before she could reply, Poppy was asleep, her gentle snores filling the space between them.

"Okay, mum. Give her a kiss, and we'll see you once she's recovered," the nurse said, giving Louise a moment before stepping back so she could move away from the bed. She glanced down at the plastic overshoes covering Louise's trainers. "Let me take those for you."

Numbly, Louise peeled them off, handed them over, and let herself get ushered into the corridor.

Her legs were jelly as she made her way back to the ward, her stomach a churning maelstrom of acid. Twice she had to pause by a waste bin, sure she was about to throw up. What had Poppy meant about the lady in black? Every fiber of her being wanted to sprint back the way she came and demand they stop the operation. Something was going to go wrong. She knew it.

No.

Swallowing hard, she braced her back against the wall, took a deep breath, and exhaled slowly.

She wouldn't let her paranoia get the better of her. It was a minor operation. Poppy would be fine.

Somehow, her feet found their way back to the ward. Pressing the button on the wall, she waited to be buzzed in. She was vaguely aware of a woman in pink scrubs beside her who dipped her head and made the sign of the cross while mumbling something as they entered. Managing a smile to the nurses as she passed, Louise slumped into the chair next to Poppy's empty bed. The sight made her shrink in on herself.

There was nothing to do now but wait.

Footsteps tore Louise from her daydreaming as a woman with dark hair approached. She straightened in her seat.

"I'm Elaine Smith, the locum consultant taking care of Poppy."

"How did it go? Is everything okay?"

"Everything's absolutely fine. Poppy's in recovery now. There was an unexpected complication, so we'll need to keep her in overnight for observation."

"Complication?" Louise shot Martin a look, her heart rabbiting inside her chest. His brow wrinkled in concern, but his eyes remained on the consultant.

"It's nothing to worry about. Like I said, Poppy's fine. She's awake now, groggy but awake and well. We believe she had a reaction to the anesthesia, which caused her heart to temporarily stop beating. It happens sometimes, but she was quickly stabilized and there were no further issues. We'll continue monitoring her, but all being well, there's no reason she shouldn't be discharged in a day or two." Elaine paused, her face softening. "I know that this must be alarming for you, but she's receiving the best possible care. Do you have any questions for me?"

"Can I see her?"

"Of course. We're going to transport her to the High Dependency Unit. If you want to grab your things, I'll take you there now."

Snatching her handbag from the floor and slinging it over her shoulder, Louise stood. Her hands shook as she gathered her daughter's coloring book and other bits, stuffing them hurriedly into the backpack, before following the consultant toward the doors. The words played on a loop inside her head.

Her heart stopped beating.

She swiped at her eyes and sniffed, unable to hold back her tears any longer. Aware of Martin keeping pace behind, she glanced over her shoulder. But he was already fixated on his phone—his fingers flying across the screen—oblivious to how desperately she needed his support at that moment.

With every step, the temperature seemed to drop, the chill seeping through skin and bone until it froze at her core. Louise shivered, chalking it up to skipping breakfast, until the consultant rubbed briskly at her own arms and grumbled.

It seemed like an eternity before they reached the HDU. At the sight of her daughter—wires connecting her to various pieces of monitoring equipment—Louise choked back a sob.

"Pull yourself together," Martin spat, his voice low enough so only she could hear.

Too overwhelmed to respond, she dried her eyes with the sleeve of her hoodie and willed the tears to stop.

Noticing their arrival, Poppy propped herself up unsteadily on her elbows. "Mummy? Daddy?" She swayed before collapsing back against the bed.

The consultant turned to regard them both. "Don't worry, disorientation is perfectly normal. It can take a while for the effects of the anesthesia to wear off. If you can, try and get her to eat and drink something."

Whatever else the woman might have said was lost on Louise as she moved to her daughter's bedside. Poppy was staring up at the ceiling, the barest of whispers ghosting across her lips.

Louise leaned closer.

"They took her away."

"Took who away, honey?"

"Myrtle."

Eyebrows knitting, Louise glanced at the ragdoll tucked in the crook of Poppy's elbow. "She's right here. Myrtle's right here."

"I had to do it. They deserved it. They took her away from me."

Every muscle in Louise's body tensed. "Do what, Pops? What did you have to do?"

"They took her away..." Poppy's eyelids fluttered shut, the words trailing off as sleep claimed her.

Goosebumps prickled across Louise's flesh. The sooner they were out of this Godforsaken place, the better.

"My grandbaby! How are you feeling, my gorgeous little girl? My goodness, look at the size of that bandage." Martin's mother swept through the ward toward Poppy's bed, practically barging Louise out of the way in her haste.

"Pauline, I didn't know you were coming." Louise turned to her husband.

He lifted his shoulders in a shrug.

Of course he would invite his mother to visit. Never mind the fact they had agreed for her to come over on the weekend, once Poppy had been discharged. Or that he knew the two of them didn't get on at the best of times. Christ, why couldn't he just be in her corner for once?

Oblivious to the fact Louise had spoken, Pauline continued. "Aren't you going to say hello to your nanny?"

Poppy looked up from her coloring. "Hello." The words were flat, devoid of any emotion.

Familiar fingers of ice crept up from the base of Louise's spine. She tried to remind herself Poppy was just tired. It had been a long couple of days for all of them. The nurses had said it might take a while for her to feel back to her old self again.

"Give Nanny a hug." Without waiting for a response, she flung herself at Poppy, wrapping her in a tight embrace.

Poppy remained motionless, her expression never changing. Not that Pauline seemed to notice as she pulled away and started fussing with the canvas bag hanging from her shoulder.

"Here, I've got you a present." She pulled out what looked like an oversized, pink shoebox and held it out. "Well, take it then, darling."

Unblinking, Poppy regarded the box before returning her gaze to her drawing.

"Look, I'll help you." Yanking off the lid, Pauline set the box down on the overbed table.

Inside was a doll wearing a glitzy pink party dress, matching faux-fur coat, and a pair of sparkly gold shoes. Its long blonde hair was held back from its face with a flower headband. Without a doubt, there would be glitter all over everything the moment it was removed.

Not even sparing the doll a second glance, Poppy pushed the box to one side, selected a red pencil, and continued coloring.

Pauline's smile dropped. "What's the matter? Don't you want it?"

"No, thank you."

"Poppy Ava Williams," Martin barked, pushing out of his seat to loom over his daughter, "don't be rude. Say thank you."

"I did."

A red stain flushed across Martin's cheeks. "Poppy, say thank you. Now."

"I did," she repeated evenly. "I said no, *thank you*."

"Poppy." His voice echoed, drawing frowns from the nurses.

"Martin," Louise hissed, "she doesn't want it."

Her husband shook his head, giving her a look like she was stupid. "She's being rude."

"I'm sure she'll play with it later. Just leave her be, she's tired."

"Look," Pauline continued, pulling the doll from the box in a cloud of glitter that drifted across the bed, "she's pretty, just like you."

Poppy ignored her.

"How about we move Daisy out of the way?"

"Her name is Myrtle." Poppy fixed Pauline with a dark look. "She's my baby. Please don't touch her."

"Well then, how about we let *Myrtle* meet her new sister. I'll just move her a little."

The moment Pauline's fingers closed around the ragdoll, Poppy let out a feral scream. She launched herself at her grandmother, sinking her teeth into the woman's arm. Pencils and sheets of paper scattered across the floor in an explosion of glitter.

"Poppy!" Louise and Martin moved as one, dragging their daughter away from the howling woman.

Blood beaded from Pauline's punctured flesh. She stared slack-jawed at Poppy, who was watching her from the cage of her parents' arms.

For a moment, all was silent.

Louise could feel the collective weight of every eye in the room on her daughter. She refused to look up. She couldn't have even if she wanted to; she was fixated on her mother-in-law's wound, on the rivulets of red tracking down her skin. Poppy did that. Her kind, sweet little girl just attacked her own grandmother.

"What the hell, Poppy?" Martin growled. "Mum, I'm so, so sorry. I don't know what came over her."

Pauline frowned down at her arm, then rose to her full height and took a step back. "That child has the Devil in her." Her hand flew to the gold cross at her neck.

Louise gasped. "Pauline! She's just overtired." Even as she said it, she knew how feeble it sounded.

"*Overtired*? She's behaving like an animal. What she needs is a good smack on the backside." Seeing that neither parent was willing to physically punish their child, Pauline huffed and snatched the doll, stuffing it back into the canvas bag. "Just wait until the vicar hears about this." She took two stomping steps in the direction of the doors, then stopped. Turning back on herself, she leaned across and ripped the ragdoll from Poppy's grip.

"No!" Poppy lunged forward, grasping desperately at nothing as Myrtle was stolen from reach. "No! My baby! You can't take my baby!" Her lips peeled away from her teeth in a snarl. She scrambled across the bed, the wires from the monitoring equipment stretched taut.

"No, honey! You'll hurt yourself!" Louise rushed forward, pinning her down as gently as was possible. Poppy writhed and thrashed in her grip. "Pauline! For

Christ's sake, give her back her doll!" A sharp, bony elbow caught her in the ribs. She gritted her teeth, aware one of the nurses had appeared by Poppy's bedside in an attempt to deescalate the situation.

Ignoring them all, Pauline tramped out of the ward.

"Mum, wait!" Martin jogged after her, the doors swinging shut behind him as he disappeared from view.

Poppy let out a shuddering moan and fell back against the bed. Her red-rimmed eyes glazed over. Her expression became eerily flat. "They took her away."

The words hit Louise like a fist to the gut. Her mind raced, taking her back to the moment Poppy first uttered them. A cold sweat formed on her palms; she wiped them down her jeans.

"Poppy?" Her daughter's eyes locked onto her, causing her heart to lurch inside her chest. "A—are you okay?"

"They took my baby."

"We'll get Myrtle back for you. But what you did to Nanny was wrong. Biting is never okay. You'll need to say sorry. Do you understand?"

"I understand."

The hollow quality to Poppy's voice turned her blood to ice.

Suppressing a shudder, she bent to retrieve the drawings from the floor. She froze in place, a gasp catching in her throat. Scrawled across the piece of paper were three figures in black, their mouths stretched in silent screams. And all around them in red, yellow, and orange were walls of flame. Fingers trembling, Louise crushed the drawing in her fist and shoved it in her hoodie pocket before the nurse could see it.

What in the hell was happening?

"I bet you're glad to be going home now, Poppy?" the nurse said with a warm smile.

"Yes," she replied, the corners of her mouth lifting all too slowly.

A wrinkle appeared between the nurse's eyebrows. "Uh, well, have a safe journey home."

Louise led her daughter away.

Poppy just needed a good night's sleep in her own bed. The operation had obviously taken its toll. As soon as they got home, everything would return to normal.

Once outside the ward, Louise released a heavy sigh. She could feel her daughter's eyes on her.

"What's wrong, honey?"

"Nothing, Mummy." Her focus drifted.

Louise followed her daughter's line of sight. One of the nurses she had come to recognize stopped just before the doors and made the sign of the cross.

"Excuse me," Louise said, "you're the second person I've seen doing that since we got here." She left the sentence hanging.

"Oh," the nurse waved her hand with a chuckle, "it's just a silly superstition."

"Superstition?"

"This used to be a convent, back in the day, before it burnt down and got rebuilt as a hospital. Apparently, the ghosts of the nuns still roam the halls, so we do that as a sign of respect. It's supposed to be good luck. I know it's all nonsense, but it's become a habit now."

Convent? Those shapes in the fire... Her throat suddenly dry, Louise pressed her hand against the balled up drawing in the pocket of her hoodie. Her pulse quickened.

Conversation over, the nurse nodded her goodbye.

"Come on," Louise said to Poppy, all too aware of the hitch in her voice, "Daddy's probably outside with the car by now."

Every step was leaden. She could scarcely remember the walk back through the hospital. It wasn't until Martin's voice finally broke through that she even realized she was sitting in the car.

"Are you going to shut the damn door or what?"

"What?"

"The door! Jesus, Louise, are you braindead or something?"

Snapping out of it, she pulled the door closed and buckled her seatbelt. The crumpled corners of the paper jabbed at her through her pocket. Adjusting her hoodie, she did her best to forget about it. Once they were back home, everything would be fine.

The world passed in a blur as they drove in silence. Louise fidgeted in her seat, the nurse's words nagging at the back of her mind. Pulling her phone from her bag, she opened Google and typed.

"Did you know there used to be a convent where the hospital is now? One of the nurses told me." She squinted at the screen as the car jolted over a bump in the road. "Apparently, it burnt down in 1852."

Martin grunted in response.

"Jesus." She covered her mouth with her hand, her eyes bulging as she read. Her husband didn't respond. Scrawling down the lines of text, she felt her heart rate increase. It was only when she let out an audible gasp that he bit.

"*What?*"

"According to the diary of one of the surviving Sisters, the fire was set deliberately by a novice. The girl was forced by her parents to join the convent to avoid a public scandal. Apparently, she went insane after giving birth..." she paused, her throat becoming tight, "when they took her baby from her."

Martin didn't react, but his eyes shifted to the rearview mirror, narrowing as they found Poppy.

He flicked the indicator up and made a right turn.

Louise watched through the passenger window as the road they usually drove down disappeared in the distance. She stiffened. "Where are we going?"

"I told mum we'd stop in for a bit before going home."

"You did *what?*"

"Poppy needs to apologize."

"Are you insane? Poppy *needs* to go home. She's tired. We both are. You know she didn't get much sleep at the hospital. She needs to rest, to decompress."

"Decompress," he scoffed, "what new-aged rubbish have you been filling your head with now? She's a child; she'll do as she's told. So will you."

"*Excuse me?*" Fire ignited inside her chest, flooding her insides until her whole body flushed with the heat of it. "Who the *hell* do you think you're talking to?"

"My wife. Maybe it's about time you started acting like it."

"Take us home."

Martin rolled his eyes and continued driving.

"Take us home. Right now."

"We'll be five minutes, tops."

"No, Martin. I want to go home. I mean it." She forced the words through clenched teeth.

Ignoring her, he glanced back up at the rearview mirror. "You want to go and see Nanny, don't you, Poppy? And say sorry for what you did?"

"Don't be a dick, Martin. Just take us home for Christ's sake." Louise twisted in her seat, angling herself toward her daughter and composing herself as best she could. "Poppy, we don't have to see Nanny if you don't want to."

Poppy tilted her head to the side, considering the question. "No, that's okay, Mummy. I'd like to go and see Nanny. I can get my baby back."

"See," Martin said, unable to keep the shit-eating grin from his face.

Louise deflated. She could feel her husband's self-satisfaction radiating off him in waves. It made her skin crawl.

He took a left, slowing the car to a stop outside Pauline's house, and killed the engine. "Come on then, let's go see Nanny."

It took everything she had to force herself to unbuckle her seatbelt and step out of the car. Sulking would only play up to Pauline's image of her as the childish girl who had stolen her son away. Well, after the things he just said, she was welcome to have him back.

The front door swung open before they even made it down the driveway, Pauline beaming as she set eyes on her granddaughter.

She was ashamed to admit it, but seeing the livid bruise and scabbed outlines of Poppy's teeth on Pauline's arm brought Louise a spiteful surge of amusement. Masking her resentment, she followed her family inside.

The living room was just as she remembered. White crocheted throws and pillows adorned the sofa and armchairs. Photos of children and grandchildren covered the walls. And there, just above the gas fireplace, was a wooden crucifix with a copper figure of Jesus hanging from it.

"Nanny, can I go play in the garden?" Poppy asked.

An emotion Louise couldn't quite decipher flickered across Pauline's face. "Oh, could you just wait a minute, darling? There's someone here I'd like you to meet first."

Louise's head whipped round. She arched an eyebrow in question at her husband.

"Let her play for a few minutes first, Mum," Martin said, his lack of shock telling Louise he already knew about the surprise visitor.

Poppy smiled, skipping out of the living room and into the kitchen. The door closed softly behind her.

Just as Louise was about to ask who Pauline wanted Poppy to meet, she heard the flush of the toilet. Moments later, a man in a black suit descended the stairs toward them. No. Not a man in a black suit—a vicar.

Louise looked from the man to Pauline and back again. "What's going on?"

"I just invited the vicar around for a cup of tea and a chat, that's all, dear."

Dear? In all the years she had known the woman, her mother-in-law had never referred to her as "dear." Then again, aside from Poppy's baptism, on which Pauline had practically bullied them, she had never been in the same room as Pauline *and* the vicar before. *Obviously keeping up appearances.*

'Hello, how are you, Louise?' the man said, holding out a hand amiably.

Accepting the handshake, she tried to piece together what was happening.

The vicar took a seat, adjusting one of the crocheted pillows behind his back. "Pauline's been telling me that Poppy's not been quite herself since her operation?"

She shot an accusing look at her mother-in-law. "Seriously?"

"It's okay, Louise, nobody's under attack here. Pauline just expressed some concerns about Poppy's behavior." His head moved in an almost imperceptible nod to the bruise on Pauline's arm.

"I suppose Pauline told you how she got that?"

"She did."

"And did she tell you that the reason she got bitten was because she took Poppy's favorite doll away from her? While she was recovering in hospital? After her heart stopped during surgery?"

The vicar frowned, confirming her suspicions. His face slipped back into a mask of serenity. "That must have been very hard on her. Do you mind if I have a little chat with Poppy?"

"Yes. As a matter of fact, I do."

Pauline's sudden intake of breath should have been expected. Her mother-in-law placed a hand over her chest as if mortally wounded. "Louise, this is a man of the cloth. Show a little respect. He's a guest in my home and has every right to speak to my granddaughter if he wants to."

"No, Pauline, he doesn't. Poppy is my daughter, something that you seem to keep forgetting, and—"

"Louise, stop," Martin growled. "She's my daughter too, and I say it's okay. You're making a scene."

"A scene?" She barked a humorless laugh. "If you want a scene, I'll give you a scene. I'm leaving. And I'm taking my daughter with me."

She strode toward the kitchen door. No sooner had she gripped the handle than Martin's hand was clamped around her upper arm, pulling her back.

Hissing in pain, she jerked away from him. "Martin, get off me! What are you doing?"

"Just be reasonable. You're acting like a crazy person. You're embarrassing me."

"I don't give a shit."

The dangerous glint in his eyes gave her all the warning she needed as he lunged for her again. She stepped to the side, slapping him across the face with all her weight. He staggered back, clutching his scarlet cheek, his mouth opening and closing like he had forgotten how to speak.

"Poppy, we're leaving," she bellowed, shoving the kitchen door open so hard it slammed against the wall.

Poppy was standing in front of the gas hob, staring intently at the microwave to her left as something rotated slowly inside. She spun, pulling Louise's attention from whatever was obscured behind the tinted door. A grin split her face as she thrust her ragdoll out triumphantly. "Look, Mummy, I found Myrtle."

"That's great, honey. Come on."

Marching back into the living room, clutching her daughter's hand, Louise ignored the indignant protests of her mother-in-law and made her way to the front door. Martin cut her off, his face red, the veins at his temples throbbing.

"You're not going anywhere, Louise. There's something wrong with Poppy ever since the operation. Even *you* must have noticed it."

She pulled Poppy behind her protectively. "She's still recovering."

"Are you stupid? The effects of the anesthetic wouldn't have lasted more than a day. She's not herself. The staring into space. The blank look in her eyes when she speaks. Our Poppy would never have attacked Mum like that."

"She's six, Martin! Six-year-olds have tantrums. What's the matter with you?" She shook her head and turned to address the vicar. "And what's your part in all this?"

The man hesitated, looking mortified. He held up his hands in a placating gesture, clearly struggling to find the words to answer her question.

"The vicar just wants a chat, that's all. I really don't understand why you're being so difficult," Pauline said. The slight lift at the corners of her mouth told Louise everything she needed to know; Pauline was enjoying this. No doubt news of her unhinged daughter-in-law would reach the congregation by the day's end, and with the vicar as a witness.

Louise glared up at Martin, only the sounds of their breathing and the muted drone of the microwave breaking the silence.

Poppy tugged at her hand urgently. "Mummy, I want to go home. Daddy's scaring me."

"You're scaring her. Are you happy now? Get out of our way."

His eyes narrowed to slits. He took a threatening step toward her.

A shrill scream burst from Poppy's mouth. "Don't hurt my mummy!"

Martin took a step back, anger morphing to shock, shock to guilt. He looked from his daughter to his mother, as if seeking further instruction. But Pauline's focus was on the vicar, who was frowning in obvious discomfort.

Elbowing her way past her husband, Louise threw open the front door. She shepherded her daughter outside quickly, letting the door slam shut behind them. Digging in her handbag as she half-jogged toward the car, she jerked her keys free.

Realizing she couldn't hear her daughter's footsteps, she turned on her heel, her heart leaping into her throat. "Poppy?"

Poppy twisted away from the front door to face her, slipping something into her pocket.

"Poppy, get in the car, honey. Quickly."

"Coming," her daughter replied in a sing-song voice, skipping toward her.

Once Poppy was secured in her car seat, Louise clambered into the driver's side and locked the doors. Her hand trembled as she pushed the key into the ignition. She took a shaky breath, the sound of her own pulse throbbing in her ears, and started the engine.

BOOM!

The deafening explosion shook the car. Louise screamed, her brain trying to make sense of what had just happened. Lurching around in her seat, she made sure Poppy was okay. Her daughter smiled back serenely at her.

Spinning back around, her mouth fell open. Thick plumes of black, acrid smoke were spewing up from the back of Pauline's house. She opened the car door and stepped out, her movements jerky and disconnected, like a marionette with tangled strings. The inside of the living room was filled with tongues of ravenous flame. And for a moment, she saw three figures, their mouths wide as agonized screams tore from their lungs, the fire already melting their clothes and blackening their flesh as it consumed them.

Louise made a strangled noise. She snatched a breath, the weight of her chest crushing her lungs. Mechanically, she pulled the drawing from her pocket, uncrumpled it, and held it up. Bile burnt at the back of her throat. She bent forward and retched, the paper slipping from her grip.

One of the figures peeled off from the rest, making a bid for the front door. It returned almost immediately, slamming its fists against the glass in a frenzy. Each blow left a bloodied smear of flesh and grease.

"Martin?"

"Don't worry, Mummy."

Numb, she followed the sound of Poppy's voice.

Her daughter fished in her pocket, then pulled out a silver key. "They deserved it. They took my baby."

The Hunter

Philip Fracassi

When I was a boy, the basement was my sanctuary.

I'd removed the bulb from the lone socket in that empty concrete room, preferring the dark. The stairs—rotting naked wood but sturdy—could only be illuminated via the open door at the top, leading to a hallway that was murky, even on bright days.

At first, the basement was a hiding place, while above, my father stomped and screamed, hunting for me. Veins thrumming with poison.

Later, it became a dare.

How long could I sit in the dark? Invisible to myself. To him.

Huddled within that perfect black, I became nothing. Ether. Pure spirit.

Even shadows need light to exist.

Without light, Father would not come down. He'd holler from the opening, angry and terrified. A mad dog barking at the void. Below, I'd sit quietly in the center of the cold concrete room, watching the shape of him.

To my father, I was formless; a rogue memory of hate stretched across the basement's expanse, pure as outer space. My eyes, perhaps, pinprick stars.

It was only after several visits to that underground world, that lightless void, that I began to feel the other.

To commune.

The first time, timid fingers pressed at the back of my neck. Cold. Dry.

I gasped but did not move. Could see nothing. Held my breath and ignored my thumping heart as she brushed my cheeks, lightly touched my closed eyelids, and pressed against my bare knees. An icy hand slid up my shirt, spreading like a starfish against my spine while I took deep breaths of moist, chilled air.

I was not afraid.

Meanwhile, upstairs, my father screamed and beat the floor with footsteps like thunder, his anger a thunderstorm unleashed in hallways and bedrooms and kitchens. After a time, once things calmed in the house above, I'd leave the basement. Slowly, quietly. I'd leave her and return to my bedroom. I'd make a sandwich, steal a Coke, hide behind a flimsy door. I'd play the part of boyhood. The role of Son. And Father would breathe heavy in his own bed, a balustrade of guardianship between cannons of violence.

Days would pass. Weeks.

Often, I'd return to the darkness in the basement. To what waited for me there, eager now, craving my warmth. I'd allow it to do what it wanted while my father hunted. Whisper in my ear, draw on my flesh with pointed fingernails.

As the life above became more ethereal, my life below became an entrapment. A cautious dialogue building toward something more concrete, more binding.

I'd wince and softly cry while she carved herself into my skin, feverishly speaking words of comfort as if both our lives depended on it.

The last time he caught me I'd been asleep in my room.

It was late, and I'd thought myself safe. But he'd kicked in the door, howling. Yanked away my blanket and threw it to the soiled carpet. His large hand clenched my ankle and yanked me off the bed. My body thumped to the floor. I reached for a hold, for something to save me, as he dragged my body into the tight hall. He strode wordlessly as I panted in terror, sliding against rough wood, naked but for boxers, one size too small.

In the kitchen, peeled lips of chipped linoleum scraped across my back. I winced but did not cry out. Still clutching my leg, eyes wild with delirious need, he searched the drawers for an instrument. Silverware waterfalls crashed to the floor; spatulas and worn wooden spoons clattered. Finally, he pulled out a knife with a black handle, the blade maybe three inches. What you might use to peel an apple.

I jerked free of his grip, flipped over, and began to crawl. Suffocating terror filled my chest and throat. But he was fast—evil things always are—and reached my legs, dropped his weight on the backs of them, trapping me. He stabbed the knife into my left calf and began to cut upward in a vertical line. A black flesh butcher muttering indecipherable words—a language born from needles—as he sawed open my leg, blade chewing through muscle.

I screamed, but the pain adrenalized, gave me strength. I yanked my other leg free and kicked heel into jaw. He grunted, loosened his hold, and I kicked again, met bony shoulder. I sprang to my feet and ran for the basement, ignoring the burning and bleeding, the damage he'd done.

I yanked open the door and made it one step. He shoved me from behind and I flew forward into the dark, arms raised in protection. I landed hard on the stairs; ribs and hip bone hit edges, breath punched from my lungs. I scurried like a spider down the last few steps across the cold floor.

"Help me," I panted.

The temperature plummeted as if one of the walls had split like a mouth to reveal an abyssal, web-strewn cave leading to a dark ocean. She emerged and pressed her hungry, ghostly flesh against mine. One long arm wrapped itself around my bare, skinny waist. Her mouth, the only warm part of her, sucked on my ear. Too many teeth nibbled at the edges. Her voice the scrape of rust off metal.

"Promise," she whispered.

I nodded, my body trembling with cold and fear. Blood flowed freely down my burning leg, and I felt my mind weaken. "Yes," I said, knowing what she wanted of me. She'd asked so many times... "Yes."

Father paced the hallway, his restless shadow a fluttering crow's wing through the basement's open door. He mumbled, argued, screamed. All the while stomping his boots, his petulant anger confused by murderous desire, his twisted brain unknotted by clean thoughts of murder.

"Coward!" I yelled. "Bitch coward!"

He broke like an avalanche, pounding down the stairs as if using six legs instead of two. Inarticulate yelps and barks sounded above beating limbs, his poisonous mouth stuffed with pigs as they were chopped and gutted.

He had just stepped off the last stair onto the concrete when the door above slammed shut, sealing us in with cold finality. Heavy, rapid breathing moved through the dark as he hunted, boots scraped concrete as I slid silently away. I found a corner and tucked into it, made myself small.

As my eyes adjusted, I could make out his form moving side-to-side, arms swiping, feet kicking, hoping to catch flesh.

She whispered something as she let me go and moved in, a spider dancing toward prey. When she wrapped her arms around him, he shrieked into the dark. He cried out for me and begged, the surge of sobriety a terror reflex, an eruption of clarity triggered by the human desire to stay alive.

As he wept and roared, she fed. I watched the dark shadow of his body compress and warp into unnatural angles. A doll made of sticks. The snap of bones were midnight gunshots mixed with the guttural squelch of pressure-split skin; a splash of blood hit the floor as if from an overturned bucket.

Satiated, she came back to me. Icy fingers carved frantically into my flesh. I laid back and spread my arms and legs as she worked.

Hours later, I emerged.

I knotted a kitchen towel around my leg to slow the blood trickle running over my heel. One wound of many.

In the bathroom, I studied my naked body, bathed in hazy yellow.

My palms were no longer creased with lines but concentric circles. Hieroglyphs had been etched into my skin—the inside of my thighs. My back. My neck. My belly.

A promise tattooed into flesh. A contract.

Where I live, there are many fathers like mine.

Fat black flies.

Adventurous Spirits

Jon Cohn

"Check out this one," Gulch said, shoving a picture on a phone in front of Peter's face.

Even though he was in the midst of navigating them down a steep dirt road in his Jeep, Peter's eyes couldn't help but glance at the image.

In the picture was a figurine standing on a table, roughly the size of his thumb. It was a meticulously painted miniature depicting George Washington crossing the Delaware. However, in this version, George was a beautiful and busty woman in what looked more like a wet t-shirt contest than a national conquest.

"This is weird in ways I can't even begin to describe," Peter said, shaking his head and returning his concentration to the pockmarked road.

"It's not weird!" Gulch protested, defending his hobby. "Do you have any idea how much demand there must be for a company to produce these? The molds for figures cost at least ten grand each!"

"Don't make this worse," Peter said as he drove through thickening Hawaiian rainforest. He was in his third year of grad school, studying anthropology, while Gulch was already in his second year of teaching European history at their old high school.

Kristen, the final core member of their childhood friend group, who was in the midst of working toward her masters in forensic science, popped up between them from the back seat. With a mischievous grin, she said, "In a way, having gender-bent generals is actually kind of progressive of him."

"Come again?" Peter asked, his face turning red.

"Think about it. By replacing his army's leaders with women, he's kind of making a statement that he feels women should have always been represented with the strength and cunning on the battlefield as their male counterparts."

"Absolutely not," Peter said. "Have you seen the boobs on lady George Washington?"

"I call her Georgina," Gulch corrected.

"This isn't an empowering representation. It's a pin-up fetishization that's reductive and just plain stupid," Peter said.

Kristen couldn't help but rub it in. "You're just mad because you have a weird stick up your ass about alternate histories." She knew right where to poke Peter to get him worked up. In her defense, his rants were always entertaining.

"It's just that the point of history is to learn from it, not to rewrite or exploit it. Of all people, you two should understand how important it is to acknowledge the actions of our predecessors instead of treating it like a game. Real people fought and died in these wars. They should be respected, not made into a game or warped into a spectacle."

Peter awaited a retaliatory remark from Gulch, but Gulch's focus shifted as Peter pulled up toward their destination.

"I thought you said this was some sort of forbidden road, away from all the tourists and stuff?" Gulch asked as the car drove into an impromptu parking lot. They had turned off the highway and driven past numerous Off Limits signs down the old Pali Road. Still, their car came to the same inevitable conclusion as every other hidden spot on O'ahu—the secret was out. Nearly a dozen rental cars had paved new trails across already-beaten vegetation.

Peter grinned. This was exactly the response he hoped for from his friends visiting him on spring break. He pulled up and joined the crowd of cars, considering for a moment he should feign disappointment, but his pride got the better of him. Peter pointed at a cluster of hikers staring at their phones as they trekked up a dirt path that hugged a mountain.

"See where they're going? That's the path that circles Nu'uanu Pali, ending in a breathtaking view of the whole valley. But that's not where we're going." Peter pointed down an embankment to the left, toward a steep drop down through a dense thicket of trees.

To his right, Gulch grinned.

In the back, Kristen squinted. "Is there even a trail down there?" While she was an experienced hiker, Kristen had been hoping she would spend more of her vacation reading on beaches. This was their third hike in as many days. She knew Peter was excited to share everything he learned studying Hawaiian history, but she was really looking forward to taking a break from academia for a week. Kristen had considered sitting this one out in favor of a swim and a margarita at a resort near Peter's apartment, but he pulled her back to his side when the promise of a "haunted trail" came up.

"It's a little tricky to get down that first bit, but that's what makes it a real secret. If the trail was easy, it would be just another tourist spot." To illustrate his point of caution, he waited until the group of strangers turned the corner of their well-beaten trail before he stepped out of the car. "With a little luck, I think we'll all be in for a real treat." The trio approached the patch of trees leading into the rainforest. "You see down this way?" Peter drew a line with his hand between a narrow crack between trees. "If you look carefully, you can see the ground's been disturbed. If you use the trees to brace yourself, you can sort of slide down."

"Sure, but you go first," Gulch said.

Peter swallowed a laugh. Gulch was up for anything as long as he wasn't the first to make a potential ass of himself. To be fair, an unfortunate tumble during a Boy Scout camping trip in eighth grade was what earned him the nickname Gulch in the first place. To his students, he was Mr. Stanton. But to Peter and Kristen, he would forever be Gulch.

After one last look to check for tourists, Peter braced his hand against a tree and eased down the bank, helping each of his friends with the tricky footing as they descended. "Look," Peter said, pointing ahead, "the trail's much easier to follow from here."

"Well, I'll be damned," Gulch said, noticing a distinct partition in the knee-high vegetation covering the forest. "For a second, I thought you were just bringing us to a nice secluded spot to kill us."

"I'd be careful mentioning death around here. The ghosts might hear you," Peter said, leading them down the trail.

"Ooh, so spooky," Gulch taunted. "Are you gonna tell us the story or just keep dropping cryptic hints?"

Peter turned back briefly with a grin. "Did you see the tourist stop we passed on Highway 61, just before getting off? That's Nu'uanu Pali Lookout, a popular tourist spot. But what really makes it interesting is that it was the location of one of the bloodiest battles in Hawaiian history."

"Now we're talkin'," Gulch said.

"It's a long story, but I'll give you the ghost-tour-guide version. King Kamehameha was on a quest to rule all the islands of Hawaii, and he was doing a pretty damn good job of it. His last stop was here, on O'ahu, against a leader named Kalanikūpule. The battle started from the southern shore of the island and ended right up on the top of that mountain." Peter pointed up and to his right, but by this point, the cover of trees made it impossible to see the huge mountain that stood only a few hundred feet away.

"Kamehameha eventually cornered all of Kalanikūpule's men at the edge of the cliff. Kamehameha had clearly won, but he didn't care. He pushed his men onward, literally forcing Kalanikūpule's army to be shoved off the edge of the cliff. In the end, nearly seven hundred men fell over a thousand feet to their deaths. Today, the spot is called Nu'uanu Pali Lookout, but the Hawaiian's call it Kaleleka'anae, which translates to 'leaping mullet.'"

"That's fuckin' gnarly," Gulch said. "Is that where we're headed?"

Peter shook his head. "Nah, that's actually where those other tourists are headed."

"What?" Gulch's voice dropped in disappointment. "Then where the hell are we going? I thought you said this trail was haunted."

"That trail is. There's a bunch of messed up stuff that's happened over the years on old Peli road; that's why they closed it. But that whole area's been trampled over and picked clean. You're more likely to find a Snickers wrapper there than any trace of history. We're going somewhere else.

"See, the leader who lost, Kalanikūpule, didn't die during the battle. It's rumored he hid with a small group of companions in a cave somewhere nearby before Kamehameha eventually found him and publicly sacrificed him to his war god. But here's the thing. No one's ever found the cave, as far as we know."

Kristen raised a skeptical eyebrow. "And you're saying you found it?"

Peter shrugged like it was no big deal. "All I'm saying is that in my time at the university, I've made friends with a number of locals who have given me a tip or two."

"And how did you do that?"

"Persistence!" Peter dramatically shot a finger into the air to illustrate his point.

"So you're saying you were an incessant pain in their asses until they told you what you wanted to hear so they'd leave you alone?" Kristen said.

"You know me so well." Peter turned back at her and grinned.

"So how do you know they didn't just lead you on a wild goose chase?" Gulch asked.

"Great question. See, I thought the same thing myself. Last week, I decided to check it out anyway, and I found this." Peter reached into his pocket and produced a single brown tooth. He passed it down the line to his friends, as if for show-and-tell.

By the time the tooth reached Kristen, she was unconsciously tonguing her own mouth, feeling for a molar that might resemble the one in her hand. "I'm calling bullshit. How do you know this is even a human tooth?"

"I've already taken it to a friend in the biology department who owed me a favor. Not only is it human, she says it's at least a couple hundred years old."

"And you think this might belong to... I'm not even going to try to pronounce his name," Kristen said.

"Either Kalanikūpule or one of his soldiers. I seriously doubt he escaped alone," Peter said.

Kristen narrowed her eyes, feeling the fingers of a good mystery wrapping around her. While Peter's life went the way of anthropology, Kristen moved into the world of forensic science. In a way, they both were after the same thing in their careers, Gulch too, as a history teacher. They all wanted to learn about the past. Even though their methods largely differed, at some point or another it always came back to digging around in the dirt.

"How far from here did you find this?" Kristen asked.

"About ten minutes from here."

Gulch let out a loud hiccup of a laugh. "You think you're going to find the lost cave of this guy and then score his secret treasure?"

"No, I think *we're* going to find Kalanikūpule's secret cave together and hopefully find some artifacts, like a shield, some garments, a tribal relic..."

"Come on, buddy, you don't have to bullshit around us." Gulch grabbed Peter's shoulders and jiggled his skinny body like Jell-o. "You want some outsiders to help you bring back a history trophy to score points with the university, right?"

"Pretty much," Peter admitted. "I think I have a fairly good idea of where the cave might be. I was going to make up a story that on my last trip down here I decided to wait so we could all discover the cave together, but the truth is, I looked and couldn't find it. I was hoping some fresh eyes might help."

They stepped into a clearing, and the Hawaiian sun immediately brought beads of sweat across Gulch's brow.

For the first time since starting their descent, they could see Nu'uanu mountain and the Old Pali trail that ran alongside it. The group of tourists were just tiny specks hiking up the side of the cliff.

"Tell you what, I'll make you a deal," Gulch said. "Since this is all about battles, you gotta give me one in return."

Peter groaned. Kristen laughed. "You're still on this?"

"Next time we're on the mainland, you gotta play Battlefield Blitz with me. And not just one game either. I mean like a full weekend of tabletop wargaming."

Battlefield Blitz was an extraordinarily complicated historical war simulation board game in which players had to literally build their armies in the form of miniature figurines. Gulch had purchased, glued, and painted hundreds of minis for this game over the years.

Peter rolled his eyes, remembering Gulch's excitement over gender-bending his leaders, and headed back into the cooler shade of the trees. "Don't you have any other games? Remember that fantasy one we used to play that had trolls with cow catapults and stuff? That was fun."

"Nope, and you gotta play as Georgina Washington."

"Hang on." Peter silenced them, his eyes hardened by concentration. Underneath the wild bird calls and the wind's constant chattering of leaves came a low droning sound,steady and quiet. "Do you guys hear that?" Checking around for his bearings, Peter figured they were still another five minutes from where the trail split where he thought the cave might be. But there was this new sound, this steady beat, that drew him into waist-high brush.

"Don't try to change the topic. Are you in or what?" Gulch asked.

"I'm serious, be quiet and follow me." Carving his own path was difficult—the plant life was tall and overbearing—but the farther Peter dug in, the more sure he became about his suspicions. "Do you hear that now?"

Drums. And not just that, but voices too, singing in an unknown language.

"What's that?" Kristen asked.

"I have no idea," Peter responded. He finally pushed his way into another small clearing, where another trail unknown to him headed directly toward the base of a small mountain, maybe a tenth of the size of Nu'uanu. From here, the sound grew tinny and garbled, as if coming out of a tunnel.

Then they saw it. An overgrown mass of vines had all been neatly swept aside to reveal the mouth of a cave about six feet in height. Inside was an inviting darkness, a promised answer to questions both asked and unasked.

"Whoa, what are you doing?" Kristen's hand caught Peter as he trekked toward the cave.

"I'm going to check it out. This is what we came for!" Peter said, as if it was the most obvious thing in the world.

"You sure that's safe? I heard that locals don't really love tourists encroaching on their personal space, and this certainly doesn't seem like a tourist event," Kristen said.

"We won't know until we find out," Gulch said, pushing forward to keep up with Peter as they entered the cave.

Without much choice, Kristen followed.

Inside the cave, the first thing they noticed was the intensifying of the sound. It reverberated off the walls, creating echoes that beat out of tune and made the ceremony sound warped and distorted.

Peter pulled a flashlight from his backpack, while Gulch and Kristen activated the flashlight apps on their phones. The cave stretched on, twisting and turning while always staying just tall enough to force the boys to hunch. After the first few hundred feet, the light from the entrance was completely swallowed into cool, damp darkness.

"Do you smell incense?" Kristen asked in response to a growing earthy scent that burned at her nostrils.

"It's sandalwood. Hawaiian's have been using it for over 4000 years for medicine, clothing, food; it's everywhere. This smell could be from garments left behind by Kalanikūpule or his men," Peter said.

"Smells too strong for that," Kristen said.

"Plus, I'm not seeing any of those artifacts you were talking about," Gulch added, snapping his flashlight around the floor.

Peter saw a faint hint of light ahead. "Turn off your flashlights. And stay quiet." He slowed his steps across the uneven dirt floor. Though as light at the end of the tunnel grew from a pinhole to the size of a watermelon, the sound of singing and drums amplified to the point where Peter suspected even a tumble as severe as the one that earned Gulch his nickname would fail to be heard.

There were shapes outside. Bright reds and yellows bounced and swayed against a rainforest background. Peter crouched as he finally reached the mouth of the cave. There was a small, round valley etched into the mountain. Sheer cliffs stood all around a sunken patch of fertile ground no larger than a baseball field. Inside was a circle of men dressed in bright capes, wearing helmets topped with feathered mohawks striped red, black, and yellow. While some played drums, others held spears, axes made of wood lined with razor-sharp shark's teeth, even a few muskets.

Several soldiers parted to Peter's left, and a procession of men and women stepped in, wearing a combination of modern day suits and traditional Hawaiian garb. They moved slowly into the circle, with several young adults no older than Peter holding the handrails of a wooden cot containing an ancient looking man. The old man's body was dressed as the soldiers around him, though his cape looked somehow cheap, his helmet made of costume material, next to the intricately-woven headpieces of the soldiers.

Gulch tapped Peter's shoulder and pointed to one of the pallbearers. "Is that dude wearing crocs? What the hell is going on right now?" he whispered.

"It's a funeral. Someone I'm guessing was either distantly related to Kalanikūpule or one of his soldiers. This must be some sort of family burial ground." Peter pulled out his phone and began recording.

"Hey, do you think you should maybe turn that off?" Kristen said. "This seems kind of like a private event we're crashing here."

"Are you kidding? I've seen 18th Century O'ahu ceremonial garb before, but never in this condition. And never in this amount. And god forbid, never worn by actual people. This is incredible. Not only has this cell been able to preserve a three-hundred-year tradition, they've managed to do it completely in secret." Peter read their faces, looking for traces of excitement. He found nothing from Kristen and turned to Gulch. "This is what we came for, right? We were going to discover a cave, maybe an artifact? Look what we've found! This is a whole treasure trove of information."

"In all seriousness, if you thought Lady Washington was disrespectful, then you should probably think about what you're doing right now," Gulch said, siding with Kristen.

"Don't start with that shit right now," Peter said, focusing his attention on his phone's screen.

"I mean it, Peter. Didn't you say like ten minutes ago that people shouldn't play Battlefield Blitz because it's taking advantage of people that actually died? This is literally the exact same thing, but none of them are hot chicks."

Peter bit his lip, standing at the cross-section of opportunity and principle. He thought of a third option—compromise.

"What if we wait for them to finish, and then afterward we'll talk with them and ask for permission to save the footage. If they want us to delete it, no problem."

Gulch twisted his lip, contemplating it. Kristen, on the other hand, was having none of it.

"Do you see the weapons those men are holding over there?"

"It's ceremonial."

"They have guns, Peter."

"From the 1700s. It's an indigenous tribal funeral, not a biker gang. I'm sure they'll be reasonable." As Peter spoke, he pinched two fingers on his phone, zooming in on one of the muskets in question.

Kristen still wasn't having it. Even though she was new to the world of forensic science, she had learned enough to know when to remove herself from a potentially dangerous situation. Even beyond her training, there was something about this that didn't feel right. Something about looking at the soldiers made her head hurt, like she was staring into a magic-eye puzzle and had crossed her eyes for too long. While they were there, clear as day, she also felt like her brain had to actively work to keep them in focus.

"I'm heading back," Kristen said, pulling her phone from her pocket and taking a step back. Her dizziness, combined with the uneven ground and sweaty palms, caused her phone to slip from her hands. The world seemed to slow down as she tried and failed to catch it. All she could do was watch in horror as it clattered its way down the rocky embankment leading into the ceremonial circle.

Kristen gasped. She shouldn't have been able to hear it over the chanting and drumming, but that all ceased in perfect synchronicity as soon as her phone clattered into their sacred space. Instead, her outcry of shock reverberated in the tight valley, making Kristen sound like she was in a dozen places at once.

"Na'u!" From somewhere in the crowd, a single soldier raised a barbed spear, pointing it directly at the trio.

"Na'u!" another shouted, gripping an ax tightly in one hand and pointing an accusatory finger with the other.

Dozens followed suit. What felt like a hundred eyes burned into them.

All the while, Peter kept his eyes glued to his phone's screen.

"Come on, man, turn it off," Gulch said. "We gotta go."

The soldiers were chanting, all in perfect unison. "Na'u! Na'u! Na'u!"

The picture on the screen trembled as Peter's hands shook. Finally, he shoved the phone in his pocket and pulled out the flashlight. "Let's go."

Peter pivoted, staring down to find the button on his flashlight as he re-entered the tunnel. The flashlight nearly fell when Peter collided with a body that felt as sturdy as a tree. Another soldier blocked the way back, but it was worse than just that.

This man was different. Instead of vibrant ceremonial clothes, he wore a red loincloth, with feathered bracers on his arms. A line of black, triangular tattoos ran up the side of his face, which was filthy. His forehead was split vertically, and a river of blood ran freely into one of his mad eyes and down his cheek. His mouth opened, revealing brown, rotting teeth, some of which had fallen out. Blood spattered from his lips onto Peter's face as he growled, "Na'u!"

Peter felt himself pulled back into the sun as three more wounded soldiers appeared from inside the tunnel. They were surrounded by soldiers on all sides.

"Maybe we should apologize to them," Kristen said, her voice reduced to a squeak under the oppressive chant.

"I don't think it will do any good." While unhelpful, Peter's words rang true as the circle closed around them. Men pointed their weapons at them from all sides, moving in step with each other to trap the invaders. When there was nowhere else to move, and they all squeezed in as tightly as they could, the soldiers stopped their advance and ceased their chant. The bleeding soldier, standing face to face with Peter, raised his ax and shouted, "Kūka'ilimoku!"

The ring of soldiers all simultaneously reached down to the dirt yet came up with handfuls of sand. Once again, the bloodied soldier cried out, "Kūka'ilimoku! Na'u!" And all at once, every soldier blew their handfuls of sand directly into the trios' faces.

The grit of the sand coated Peter's eyes. It was as if the whole world fell away when the pain from the sand hit him. He fell to his knees, trying to blink it away but only causing more stinging as his lids scraped like cheese graters against his corneas. By the time he worked up enough tears to clear his fuzzy vision, he wondered if he could believe his eyes.

There was no one there, save for him, Gulch, and Kristen.

"Jesus H. Fuck that hurt!" Gulch cried, still reeling from the pain.

Kristen, on the other hand, stood in silent shock, surveying her surroundings and feeling her sanity growing brittle. What had once been blocked from their view by the collective of soldiers was a small grove containing several dozen pyramids of rocks. One stack, closest to them, sat upon what Kristen knew all too well to be a fresh grave.

"Peter, what the hell just happened?" Kristen demanded, noticing his face wore an expression closer to terror than shock.

"Night Marchers. Oh god, we have to go." Peter clicked on his flashlight and hurried toward the cave where they entered before.

"Care to elaborate on that? Where did they all go?" Kristen's voice boomed with the aid of the tunnel's walls.

"Yeah, and do you mind slowing down? Those bastards blew sand into my eyes! What a dick move!" Gulch said.

"How are you not more concerned by this? Am I the only one who just saw what happened?" Kristen snapped.

"Of course I'm concerned," Gulch said, "It's just that my eyes hurt really goddamned badly, and it's hard to be worrying about two things at once."

Kristen grunted at Gulch's apathy, only further driving her toward feeling like she was going mad. "Peter, you better tell me what the hell the Night Marchers are right now, or I swear to the Lord above, I'm going to rip that flashlight out of your hands and beat you to death with it."

"You wanted to see ghosts, right? Well, we just pissed off a whole bunch of them. Night Marchers are, to locals at least, not something to mess around with. If they spot you, or if you get in the way of their march, they'll kill you."

"This may sound like a stupid question," Gulch said, rubbing away the last of the sand from his eyes. "Shouldn't Night Marchers typically only be out at night? It's, like, one in the afternoon."

"Traditionally, yes. Most stories of encounters with the Night Marchers do take place at night. But there are stories about ancestors of decorated warriors being laid to rest by Night Marchers during daytime ceremonies. I'm pretty sure that's what we just stumbled into."

Kristen's heart pounded as she followed Peter's light through the tunnel, feeling claustrophobia tear away at her ability to keep the mother of all panic attacks at bay. "Alright, just one more question. What was that word they kept saying?"

"Na'u," Peter said, almost sounding guilty. "It means 'mine.'"

"Cool, so we're all tagged for death by killer ghosts now, is that what you're saying?"

"If you believe the legends," Peter said, trying and failing to sound like he wasn't equally buying into this.

Because this was insane, Kristen figured. What they just collectively saw was something that had no rational explanation.

"There it is," Gulch said, as if he caught Peter in a trap. "Don't you see, Kristen? This is all Peter and his friends. They staged the whole thing."

"Oh, come on. You don't actually believe that, do you?"

"Between a prank and killer ghosts? Yeah, I do. I'll admit it wasn't cool blowing sand in our eyes, but we were blinded for, what, at least a minute? Plenty of time for them to sneak out a back exit or something. It's just a joke, right?"

Peter didn't answer, instead splitting his attention between navigating the tunnel ahead with his flashlight and rewatching the video on his phone.

Kristen, choosing to ignore Gulch's denial, focused back on Peter. "How do we stop them? There has to be something in Hawaiian legends about stopping Night Marchers once you've been marked."

"There's a lot of different legends. One says you have to get an ancestor of the tribe to speak on your behalf and get them to forgive you; another has you collecting some sort of plant as a tribute, and another has you lying on the floor face down."

"Oh come on, now you know he's making this shit up. Just watch, tonight he'll have us all lying face down in the dirt as his buddies take pictures of us looking like idiots. Besides, what happened to the dude in crocs? Was he a ghost too?"

"It's not a prank!" Peter finally snapped. "I don't know what we just saw, and I'm doing my best to come up with some sort of explanation."

"Then what do we do?" Kristen asked.

Peter swallowed. It did nothing to soothe his dry mouth or throat. "The people who told me about this place—how would they know about it unless they were somehow connected? Maybe they can speak for us to show that we're sorry."

"Maybe you should start by deleting that video." Kristen pointed to what was still playing on his phone.

Peter clicked it off and shoved it into his pocket. "If they're ghosts from the 1700s, they have no idea what a phone even is. I have actual proof of the supernatural. If we do survive the night, the world needs to see this."

"No, and in fact, I would say they shouldn't. You want to talk about respecting history versus changing it? How soon after you put out this video is this cave going to be full of tourists? Bodies will be dug up by grave robbers, and this cultural tradition dies. Do you want to be responsible for that just so you can get a pat on the back from the university?"

Peter gave her a hard look, then turned away to keep moving. "I'm not making any decisions right now, but deleting the footage isn't the answer. Come on, the entrance to the cave should be just around the corner. If we hurry, we can make it to my source's house by nightfall."

Except when they turned the corner, they found nothing but more tunnels. They hurried down to the next turn, and the next.

"This isn't right," Gulch said. "We should be out by now."

They pushed ahead, seeming to speed up around every corner until they were all but sprinting in the darkness. Finally, after what felt like ten minutes of snaking corridors, they saw an opening creep into view. It should have come as a relief, but instead, it only served up a fresh wave of dread.

It was dark outside.

"What the hell?" Gulch checked his phone. "How could it already be eight? It was one when we stepped into that cave. There's no way we've been wandering for seven hours."

"Still think it's a prank?" Peter asked without a trace of humor. "Let's just get to the car and put as much distance between us and this cave as possible."

"That's easy to say on an island the size of Phoenix," Gulch said.

While it was harder to catch the trail in the dark, Peter was able to find the wake of damaged and disturbed plants he and his cohorts created on their way in. Reaching the trail, then the car, was a relative breeze since they all had adrenaline on their side. What brought an extra spring to their step was a quiet but insistent beat they could all hear in the distance, though none of them dared to mention it.

Once they climbed the embankment of trees, they piled into the car, with Peter at the wheel, Gulch beside him, and Kristen in the back. As he twisted the key in the ignition, the blaring sound of a conch shell rang out through the night.

"That can't be good," Gulch said.

Peter flipped the car around and tore across the dirt trail, climbing toward Highway 61. No matter how fast he drove, the sound of drums only grew louder. Peter turned on the radio to try to drown it out. Through static crackled a chant, this one sounding more gruff and aggressive, like a mantra warriors carried into battle. Fighting frustration and fear, Peter attempted to change the station on the radio, searching for something to ground him to sanity.

"Look out!"

Gulch's cry brought Peter's attention sharply toward the road. A pair of red-and-yellow-cloaked warriors stood there, each holding a spear out in front of them. In a split second reaction, Peter swerved to the left.

While he managed to avoid one of the spirits on the highway, the Night Marcher on the left passed through the car as if he was made of nothing more than fog. His spear, on the other hand, seemed to be made of something else entirely. As the warrior slipped through the hood and into the cab of the car, his spear impaled Gulch through the neck. As the car careened through the ghostly bodies, they took a souvenir with them. Through a blood-soaked but otherwise undamaged car, Peter looked in the rearview mirror to see the body of his childhood friend hanging loosely from the end of a spear in the middle of the road.

"Peter!" Kristen shouted. Surely she was screaming about the same impossible thing he just witnessed.

He was wrong. Instead, Kristen was shouting for Peter to look out for the locked fence just ahead, indicating Nu'uanu Pali Lookout. The car slammed into the fence, knocking it over but, in the process, shredding the tires of the car with four ear-splitting pops. Peter and Kristen were jostled around as the car rolled to a stop on its own, a mere fifty feet from the cliff where 700 of Kalanikūpule's men once plummeted to their death.

Kristen threw open the back door of the car and ran toward a tiny kiosk nearby, hoping to find some form of solace inside.

"Wait!" Peter called, knowing the building would offer no protection. He looked behind, at the road they came from. It was filled with a procession of dozens of Hawaiian warriors, marching toward them with all manner of deadly weapons. Even in his panic, he couldn't help but take a moment to notice none of the Marchers touched the ground. Their bare feet hovered at least six inches from the ground as they stepped in time. "Kristen, you have to get down!" Peter called as he threw himself to the dirt, shutting his eyes and staring straight down. He heard Kristen rattle the doors of the kiosk. Failing that, he listened to her beg for forgiveness as she ran toward the cliff's edge. Despite hovering above the ground, Peter could hear the sounds of their footfalls all around him as they passed over his body. It took everything he had to keep himself from looking up at the madness around him.

At one point, the procession seemed to pass him, having marched on toward Kristen. Her cries grew more urgent, begging them to please stop. Next came the sound of small rocks tumbling down a thousand feet of sheer cliff.

He just couldn't help it. Peter opened his eyes and looked up just in time to see a warrior kick Kristen off the side of the cliff. Her scream didn't even last a whole second until the first of many sickening thuds and crunches cut her off.

It was his intention to only look for a second, but as he watched her fall, he knew he sealed his own fate as well. Eyes burned in the darkness as a single soldier marched up to him. At first, he thought it must be the bloodied soldier he encountered at the cave. But he was wrong. Still, the man looked familiar. Just as he raised the shark-toothed ax over his head, Peter made the connection. It was hard to recognize him at first because he looked so much younger, so much stronger than the corpse of the old man who was laid to rest earlier that day.

"I'm sorry," Peter said, looking the dead man in the eyes.

The warrior reached into Peter's pocket, pulled out his phone, and crushed it in his hand. With a smile, he said, "Na'u."

Little Girls

Justin Boote

Henry's heart skipped a beat as they entered the dusty, old room, his eyes darting everywhere as he looked for any signs of ghostly apparitions. They were in the dead man's bedroom, a huge four-poster bed sitting in the middle of the room against the wall and a large closet that could easily hide three or four people inside. He had visions of the wooden doors creaking open of their own accord in the middle of the night, a rustling inside perhaps, wondering if they were clothes that were moving from side to side in there, or something else. Something dead.

"And in here is where Matthew Cartright died, right there in bed. He had been stabbed over eleven times by the intruder, who was never caught. Legend has it that every night, at exactly midnight—the time he was murdered—you can hear his screams for help echoing around the great mansion.

"And not only that, but his mutilated body also wanders the corridors, looking for his killer." The guide smiled as she took in the beaming faces, murmurs of approval, and nodding heads of the seven visitors.

A trickle of morbid delight ran up Henry's spine as he envisaged the grisly episode, imagining hearing that ghastly scream in the middle of the night and seeing Matthew's shimmering ghost float past. He would pay a large amount of money to be able to stay here for the night and fulfill his wishes, but unfortunately, people still lived here and a guided tour was the only concession.

"Are there photos?" he enquired of the lady. "Documented evidence?"

"Oh yes! Downstairs you can flick through the photo albums of all the ghostly sightings made over the years. We have postcards and posters available for sale as well, by the entrance, plus a non-fiction book written by the owners from the time they arrived here to present."

Henry's head was going to explode. These people were living in his version of heaven, cohabitating in a mansion with a real ghost and making a good amount of money out of it at the same time.

He wanted that. Henry would sell his house, if he could, and do the same—buy a haunted house, stay up all night taking photos, then when he had enough material, write a book about it. He saw himself on television, promoting the book, answering questions about how terrifying it must be, and he would jokingly say yes, it was pretty scary, but he felt it his duty to continue living there so the house wasn't torn down. It would all be a lie because it wouldn't be scary at all.

It would be perfect.

But it wasn't going to happen.

Rachel and Joey were the reasons it was only ever going to be a dream. His wife would suggest he visit a therapist if he so much as mentioned the idea to her—and then probably petition a divorce—and Joey, at six-years-old, would be utterly terrified, no matter how much Henry tried to convince him ghosts were, in fact, harmless. Instead, he was forced to go on ghost-hunting trips to feed his hobby and fantasies.

He had been a fanatic of all things supernatural since his father died when he was young and had been convinced the man visited him from his grave. At the time, he had been pretty scared every time he woke up in the middle of the night to see his father standing over him, or a dark figure standing in the corner, two bright eyes like stars staring back at him.

After a time, he came to realize nothing ever actually happened to him except those first few seconds of terror, when he would scream for his mother and she would come running to find him shivering and crying in an empty room. He learned his father had not come back to hurt him, either physically or psychologically, and that perhaps he just yearned to see his son a few more times before he moved on.

It became romantical, the notion of his dad not wanting to leave just yet, and by the time finally moved on, Henry looked forward to the ever-decreasing visits. He was sad when they finally stopped, but that memory of childhood never left him. He was hungry for more.

The tour ended, and Henry dutifully bought a copy of the book to read later.

He was mildly depressed when he got home—back to the reality of parenthood and adulthood. Fortunately, he worked mostly from home as an architect, planning on his computer the next building to be constructed, so he could sneak in chapters of the book on occasion with no problem. Rachel knew not to disturb him when he was working, and that was what he was going to do. Besides, it was Sunday and his day off.

Before he could get settled, Rachel was waiting for him, Joey playing nearby.

"Hi, honey, how was the tour?"

"I want to live there. I'm going to sell this house and make them an offer. Did you know the original owner was stab—"

"Enough, Henry, I don't want to hear about it. You'll scare Joey. But, as it happens, talking of moving home, I just got off the phone with my parents. They're going away for two weeks and wondered if we could stay at their place and take care of the cat for them. Joey has finished school for the summer holidays as well, and you could bring your laptop, of course, so you don't miss work. What do you think?"

Henry thought it was a very good idea. It was only a three-hour drive from their home. The house was huge, with a back garden that connected to a small woodland area. Whenever he went there with Rachel, he loved sitting in the garden and watching deer and such creep onto the land. He couldn't think of a better way to relax after work. He even got on well with his in-laws, which was a bonus.

Plus, not too far away was a medieval castle that had been turned into a tourist attraction. Wandering around the old rooms, his imagination went wild contemplating all the gruesome deaths that must have occurred during the centuries and, subsequently, the ghostly reminders at present.

The big, silly grin on his face told Rachel everything she needed to know.

They arrived the next day. Even Joey was excited to get there—there was a swimming pool in the front garden, plus the chance to play out back all day without a care in the world. The only thing Rachel and Henry would have to worry about was ensuring the cat didn't starve to death.

The house was almost as big as the one Henry visited on his tour, and probably just as old. Three floors housing five bedrooms, plus an attic, one could get lost in the place. The first time he ever came here, shortly after meeting Rachel, he had been in awe. They stayed there all weekend, and Henry had wanted to stay up all night to carry out his own nocturnal vigil for anything ghostly, but Rachel refused to let him. Her parents were light sleepers, and if they heard someone wandering the house in the middle of the night, he was likely to get shot. Reluctantly, Henry had to agree on that one. He could wander to his heart's content during this stay.

It was evening by the time they got settled in and unpacked, then found the cat's litter and food trays. Joey was soon worn out after running around the garden for a while. By nine, he was already fast asleep on the couch beside his parents as they watched television and shared a bottle of wine.

"I think I might go to bed myself. I'm shattered," said Rachel, yawning. She tied her long, dark hair into a ponytail and set down her empty glass. More than two glasses of wine always made her tired—she had practically given up alcohol after Joey was born and only drank at special occasions. This was a special occasion.

Henry faked a groan. "You're not going to bed already, are you? Our first night here? I thought we might celebrate in other ways."

This was a little white lie. What he really wanted was for both his wife and Joey to go to bed so he could spend some time alone in the place.

The sly grin on Rachel's face suggested she had seen through him as well. "I know exactly what you're thinking. I swear, if you break anything or get lost, I'm not coming to look for you, and you can explain to my parents when they get back."

She stood up, kissed him, and half dragged Joey to bed, winking at Henry as she left. Henry poured the rest of the wine into his glass and settled back to take in his surroundings.

An hour later, he was ready to begin his tour. But despite the adrenaline rush and the sense of adventure and discovery, he found himself yawning too. And he came to the ominous realization that having fallen asleep so early, both Joey and Rachel would be up earlier than usual tomorrow and Joey would be excited to go out and explore.

"Okay, dammit. We'll start tomorrow night," he muttered to the empty room and, somewhat regretfully, headed up to bed.

Even though he was drowsy, his head was still swimming with possibilities. A house this big, this old, he lay there fantasizing about discovering a skeleton bricked up behind a basement wall, perhaps old relics buried in the basement floor and the owner still searching for them. He imagined the distant howling of some old woman that...

There was a series of thuds coming from outside the bedroom, as though someone was walking down the stairs. His immediate thought was Joey had woken up, gotten disorientated, and was looking for his parents. Henry quickly jumped out of bed and headed out after him.

"Hey, Joey, that you?" he hissed, not wanting to wake Rachel. But when he looked down the stairs, there was no one there. He strained to hear if Joey was wandering about downstairs, yet the only sound was his breathing and the dull ticking of the grandfather clock in the hallway. Confused, he went to check Joey's bedroom, next door to his. Joey was in there fast asleep, snoring gently.

Confused yet more, he headed back to his room and climbed into bed. He had been imagining things, his fantasies getting the better of him. When he was finally falling asleep and unable to separate reality from fiction, the bedroom door creaked open and two tiny pinpricks of light peered in.

The next day, he had completely forgotten about the thudding on the stairs, mainly because before he was even awake, Joey came barging in, excited about spending the day outside and exploring the woods and swimming in the pool later. Rachel and Henry dutifully got up, made breakfast, and were soon heading out.

A river ran through the woods, so they followed its path. Henry pointed out all the deer and animals they saw, the occasional heron flapping huge wings overhead, while they sat and ate sandwiches on the riverbank. In the afternoon, the sun hot and bold in the sky, all three of them splashed and swam in the swimming pool. By dinnertime at six, all three were once more exhausted.

"You know, we should come here more often," said Henry as they ate dinner. "Maybe even... move in with your parents?"

"Uh huh, no way! I didn't leave home at nineteen to move back again at thirty-two. You can come and live here if you want. I'll stay where I am."

"I wanna come and live here!" said an excited Joey, perhaps thinking his dad was being serious.

"See!"

"Good. Then you both stay—more peace and quiet for me."

They finished dinner, then Joey asked if he could go play in the games room his grandparents had set up for him shortly after being born. There was a game console in there which would keep him busy for hours if they let him, so they happily left him to go play while they fed the cat then settled down on the couch.

They were watching a movie after checking on Joey when Henry thought he saw something flash past the living room door. Thinking it was Joey, he got up to check, worried he might knock something over. But as he looked up and down the hallway and saw nobody, a leather soccer ball came thudding down the stairs toward him. Instantly, he recalled the incident from last night. More importantly, Joey was strictly forbidden from playing upstairs by himself. They noticed the cat had a habit of lying at the top of the stairs or would occasionally dash up and down them when playing. To trip over the damn thing would be so easy...

He was about to fetch his son when Joey appeared from the games room at the far end of the hallway. Henry's heart thudded at roughly the same cadence as the soccer ball. Butterflies awoke in his stomach and floated around, tickling his insides.

"Joey? Have you been in there playing all this time?"

"Yes, Dad. But I'm bored now. Can I come and watch a movie with you and Mom?"

Henry barely heard him. He stared at the ball at his feet, then back up the stairs. "And you haven't been upstairs?"

"No, you told me not to."

"Okay, yeah, let's watch a movie."

His imagination was getting the better of him again, so he was hardly aware of the movie they were watching or that Rachel was telling Joey it was time for bed. He had been fantasizing this was the incident that would start off his book about the haunted house, that solitary soccer ball bouncing down the stairs. He was still lost in his thoughts when Rachel announced she was off to bed herself.

"Don't stay up too late," she said, "and don't get lost if you go traipsing about. I'm not coming looking for you."

She kissed him then headed upstairs, leaving him once more alone with just the monotonous tick tock of the grandfather clock to keep him company. After the seemingly innocuous incident with the ball, he was more determined than ever to check out the house. He poured himself a shot of whiskey to calm his nerves and headed upstairs.

The attic was full of junk, most of it covered in white sheets like cartoon ghosts. As he moved around, the dust brought a constant desire to sneeze. The window was filthy and covered in grime, making it almost impossible to see the landscape outside, regardless of it being pitch black out there. His imagination conjured dozens of possibilities, of what might have been and what was.

After a few moments, he left the room and moved along the landing, his ears straining to pick up the slightest sound, his eyes darting everywhere. The rest of the rooms were all ordinary, mostly bedrooms, or locked, and he had no desire to try to open them.

He figured the next stop had to be the basement. Basements in old houses always stored dark secrets, and he thought it highly unlikely it wasn't the case here. Hadn't his father-in-law once told him the previous owners, many decades ago, had died here? That was as good a reason as any.

He was moving slowly down the stairs when suddenly he stopped. What sounded like distant, muffled moaning was coming from behind him. The hairs on his neck prickled and his heart jumped into his throat. Henry froze, one foot comically in the air still as if he had been frozen in place. The sound, like a child sobbing under a blanket, was coming from the room to the far left of the landing. A prickle of hesitation trickled up his spine. The idea his fantasies were actually coming true gave an edge he wasn't so sure was quite as exotic anymore. Still, he turned back and headed in the direction of the sound.

It was coming from a guest bedroom that was empty except for a double bed and a large closet. It was definitely the sound of a child crying. For a moment, he wondered if Joey had gotten up again and got lost, but this sounded more like a girl. He took a deep breath, not entirely sure he was ready for this after all, and swung the door open.

The crying stopped immediately.

Henry looked around the room, in the closet, and under the bed, yet there were no signs of any children or spectral apparitions. The only difference was a faint aroma of earth that had been freshly dug after a storm. It was only faint, but he knew it hadn't been there before. This time his whole body rippled with excitement.

He stayed there a few minutes longer, desperate for a shadow to dart across his vision, or for something to move, or a cold gust of air to suddenly brush past him. But when nothing happened, an instance of regret and disappointment replaced the excitement. He left the room to check the basement.

He was halfway down the stairs when, from apparently nowhere, another soccer ball bounced past him and rolled to a stop at the front door.

It was a different one from last night—a cream-colored ball—but even so, he stared at it as though he had never seen a soccer ball in his life. Giggling echoed around the house, then that faint sobbing again. A myriad of emotions washed over Henry. He pinched himself to make sure he hadn't fallen asleep on the sofa, but the rapid pulsing of his heart had nothing to do with any dream. He thought of rushing to wake Rachel, grab his phone to record the sounds he was hearing, call out to whomever it was haunting the place, for there could be no denying that his greatest dream had just come true. There had been no balls lying around upstairs, the cat was staring from the couch, and both Joey and Rachel were fast asleep. It was a ghost—a real goddamned ghost!

"Hello?" he called out timidly. "Is there anyone there?"

Thoughts of a book were already floating around his head before he made it to the bottom of the stairs and tentatively picked up the ball, as if it might bite him. As he held it, the fleeting glimpse of a shadow running past the kitchen door caused him to drop it. It looked like the outline of a small child, head ducked so he couldn't recognize who it was. He ran after the figure, heard chuckling coming from behind him in the hallway again, and rushed back out.

The basement door was wide open.

His nerves were live wires. His heart was going to explode like a grenade in his chest as he contemplated the invitation, for an invitation it had to be. There was no way that door should be open; in fact, he remembered Rachel telling Joey under no circumstances was he to go near it and thought he remembered her locking it with her spare set of keys. The stairs were old and dangerous, and the place was surely full of bugs and spiders, which would give Joey nightmares for weeks.

So, someone wanted him to go down there.

Feeling slightly uneasy about the prospect, he flicked on the light switch and headed down, holding the wooden banister carefully so he wouldn't slip. It was dark and murky down there, full of junk, and Rachel had been right about the spiders—they flitted about everywhere, and there were some damn big ones too. But his focus was more on any unnatural shapes or shadows that might be lurking.

Then he saw it. A shadowy figure, motionless and watching him, stood at the back of the huge basement filled with boxes and old gardening tools. At least he assumed it was staring at him, for he couldn't discern its head. The figure, perhaps the size of a young child, had arms by its side and shoulders that were easily visible, but where the head should be was a jagged, horizontal outline.

Henry was paralyzed, unsure what to do or say. In the dull, grimy light, it was too hard to see anything with clarity—it might have been a coat rack there instead, so easy to confuse with that of a person. But when an arm raised and waved to him and the figure started giggling, there could be no mistake—it was the (headless?) ghost of a child.

The nerves in his stomach abated, and a warm sense of relief washed over him. There was nothing to be frightened of. It was just a youngster who had perhaps gotten lost on their way to Heaven and was still running about the house, having some fun.

He smiled and waved back, was about to say something, when the apparition sank back into the murky shadows and disappeared. Henry called to her—for he was sure it was a girl from her girlish laughter—but when there was no reply, disappointment returned briefly until the sheer magnitude of what he witnessed dawned upon him.

It took almost two hours until he was able to fall asleep.

It also took a long time debating whether to tell Rachel the next morning.

When she asked him how his nightly excursion had gone, he was lost for words, mainly because he knew she would be freaked out by the sudden appearance of ghosts in the home, despite it being obviously a friendly one. Instead, he asked her about the history of the place, particularly how the previous owners had died and if they had children.

"I don't know. How would I know that? I remember something my dad told me years ago about the family found dead, and yes, I think they had a daughter, but I didn't ask anymore. I didn't want to know. Why?"

Good question. Should he tell her? Hell, why not.

When he finished, she scoffed and laughed. "You don't expect me to believe that, do you? It's your imagination, wishful thinking. If there were ghosts here, my dad would have said so. And don't you dare say anything in front of Joey."

She refused to discuss the topic further, saying she was going to feed the cat and take care of the box.

They spent the rest of the day in the village, shopping and doing general sight-seeing, but Henry's mind was elsewhere. He was already thinking about tonight and making contact again, but it was the fact the spirit's head had apparently been missing that troubled him. He assumed it must have been the lack of light that made it seem that way, for the girl had giggled and laughed at him. It would have been impossible without a head, wouldn't it? He decided he would take a small flashlight this time around and hope to catch a better look at her, try to get her to tell him why she remained behind.

When night came and the inevitable call to Joey to go to bed arrived, Henry could hardly wait for Rachel to follow. She had been hinting they should go to bed together, take advantage of the huge bed, but he really didn't want to. All he could think of was the little girl.

He thought of lying to her about feeling tired, but instead opted for the truth—he wanted to find the little girl and prove her existence somehow. She was, after all, just a friendly ghost, like Casper, so obtaining a photo of her should be easy. Rachel muttered something about living with an eccentric and headed off to bed, disappointed.

It was just thirty minutes later when, still in the living room waiting for his cell phone to charge, he heard the thudding on the stairs and the creaking of the basement door opening. He jumped up, grabbed his phone, praying it had enough battery, and rushed to the hallway. He was just in time to see what he thought to be soccer balls bouncing down the steps of the basement. Having forgotten to turn on the lights, he was somewhat unsure.

Excited, yet nervous at the same time, he moved to the basement and peered down. There they were, the soccer balls rolling around down there—five or six maybe. A childish giggling echoed around the dark room, followed by a loud wail that ended abruptly, as if someone had clamped a hand over the owner's mouth.

Henry switched on the beam from his phone and gently walked down the steps, yet as soon as the beam came on, the balls disappeared. In their place were tracks where they had been rolling about in the dirt. Something small and dark dashed across the room, just out of reach of the beam.

"Hello? Little girl, is that you? You don't have to be afraid. Show yourself."

He switched on the phone's camera and waited.

Another shadowy figure twitched in the far corner, two small pinpricks of light flickering like stars from what he assumed to be its head.

"Hi. Come out, I won't hurt you."

There was a scuffling sound, as if someone was scraping back the soft earth covering the floorboards.

He reached the bottom of the steps and shined his phone around, revealing nothing but boxes and junk, but each time as he scanned from left to right, something moved in his periphery—shadows darting about everywhere like bats on a pitch-black night.

The door to the basement slammed shut. The light app on his phone switched off, leaving him in total darkness.

Something light and cold touched the back of his neck, making him yelp in shock as he spun around. His hair was tugged gently, causing him to yell. Soft giggling came from all around him.

They were playing with him, lost little girls bored and wanting some fun. He chuckled knowing no harm was going to come from them.

"Hey, stop that! Turn on the lights again. We can't play if I can't see you."

As if in answer, he was roughly pushed and fell down, smashing his face into the earth. The giggling continued.

"Hey, that's not funny," he said, spitting dirt from his mouth.

Something heavy on his back pinned him down, like when Joey liked to playfight with him. He tried to push himself up, but the weight was even heavier, as though there were two children sitting on him, making it hard to catch his breath.

"C'mon, I can't breathe," he gasped. "This isn't funny anymore."

But it wasn't until he felt something thin and sharp run across the back of his neck, causing panic to settle in, that suddenly the lights came back on. He found himself alone in the basement, panting heavily as he pushed himself back to his feet.

"Hey, where are you? That wasn't funny, you know."

Henry waited for an answer, but when all he got was soft, distant chuckling, he headed back upstairs, still unnerved about the whole experience. It took three large shots of whiskey for his nerves to settle and finally see the funny side—poor kids just wanted to play and got carried away.

The next day, Henry said nothing about being pushed over but told Rachel about seeing their flittering shadows in the basement and the distant laughter. She did not seem to find it as amusing as he did.

"Henry, I don't want you talking about that anymore. You're freaking me out. I'll start seeing things myself, and then Joey will get worried. Just... keep it to yourself. The idea of living in a haunted house, albeit only for a couple of weeks... I'll go home and leave you here with nothing but the cat. So just... shut up."

Henry's grin wavered and vanished. He couldn't understand how she wasn't as enthusiastic as he was. The book he had been dreaming about for years was going to happen! A little bit of research into the history of the house and he would be ready. All he needed to do was find out what the girls wanted.

There was a scream from upstairs—Joey.

They rushed upstairs to find Joey sat frozen on his bed, sobbing hysterically.

"What is it? What happened?" yelled Rachel.

"There was a girl in my room that came out of the closet, but she didn't have a head. She just stood there and pointed at me, and there was blood running down her chest from her neck and…"

Joey could speak no more as he hugged his mother in terror, who glared at Henry in a "See what I mean?" fashion.

His research showed the original owners of the house died in mysterious circumstances, so in that, his father-in-law was right. What he neglected to tell him was they had also been suspected of being involved in an illegal child-trafficking ring. Several children had gone missing over a few months near the area, never to be seen again. Henry sat back, horrified. He wondered and tried to recall if his in-laws had personally known the original owners but couldn't remember.

He thought about Joey and what he described, and how he had thought the first ghost had been missing its head. It had to have been Joey's imagination; perhaps he had heard Henry telling Rachel and subconsciously visualised it while playing. They weren't scary ghosts; they were just bored little girls wanting to play. But he also had to consider whether there was a connection to the missing kids and what he had been witnessing these last couple of nights.

Was that why they hadn't gone to Heaven? They wanted their whereabouts to be known so they could be buried in peace?

If so, he had to help them. He thought of telling Rachel the news, but she was being grumpy around him and wanted to hear nothing more about ghosts. This would make her pack up and leave, of that he was positive.

That night, Joey insisted on not sleeping alone, so Rachel took him to their room, while Henry was to sleep in the spare room. That was fine with him. Once they were asleep, he grabbed his phone and headed toward the basement. He needed some kind of evidence to present to his father-in-law, and subsequently the police, or they would think him mad.

Just as he reached the door, it swung open for him like it was waiting for him. Giggling and what sounded like whispering came from down there. Then he heard hissing, as though someone was telling them to be quiet. Not wanting to startle them, he refrained from turning on the light app and peered down the stairs. Those soccer balls were once more rolling around of their own accord. Were the ghosts playing with them? What was their significance? Regardless, it was evidence. He turned on the camera and started recording them but soon realised that without the light, they would be hardly visible. He turned it on and quickly held the phone up.

And dropped it.

He stood there not quite believing what he was seeing. Maybe he was asleep on the couch again. What he was staring at were not soccer balls, but human heads. Children's heads with long flowing hair and dark, sunken craters for eyes and rotten holes in place of their noses. Their mouths were wide as if offering silent screams, teeth grey and rotten like gravestones.

Loud wails reverberated around the basement like distant lost souls. Giggling answered the eerie howling, then it was Henry's turn to cry out when he was suddenly pushed down the stairs, crashing onto the earth. Stunned, he lay there for a few seconds, while shadows flitted back and forth like children playing hide and seek. When he looked up, he was horrified to see what he first assumed to be rogue tree roots poking up through the soil, until he realized they weren't roots but skeletal arms and hands, so tiny and delicate they could only belong to children.

One of the dancing figures stopped and stood before him, slowly taking on a more physical form until he could make out the dainty features of a young girl. Her face was badly misshapen, as though while transforming into something more tangible, she had forgotten to rearrange her face properly. One eyeball dangled on her cheek, and the other was missing. Her mouth was slightly out of sync with the rest of her features, a little too far to the left, until he noticed her mouth was a long slash, as if a knife had cut her open a bit farther.

"Have you come to play?" she said in a voice that suggested two people talking at once, their voices slightly overlapping.

Henry tried to push himself to his feet and run, but his limbs betrayed him. All he could do was scrabble at the earth with his hands and feet, as though trying to dig himself a great hole. Which perhaps he was.

"Why won't you play with us?" asked another girl who appeared before him. "We're so lonely down here. Would Joey like to come and play? He said he would if you let him."

Henry was sobbing, but at the sound of his son's name, renewed vigor coursed through him. He pushed himself to his knees, yet something seemed to be preventing him from rising, a weight on his back that, when he turned and looked, belonged to another of the children. This time, the head was missing completely. Her arm was holding him down firmly. Somehow, he knew that despite being decapitated, she was looking at him and smiling. He could see her in his mind.

"What do you want? Leave my son alone."

Then he thought about the rest of the newspaper articles he had read. A few of the victims had been found near the area, decapitated in two cases. It occurred to him again there could be a relationship between those victims and the headless ghost girl. The first one he had seen he swore had been a trick of the light, but his son? Kids were prone to exaggerating. But it still didn't explain why they were here, not playing with him anymore but threatening him and Joey.

"But we're so lonely. We want new friends to play with. We can't leave here anymore. He won't let us."

"What do you mean, he won't let us? Who?"

"The man who brought us here."

Henry tried to think as he continued struggling and failing to stand up—the weight was too heavy on his back. The only people he could think of were the original owners, who had apparently died here. Could they have had something to do with it, the child trafficking ring being so close? Regardless, that was irrelevant in that moment; he didn't like the way they wanted to involve Joey. What Joey had seen in his room turned out to be real, after all.

"We want Joey. And we want him now," said another shadowy figure beside the girl. "He belongs to us. We've wanted him all along, ever since you first came. But then you left again before we could take him. All children in this house belong to us. The man said so."

Henry was stunned, horrified. He was still squirming in the dirt, swiping at the girl pressing him down and hitting nothing but air. He stopped for a moment out of pure shock. He hadn't considered anything else other than a lost little girl who wanted to play with him. He was going to write a book about the friendly ghost; he had wanted Rachel to be a part of it at first, but reconsidered as the girl's eyes began to glow like growing flames, illuminating the room, revealing all the other girls around her, some decapitated, their filthy white dresses now splattered in their dried blood, all grinning—not mischievous smiles, but sinister, malevolent. They had tricked him. These kids had died in this house, and the person responsible for it—the previous owner—had died here too, keeping them prisoner with him and using them to attract more children. Children like Joey, who last night had been terrified of the thing that emerged, headless, from the closet.

The thought of Joey being in danger spurred him even more. He thrashed and writhed on the floor, while the girls giggled. Yet some supernatural force stopped him from even rising a few inches.

There was a loud thud from the upstairs, and immediately the girls were silent.

The fleshless skulls of the children were poking through the soil, rising like the dead from their graves.

Another thud came, then he heard the quiet laughter of a small child—Joey. The basement door opened, and Joey stepped in, still in his pajamas and holding a young girl's hand, both giggling as though sharing a secret.

Henry tried to scream, to tell him to run to his mother, but he had a mouthful of dirt. He was being slowly pushed farther down into the dirt as though it was quicksand and he was sinking down and down.

"This is where we play," said the girl holding his hand, who looked perfectly normal, not a ghost at all—she might have been Joey's sister. "This is where we've always played. You can play too."

Henry fought with everything he could, sputtering as he tried to yell at Joey, his mouth and eyes full of dirt. He was almost completely buried and was going to remain here forever with the little girls. If ever a book was to be written about the ghosts in this mansion, he would have a main role to play, not be the author after all. But that was all irrelevant. As his head and the rest of his body was finally pushed below the earth, and his last breath was caught in his lungs, he heard the girls telling Joey how much fun they were going to have. A game that would last forever.

The cat sat at the top of the steps, staring down at the melee and swishing its tail back and forth.

Home Again

Debra Castaneda

It's my first night in my new, tiny home. The ads called it affordable, sustainable, easy to maintain.

But it's a prison, and I'm its captive.

I stare out the window and pound my fist against the glass, hoping to get someone's attention.

But no one can hear me.

I wave frantically, but my neighbors can't see me, either.

The front door won't open. Neither will the back door.

I'm trying hard not to panic, but there's something in here with me.

People are gathered just outside, in the common area. They're having a party to celebrate the opening of Meadow Village. They might as well be miles away.

My place is a mess.

It shouldn't be.

Before moving in, I downsized, culling my belongings until I had just what I needed and nothing more. I was determined my new life would be free of clutter and waste, free of old, bad memories—an escape from the chaos that once consumed me. The chaos of a husband lost to addiction.

I spent the last several days moving into the cozy space of my new, tiny home, making sure everything was in its place, each item carefully stowed away.

But now, as I stand frozen in the center of the room, I see my belongings scattered around haphazardly, as if someone had sneaked in while I showered and tossed everything about. There is malice in this. Even rage.

My heart beats too fast as I take in the scene before me.

The few books I arranged on the built-in shelves lay strewn across the floor, their covers bent. My favorite mug is shattered on the floor. Every item of clothing I own is strewn around the room, some of it shredded. A tangled mess of panties and bras fills the sink. The Mexican casserole I made for the party is ruined; refried beans spill over the sides, black olives and bits of green onion are scattered on the counter.

There's a handprint in the center.

There's nowhere for an intruder to hide, but someone did this. I can feel eyes watching me.

I panic and lunge for the door, pull on the knob again. It still won't open. I try pounding on the window again. Charlotte, a red-headed young woman who owns the house next to mine, is facing my window talking to Isaiah, the impossibly-tall beermaker with locks.

"Help! Help!" I yell, but Charlotte doesn't notice. No one seems to hear me.

I'm turning around slowly, taking in the mess, the rhythmic sound of blood rushing in my ears. Then I hear something.

Creaking. The ceiling. The walls. The floor. The bathroom door slams closed, kitchen drawers fly open and bang shut.

I scream.

Then I see it, a shape huddled in the far corner, squatting between the platform bed and the wall. When I blink, it's gone. Another movement catches my eye. It's skittering up the wall, a dark, shadowy blob that melts into the wooden slats of the ceiling.

Earlier, my neighbor Bob offered me mushrooms. He's a retired professor who teaches classes about psychedelic mushrooms.

"Maybe another time," I said.

So I was stone-cold sober, a bottle of pinot grigio for the party unopened in the fridge.

I lurch back to the window. People are gathered at the edge of the meadow, probably talking about a communal garden. We're creating something here, a new style of community where we'll rely on each other for things. Barter, like the old days. First a garden, then a rec center, an art studio, and a workroom.

I teach textile design at a private college. Clothing will be my contribution.

Why has no one come to check on me? Then I remember. Because we decided privacy was paramount. We would give each other space. We would not be intrusive.

I am not being ignored or forgotten. They are respecting my space. Maybe I changed my mind, decided to spend my first evening alone, drinking wine and reading.

The house is creaking. Loudly. Tears blur my vision as I try the window again, pushing down on the lever as hard as I can. It breaks off in my hand, and my guttural scream of desperation echoes through the room.

The window casing is new, but the glass is old, thick, and slightly wavy. Everything in the tiny house is old—parts reclaimed from a historic home deep in the forest of the Santa Cruz mountains. That was part of the appeal—recycled materials, old world craftsmanship.

The old home was famous for all the wrong reasons. A San Francisco railroad baron built it for his family, a vacation home in the woods. He, his family, and a staff of three were all murdered, butchered, their bloodied bodies hung from the trees.

Who killed them remains a mystery. The house, a Victorian masterpiece, changed hands many times over the years. It was rumored to be haunted but was too remote for the buses of the Santa Cruz Haunted House Tour.

Eventually, a developer bought it, disassembled it bit by bit, trucked it down Highway 1, and used all the best parts to build our tiny homes.

The framed photo of the Specter Mansion—a gift from the developer—falls from its hook next to the front door. The glass cracks. The frame flies across the floor, guided by an unseen force, and smashes into my knee. A shard of glass slices through my skin, and I cry out in pain, in terror.

With a shudder, I realize what happened at the Specter Mansion in 1889 is connected to what's happening now.

I feel it in my bones.

"Go away! Leave me alone!" I scream at my tormentors.

Then comes another chilling realization: they came from the mansion. They are embedded in the walls, lurking within the very materials used to build them. They didn't follow me here.

And they can't leave.

Hours ago, I reveled in the coziness of my new home, the clean lines, the warm light, the gleaming wood, the charming porthole above the arched front door, the wrought-iron hardware.

Now I am alone, trapped with ghosts who are trapped with me.

I hear a scratching sound. The hair on the back of my neck lifts as I realize it's coming from behind me, where the ceiling meets the wall.

I don't want to look up there.

The built-in dining table breaks loose from the wall. An iron fleur-de-lis—the only keepsake from my wreck of a marriage—comes flying at me. It bashes into my temple and knocks me to the ground.

I'm looking up at the ceiling, a sharp pain radiating through the side of my head. There's a shadow in the corner. It has no face but is still leering at me.

I cringe, expecting it to descend and smother me, but it doesn't move. The last bit of the day's sun warms me, the light streaming in from the skylight. Maybe the light will protect me.

The skylight. It's just big enough to climb through, but that won't be easy. At fifty, I'm not as nimble as I used to be. It doesn't matter how carefully I eat or how much yoga I do, age catches up.

I sob as I place a footstool on the bed. When I climb on top of it, pressing my hands against the wooden slats of the wall for balance, it wobbles on the mattress.

The ceiling is mere inches above my head. With a deep breath, I put a foot on a bookshelf, hoping it will support my weight.

It does.

With trembling fingers, I reach up to the skylight, fingers brushing the lever. Relief washes over me. I can do this. I can make it.

My tiny house is finally quiet, like it's waiting. With a final burst of determination, I manage to push open the skylight, the hinges squealing in protest.

I'm trying to figure out how I'm going to hoist myself up when an invisible hand grabs my ankle and pulls me downward. I'm falling.

My body bounces against the bed, then slams to the floor. A jolt of pain shoots through me. My vision swims, then blackness.

When I wake, the room is dark and icy cold. My head throbs as I struggle to sit up, the taste of iron in my mouth. I must have bitten my tongue.

I become aware of a fury of sound and movement—wood groaning and splintering. My tiny house is bucking and heaving like a boat in a storm. Through the cacophony, I hear the distant sound of children's laughter.

"What's happening!" I scream, but no one answers.

With a burst of terror-fueled adrenaline, I roll to my knees and reach into the darkness, desperate for somewhere to place my hand, to push myself into a standing position. But there's nothing. No bed. No wall. Just blackness and emptiness.

Impossible. I can't go more than a few feet in my tiny home without bumping into something.

Panic threatens to overwhelm me as the floor gives another violent lurch beneath my feet. Maybe the building has broken apart and I'm outside on the ground.

But the surface beneath me feels like wood, not dirt.

A light emerges in the distance, too far away to be within the confines of my home, and a sinister whisper reaches my ears.

I force myself to stand, ignoring the searing pain in my back, and stumble toward the light. I make my way forward and see a long hall lined with closed doors.

One opens, and my body gives a violent jerk in surprise.

It's Charlotte. I think. It's her shape and size. She moves into the hallway, hands pressed against her mouth, looks around, and gives a little scream when she spots me.

"Melissa?" she says. "Is that you?"

I wobble toward her and place a shaking hand on her arm. "It's me."

Her eyes widen as she looks at me. "Where are we?"

The answer rises in my throat like a long-suppressed scream.

"The Specter Mansion," I whisper. "We've been here all along."

She stares with uncomprehending eyes.

"After the party, when you went home, did you see anything odd? Did your house begin...breaking apart?"

She nods. The whites of her eyes seem to glow with fear.

My eyes adjust to the dim light. I can see the walls, and I recognize the porthole windows from above our front doors. They're in a long row, but they're papered over.

"Charlotte, I think the house put itself back together again."

Her mouth opens and closes soundlessly. She's too confused or too scared. She breathes heavily, bent over, hands resting against her knees as if she's just finished a marathon.

Another door opens, and a tall figure appears, locks running down his back. Isaiah. He's stooping. His head swivels, then he shuffles toward us.

He greets Charlotte, but his mouth drops open when he sees me. His expression goes blank.

I touch my face and feel a warm stickiness. When my fingers come away, they're red with blood.

"The haints were in the walls," he says gruffly in his Southern accent.

Charlotte gives a little cry. "They came out of the ceiling."

Isaiah cranes his neck, peers down the stretch of hallway. "I don't know how we ended up here, but this has gotta be the Specter Mansion."

Charlotte sobs. "How can this be happening?"

I shake my head. "We have to find a way out." My voice trembles.

Isaiah nods, his brow furrowed. "You're right. This is some crazy-ass shit. Let's go."

We huddle together and press forward, arms linked. We pass a staircase. A voice calls to us from the floor below. Charlotte stops. I can feel her body quivering next to mine.

"Don't look," Isaiah says. "Keep moving."

The next few yards take forever. But the light is getting brighter. I see a large window up ahead. My chest swells with hope. We walk faster.

From somewhere off to the side, a figure emerges. I recognize the shaggy head.

"Bob."

At the sound of his name, Bob spins around, then calls out. "Oh, thank god. Are you real? I thought I was tripping out."

We move toward him, but when Isaiah reaches out in greeting, Bob recoils. "What happened to you?" His eyes dart between us.

For a moment, I think he's just talking to me, seeing my bloody head. But in the light, I get a better look at Charlotte and Isaiah.

They've changed. Charlotte's red hair is faded, streaked with silver, her face lined. Isaiah's forehead is covered in deep creases, his locks now completely gray. Bob's wild hair is white and soft. His eyes are rimmed in red.

I turn to Isaiah. "How old do I look?"

"I'm bad with ages," he says faintly. "Seventy, maybe."

I suddenly feel lightheaded. "We've aged. How long have we been here?"

Charlotte is crying now.

Bob puts an arm around her shoulder and stares in the direction of the light.

I can hear faint voices, but I can't make out the words.

"Listen," Isaiah says.

The wrinkled faces of my companions are pinched with the effort of listening. Then I hear it. A distant rumble, a grinding, a clanking. The floor beneath our feet vibrates.

"Bulldozers!" Bob rushes toward a door at the end of the hall.

Charlotte cries out in alarm.

Isaiah follows. "What are you doing, man?"

I hobble after them.

In the large foyer, Bob pulls on the front door. The room is filled with old furniture covered in dust. Shadowy figures are pressed against the walls, writhing and hissing, avoiding the light seeping through the dirty windows.

Isaiah picks up an embroidered pillow and hurls it at the ghosts. "Get the fuck away from us!"

His profanity cuts through my fear and propels me toward a window. I rub away the grime with my sleeve. The glass is cold to the touch.

Outside, there's a wide porch and, beyond, a dead, weed-choked garden, a broken fence, and an expanse of meadow. We're not in the forest where the house was built, but in the meadow, the place where the Specter Mansion had been refashioned into tiny homes.

Behind me, Charlotte screams. She clutches my arm and shakes it.

I see it now.

A man in a neon-yellow vest and hardhat shouts, "Let's get this party started, people!"

There is no party, only a wrecking crew. It's come for the Specter Mansion, and all of us.

And suddenly, I understand.

We are doomed to spend eternity within its walls, to join the shadows that haunt its halls. Cursed to await whatever dark fate the house has in store for us.

We cry and hold hands as the bulldozers advance. We will be ghosts, together.

Don't Whistle Back

MJ Mars

Jordan watched the action recording on his cracked iPhone screen as Seabiscuit scrubbed at the ground with the toe of his Converse, rubbing out the chalk outline of a hop-scotch course his little sister had painstakingly drawn earlier that morning. With each crescent-moon smear, his sock rolled a little farther down his calf until it pooled like a deflated balloon around his ankle.

Moving his phone closer, Jordan zoomed in on the urban destruction. The edges of Seabiscuit's white shoe grew more colorful by the second as it scraped through pastel pinks and greens, obliterating the tenth square in the game.

"We need some boring domestic stuff at the start, but it has to build tension," Seabiscuit announced when they decided to go ahead and film their found footage movie. He grinned a wicked little smile when he saw the chalk diagram and seized his opportunity to create some so-called "domestic tension."

Jordan swung the camera and panned out at the sound of Little My, whose real name was Monika, hurtling out of the house. For a moment, she stood with her tiny hands clenched into fists, observing the destroyed game, the lens blurring her pink dress for a moment as the camera struggled to reclaim focus. Her face crumpled into an exaggerated pout. Without saying a word, she ran back into the house.

Sighing, Jordan looked over at his bike, knowing it was probably in their best interest to be moving on. Before he could broach the subject with his oldest friend, Seabiscuit's dad came onto the porch and looked down at the pavement.

"Sebastian! What the hell? Can't you boys think of anything better to do than torment your sister?"

Jordan backed away, keen to distance himself from the accusation, but Seabiscuit advanced toward his father and clicked his fingers behind his back like an arrogant diner summoning a waiter. It was a move that said, "Film this." So, he did.

"It's just chalk, Dad," Seabiscuit argued.

"Grow up, Sebastian." Wilf Horner realized he was being recorded and stepped toward Jordan. "What do you think you're doing?"

"We're making a movie, Mr. Horner."

The man snorted and looked back to his son. "I'm sure Ridley Scott is quaking in his boots. Go and do it somewhere else. And stop upsetting your sister!"

Knowing better than to cut the recording, Jordan walked backward, capturing his friend's scowl, with Mr. Horner heading back to the house in the background. Little My was watching from the window, and he zoomed in on her. She held up her middle finger, making him smile. Even though Seabiscuit would be annoyed at her, even he couldn't deny it would make a great end to their opening scene.

He placed the phone in his back pocket and lifted his bike from the ground, throwing his leg over the bar and waiting for Seabiscuit to quit ranting about what a spoiled brat his sister was and what an asshole his dad was and, even though she hadn't done anything that morning, how his mom was an overbearing banshee and he couldn't wait to move across the country when he was old enough.

Eventually, exhausted from his moment of angst, the boy hopped on his bike and immediately set off pedaling, taking Jordan by surprise. He followed, standing up on his pedals to build enough momentum to quickly catch up. There was no need to ask where his friend was headed. They were going to the boat in the woods, a secret project they had been working on all summer and the main focus of their movie.

Well, that wasn't quite the whole truth. The Whistler was the focus of their movie. But if they were going to get anywhere near the strange little island where the local urban legend was said to reside, they would need a boat.

Luckily, and kind of creepily, earlier in the year, they had found one.

It had been the first day of the summer break and the boys had been restless. They went looking for adventure in the overgrown plantation around the edge of the lake.

It was an area the kids of the town both avoided and gravitated to, depending on their sensibilities. Beyond the risk of tetanus from the junk that lay hidden in the grass, the drunk and lairy older teens who could be unpredictable when they stumbled upon unwelcome trespassers to their turf, and the swampy grasslands being a haven for mosquitoes and other biting bugs, the tiny central island of Backwater Brace was a looming presence across the lake. Nobody knew too much about the strange oval island other than the rumors it was haunted by a malevolent presence that had more than three kills under its belt.

The story went that, during the 1950s, there was a year of heatwaves that dried the plantations enough to make the edge of the lake a hotspot for teens to congregate who could drive up and park, lay out their blankets and sunbathe, make out, and listen to music until night fell. Once the sun went down, their attentions turned to Backwater Brace. By the end of the summer, three teens had been found dead under strange circumstances, and nobody went back to the island ever again. A rumor was passed down firmly from parent to child from then on; avoid the island at all costs. If you should ignore the warning and row over and happen to hear a whistling sound, whatever you did, *don't whistle back*.

Jordan and Seabiscuit were practical kids. Although the local legend was kind of exciting, they guessed that the kids who died in the fifties had picked up some kind of disease over there or been bitten by a critter and not gotten the help they needed. Parents made up monsters and ghouls to stop their children exploring where they shouldn't since the truth and common sense were rarely a good enough deterrent. But the incident had been seventy years ago, and times had changed.

Plus, the boys had a movie to make.

The Whistler was the perfect subject for a found-footage feature.

That first day, the boys had been roaming the lakeside, figuring out angles and wondering how in the hell they would ever make it over to the island to film the main part of the movie, when Jordan tripped over something hard and firm in the long grass. He landed on something rounded and hollow, knocking the wind out of himself. While he was hunched over with his hands on his knees, recovering, Seabiscuit set about unearthing the treasure that Jordan had quite literally stumbled upon.

A boat.

A dilapidated, hole-strewn, unseaworthy rowboat, but a boat, nonetheless.

When they turned it over, they saw the faded paint outline of its name, *The Swift*, and a crude compass carving in the wood of the central seat: VR + NL 1956.

"Holy shit!" Seabiscuit exclaimed. "It's from that summer! Help me turn it back over."

Jordan groaned, sore and confused. "Why are we doing this again?" he asked as they returned the boat to the dented earth it had been sitting in for years and Seabiscuit worked to cover it with the twigs and long grass that had kept it mostly preserved.

"Here's our discovery scene! We find the boat that the kids used back in the day. It's perfect."

Jordan couldn't help but agree that his friend's logic was sound. It did make a cool scene in their movie and would fix the issue of how they got across to the island once they eventually managed to patch the damned thing up. But he couldn't help but feel a creep of unease as he filmed Seabiscuit excitedly "finding" *The Swift*, taking a close-caption shot of the seat carving when they turned it over. He didn't know much about boats, but he knew it was unlikely one would have survived out here that long.

One thing he did know a bit about was urban legends. And if something fell into your path that seemed too good to be true, it usually meant something wanted you to find it.

He pushed the thought away as Seabiscuit excitedly turned to the camera and beamed with forced surprise. "Whoa! Would you look at that? This must have belonged to the kids who died that summer."

It sounded fake as all hell, but they could always dub it over, Jordan thought as he panned past Seabiscuit's shoulder, settling on a shot of the island as the sun began to set.

They read countless online articles about how to fix up a boat and managed to find most of the items they needed in Jordan's parents' garage. The things they didn't have they begged, borrowed, and even stole from friends and neighbors, keeping the camera rolling the whole time for their "patching up the boat" montage. Jordan knew the section of the movie showing them restoring the old rowboat would be a minute or two max and felt cheated that the true extent of the blood, sweat, and tears that went into the project would never be shown to the audience. He hated every minute of the refurb.

However, the moment they finally pushed it out onto the water and held their breaths, filming to capture whether it sank or stayed afloat, he had to admit it was worth it, even if every one of his fingers had been covered in splinters, cuts, and bandaids at some point during the process.

"Would you look at that!" Seabiscuit exclaimed, his character's go-to phrase throughout the movie. He put his hands on his hips in triumph. "Now we can make it to the island."

"When are we going?" Jordan asked.

Seabiscuit turned to the camera, grinning. "Tonight, of course. I don't want to wait any longer."

Jordan felt a dip of dread in the pit of his stomach and, as soon as he shut off the video, said, "Are we really going over tonight?"

Looking at him as though he had three heads, Seabiscuit replied, "Of course we're going tonight. It's going to be a clear one. We can get some great shots. Why wouldn't we go tonight?"

It was a valid question, but one Jordan couldn't bring himself to answer. He was being a baby, but something about the movie project had him suddenly spooked. With the boat fixed, it was suddenly all too real. There was no going back.

Jordan slipped out of his house at nine p.m. and cycled to Seabiscuit's.

His friend was waiting behind the hedges and wheeled out his bike when he saw Jordan coming. He was recording, the light from his phone screen shining back in his face.

"Ready to get this fucker on film?" Seabiscuit asked.

Jordan tried to keep the fear from his expression, especially as it was being recorded. He forced some bravado. "Hell yeah! Let's get this son of a bitch."

Seabiscuit filmed sporadically as they rode to the plantation, capturing empty crossroads as they whizzed through the red lights, the run-down buildings in the district nearest their destination, and the thickets of trees as they descended into the overgrown mess of the lakeside.

They dumped their bikes in the grass, tying a red knot to a tree branch close by so they would know where to look on their way back to the road.

Recording, Seabiscuit held up his arm and took a close-up of a mosquito landing on his bare skin. He filmed for a while, knowing the bug was drinking deep but sacrificing future discomfort for his art. When he got the shot, he smacked the back of his phone down, crushing the bug. His own blood popped from the insect's abdomen and splattered against his phone case.

Feeling a little sick, Jordan turned away and scanned the beaten-down pathway through the thickets. He hoped there were no other kids hanging out that night. Although they had only been messed with a couple times during the day, he knew nighttime would be different. He had heard of kids at his school being dunked in the lake and worse. Whatever happened to

Alice Hawkins, she never returned to the school and her family moved to a new city soon after.

Despite the hot summer air, Jordan shivered.

"Get your phone out, dipshit," Seabiscuit instructed. "I need you to film me pushing the boat back out."

Jordan did as he was told. He waited until Seabiscuit set up a standing light, then recorded his friend uncovering the rowboat from the tarp they had used to hide it and grunting as he pushed it to the shore.

"Are you getting in?" Seabiscuit asked dramatically, pointing to the middle seat, the one with the kids' initials etched into it.

Careful not to drop his phone, Jordan moved to the boat and stepped in, bracing his other foot against the shore until he gathered his bearings. He clambered in, quickly sat down, and focused on Seabiscuit.

Seabiscuit turned the light off for the time being, but he was setting the lamp up at the front of the boat so it would shine on the island as they approached. Once he was satisfied the light was secure, he hunkered down and pushed the boat off, his feet sloshing through the water. When he climbed in, he kicked water up into Jordan's face. It tasted like decayed leaves, grit, and stagnant puddles.

Jordan swiped his arm over his mouth and spat over the side of the boat.

As though he had been rowing all his life, Seabiscuit steered the boat away from the grounds and used an oar to spin it around so both he and his lamp were facing the island. He flicked the light on, illuminating the almost-still water of the lake.

To distract himself from his fear, Jordan threw himself into filming the best shots, capturing the moody angles of Seabiscuit's shoulders rounding as he pushed out the oars, the strange island edging closer in the top of the shot. The island looked uninviting, thick with shadows. It was completely still. The nearer they got, the more the sound from the lakeside dimmed and all they heard was the gentle splashing of Seabiscuit's rowing.

"It's quiet," Jordan said.

"It was," Seabiscuit retorted, hinting Jordan shouldn't be interfering with the filming.

"No, I mean, I didn't realise how noisy it was back there with the insects and the birds. But over here there isn't anything. You'd think there'd be more here since it's never disturbed."

Seabiscuit gave the notion the smallest thought, then shrugged his shoulders, dismissing it. He held out his arm and gestured to the mosquito bite that was beginning to bloom. "Maybe that's why there's less insects. Less idiots to suck blood from over here."

It was a fair point, but the silence of the island unnerved him.

The boys sounded too loud, even in their tiny rowing boat, the lifting oars sending thunderous droplets down on the still lake water, the keel forcing waves onto the undisturbed embankment. If there was anything lurking on the island, the boys had announced their presence already.

They moored, and Jordan recorded Seabiscuit securing the boat to a rock. It was probably unnecessary with the water being so still, but it made for a good shot, and it was better to be safe than sorry. There was no way they wanted to get stranded on the island overnight.

Although Jordan was invested in the movie and tried his hardest to concentrate on filming, he had to fight the urge to constantly check over his shoulder. The island behind him felt like one huge threat, and it was hard to trust in flight mode when there was a lake between him and safety.

Still, Seabiscuit wanted to get the most important scene out of the way—an exposition piece to go at the very start of the movie documenting the island's history. He stood at the edge of the lake, speaking in a low and calm voice Jordan had never heard from his friend before.

"Is The Whistler real? That's a question that's been asked in the town over there across the lake for over seventy years, ever since two teenagers came to explore this island, Backwater Brace, in 1956. They returned safely to their homes on that fateful night, but the next morning, they, along with a sibling of one of the boys, were found deceased under peculiar circumstances. Ever since then, the island has been off-limits, this island that we stand on today. So, what are we doing here, you might ask? We're going to try and find The Whistler. And if we hear him, there's only one rule. Don't whistle back."

Jordan stopped recording and lowered the phone.

"How was that? Shall I do it again?" Seabiscuit asked.

About to answer, Jordan froze when a long, low whistle sounded from the trees behind him. He instinctively lifted the phone again and spun around as he hit record, catching the final fading beat of the chilling note as he swept the camera back and forth across the treeline.

Nerves raw, he almost dropped the phone when a second whistle sounded loudly right behind him, close to his ear.

He whipped around to find Seabiscuit standing with a curved thumb and forefinger pushed into his lips, whistling back. "What the fuck are you doing?" Jordan whispered.

Seabiscuit took his fingers out of his mouth with a wet popping sound and beamed at the camera. "We want to see if The Whistler is real, right? Well, there's only one way to make him come to us."

"We got the whistle. I managed to film the whistle. That was enough. Why the hell did you whistle back?" Jordan's panic suddenly made him feel years younger, the tremor in his voice from the threat of rare tears causing his throat to tighten. He felt out of control, as though Seabiscuit was at the wheel of a car that was plunging over a cliff and he was in the backseat with the doors locked.

Seabiscuit gawped at him. "You big baby. What are you so scared of? It's probably just the way the wind comes through a couple of branches, or a weird owl or something. That's what my dad always told me. There's no such thing as ghosts, Jordan."

Feeling like an idiot, Jordan regained his composure as Seabiscuit stomped to the treeline, lifting his phone and taking B-roll of the moon peeking through the canopy. He had been so caught up in the legend he forgot what they were doing there in the first place. They weren't really hunting a ghost. They were making a silly found-footage movie. It wasn't real. "It's not real," he murmured to himself.

But when he looked to Seabiscuit, ready to apologize for getting spooked by the island, he saw his friend was staring at him wide-eyed. He had dropped his phone at his feet and was trembling all over, so violently his teeth chattered.

"Sebastian?" Jordan hadn't used his friend's real name in years, but it came out of his mouth instinctively. "What is it?"

"He's standing behind me," Seabiscuit whispered.

Jordan couldn't see anything, but when he strode forward and grabbed his friend's arm, ready to pull him to the rowboat, he felt an icy chill coming from the space behind him. It felt *dark* in the treeline, an ominous blanket of peril that shook Jordan to the core.

Flight mode kicked in.

"Come on, let's get to the boat," he said, tugging at Seabiscuit's arm and dragging him to the small boat, all thoughts of filming out of his mind.

In their haste, both boys pushed the boat into the water and climbed in from the shallows. This time, Jordan was at the front and Seabiscuit took the middle seat.

Just as he pushed off with the oar, the boat rocked again and the seat at the back creaked as though a third party had joined them in the hull.

Seabiscuit wailed. "Jordan...he's behind me!"

Staring across the lake, home seemed so far away. He didn't dare turn around. Instead, he raised his phone, the action that had defined his whole summer, flipped the camera view, and hit record.

In the screen, he watched his lightweight jacket come into view, the angle rising over his throat and his tense mouth. He looked very pale in the moonlight. He extended his arm, filming Seabiscuit sitting quaking so hard the whole boat vibrated on the water.

The phone screen showed tears sluicing down his friend's face, his shoulders hunched up to his ears. He was making himself as small as possible, trying to hide from the thing sitting directly behind him. A thick, black shadow stuck out from Seabiscuit's left-hand side.

Jordan shifted the angle of his hand, trying to capture the space at the stern of the boat. He braced himself with his other hand and felt splintered edges in the seat that had been smooth wood just moments before. He looked down at the seat.

SH + JD 2024.

Gasping, he lifted the phone and saw through the reversed display the dark shadow rise behind Seabiscuit.

A long, low whistle filled his ears.

Little My snuck to the fridge and hunted for the good stuff. It was way past her bedtime, but she heard her parents snoring, and her stupid brother had been out with his equally dumb friend, Jordan, all night. He thought nobody knew, but she saw him wheel his bike out and hide behind the neighbor's hedge. When she told their dad over breakfast the next day, that would be the end of Sebastian's summer. He would be grounded for months.

She felt a little bit guilty, but only for a moment. Their dad had been hard on them both those last few weeks, but Sebastian acted like it was only ever him who got in trouble and that it was always her fault.

Well, let's see what he was like when he finally had something to blame her for.

She grinned and pulled out a plate of chicken hunks that had been carved from the roast that evening and covered in tinfoil. Picking up a bright-white hunk of breast, she stuffed it in her mouth and chewed happily. She felt like a grown up, wandering the house on her own at night. She was never scared, and she was proud of herself for being tough.

She carried the plate through to the living area, snapped on the lamp, and froze.

Sebastian sat on the recliner, the back of his head visible over the headrest.

Ugh. He was back. But what the hell was he doing just sitting there in the dark?

"Seb?" she whispered. When he made no move to answer, she started to get annoyed. "Don't ignore me, asshole. What are you doing over there, getting Jordan to suck you off?"

Her knowledge of the world mostly came from her brother and his friends, which meant she was wise beyond her years when it came to gross boy talk. She liked to say those things back to them, too, enjoying the shocked expression on Seb's friends' faces when she cussed or used rude terminology when she was insulting him. It annoyed Seb to see her commanding the attention of his friends, so she knew it would get a rise out of him.

Still, he didn't even flinch.

She set the plate on the sideboard, munching on a piece of chicken, and walked around to the front of the chair.

For one shocking moment, she thought she was right. Jordan lay hunched over between her brother's legs. Only, they weren't Sebastian's legs. They were oars. The wood had been forced through the stumps of her brother's torn off shins, the paddles poking out from where his arms should be, forming an X through the inside of his chest. Jordan's head was lying in Sebastian's lap, facing her, his expression one of abject horror.

Dazed and in shock, Little My peed, the hot gush pooling at her feet and mixing with the blood that had dripped and spread under the chair.

Her ears filled with the sound of a long, low whistle coming from somewhere in the house, and before she could even stop herself, her lips pursed to mimic the action.

She whistled back.

The Bayshore Butcher

Timothy King

"Hey, everyone! You're here with Aubrey and the rest of the Terror Team," Aubrey said as she waved at the camera. She was doing her best not to squint in the harsh Florida sun.

Jim moved slowly to the right, making sure to capture the entire house with his camera. When he nodded, Hannah stepped into the frame. "And we're here at the home of the infamous serial killer The Bayshore Butcher." A wide smile stretched across her face. "Guess who has exclusive access to the entire house? That's right—us! We'll even show you the spot where The Butcher took his own life during a showdown with the Tampa Police Department."

With another nod from Jim as he navigated the camera back toward Aubrey, Alexandra stepped into view. "But first," she held up her hand in a stop gesture, "like and subscribe for more paranormal and macabre videos from your favorite Terror Team!"

"Cut!" Jim ended the recording and slung his camera over his shoulder. "That was fantastic. I think we got it in one take!" He power-walked back to the team's old panel van, which rested partially in the road and partially on the curb. The sliding door was open, revealing a mess of computer and recording equipment.

The team's computer whiz and video editor, Amanda, poked her head out. "One take, huh?"

Jim nodded and ejected the card from his camera, passing it to her. "See if you can post this to TikTok or something. Maybe it can generate some buzz."

Amanda nodded. She reached out to take the card. The sleeve of her shirt lifted slightly, revealing the word veteran. The two had been working together for several years, first on an indie film crew and then on the ever-growing *Terror Team* YouTube channel. He realized he had never asked her about the tattoo and decided he would make it a priority whenever they had some free time.

"Everything's set up inside!" Kayla called from the open front door.

Jim gave her a thumbs up. "We'll be there in a minute!"

Jim marveled at just how quickly this crew had taken the internet by storm. All it took was convincing this group of misfits to break into a haunted church and let him record it. That was six months ago, and the channel already had a half-million subscribers and a very popular merch store. Breaking himself from his revelry, he clapped his hands.

"Alright, people, the sun is going down, so I want to get a couple of quick shots touring the house before we get to the Ouija board scene. Everyone remember their lines?" Jim adjusted his glasses and rubbed at his beard.

The crew answered with a chorus of yeses and sures. Aubrey gave her trademark smartass response of, "Yes, Father."

Jim just shook his head, replaced the card in his camera, and ushered them all toward the house.

The outside of the home looked like all the others along Bayshore Boulevard. It was tan, with two stories and a small fence around the property. It was wholly unremarkable, save for its prime waterfront real estate and its horrific history.

Jim entered the home for the first time. Despite being an avid horror movie connoisseur and the Terror Team being his idea, he always got freaked out by the locations they visited. He preferred to spend as little time in them as possible.

A short hallway stretched out before opening into a living room and kitchen. The walls had a fresh coat of tan paint on them, and the wood floors appeared to be brand new.

He walked into the living room, where the rest of the crew was waiting with the home's new owner.

The gentleman stood up from his position on the couch and outstretched a hand toward Jim. He was far younger than Jim expected. Judging by his black hair and muscular physique, Jim thought the guy could be in his late twenties.

"Collin," the homeowner said, introducing himself.

Jim shook his hand and returned the introduction.

"Well, everyone, let's get started!" Jim positioned his camera on a small gimbal and stood at the end of the hallway, facing the front door. Hannah stood in front of the door and brushed her dark hair over her shoulder. He was about to give the signal to start recording when something caught his eye. "Stop!" He moved around from behind his camera and marched down the hallway to where Hannah waited. Grabbing the curtains next to the door, he threw them open with an excessive amount of force. "I told you, I like natural lighting," he snapped.

"You pedantic fuck," Kayla muttered under her breath. She turned off the key light she was operating.

Returning to his position behind the camera, Jim gave her a death glare. He turned his attention back to Hannah.

When the signal came, she went into full reporter mode. Walking slowly toward the camera and dragging her finger along the wall, she recited her lines. "We're now in the home of Robert Ratliff, better known as The Bayshore Butcher. Throughout the late nineties and early two thousands, he abducted young women as they jogged up and down the beautiful stretch of road in Tampa known as Bayshore. He'd bring them back here," she waved her hands toward either wall, "and these walls would bear witness to his horrendous deeds." She stopped a few feet from the camera, like they practiced so many times before, holding a stoic look while gazing into it.

Jim ended the recording and smiled. "Flawless execution!" He turned toward the others in the living room. "Kayla, I'm worried about the lighting in the attic; the sun is going down fast. Do you think it'd be a good idea to cut right to the Ouija board scene?"

Kayla shrugged. "Yeah, that should be fine. We could always come back tomorrow and grab some B roll or add a little more back story."

Jim motioned for her to lead the way. She proceeded up the stairs, followed by the rest of the crew and the homeowner. They made their way down the poorly-lit hallway on the second floor. It was clear the new homeowner had not started renovations on this part of the house. Yellow stains coated the formerly-white drywall, leaving the place smelling like the rancid stench of cigarette smoke. They reached a wooden staircase that led into the attic.

The attic was barely big enough for everyone to fit in, but they would have to make it work. Aubrey stood in the center of the room next to a massive dark stain in the wood. Jim pointed the camera at her and nodded.

The lights Kayla had set up glistened off Aubrey's nose ring, and Jim prayed Amanda could fix it in post-production.

"This," she said, then pointed at the stain, "is the exact location where one of the most infamous serial killers in history ended his own life. A nearly ten-year-long manhunt finally led the police to this house." Aubrey spun, taking in the attic before looking over her shoulder at the camera. "Faced with the prospect of spending the rest of his life behind bars, he took the coward's way out."

Alexandra emerged from the shadows. Jim cursed himself as the light reflected off of her nose ring as well. She carried a Ouija board in her hands. Holding it up for the camera to see, she said, "The untimely demise of The Bayshore Butcher left the families of his victims without answers, but we intend to get some tonight." She walked across the room to where Aubrey and Hannah were standing.

Jim walked around the trio, creating a dramatic effect as the light shifted and shadows danced across their faces. Grinning ear to ear, he killed the recording.

"Holy shit, you guys. This is golden," Jim said. He motioned for the homeowner to come closer. "Kayla said you're interested in taking part in the Ouija-board part of the video?"

Collin nodded his head. "I actually bought this house looking for more information on The Bayshore Butcher. What better way to get info than to ask the man himself?" The younger man chuckled nervously.

Jim studied him for a minute before relenting. "Alright." He sighed deeply. "Let the girls do all the talking, though. They're professionals."

Collin threw his hands up in surrender. "Fine by me. I'm just happy to be a part of it." The smile drained from his face. He leaned in closer to Jim and retrieved a black notebook from his pocket. "I was looking for the right time to tell you about this," he whispered, "but I found The Butcher's notebook while remodeling the kitchen. I know I should turn it in to the police, but I thought you might want to take a look first?"

Hesitantly, Jim took the notebook. He turned it over in his hands, examining the old, worn-out leather. Flipping it open, he skimmed a page. It was a detailed account of a victim's movements in the weeks leading up to her disappearance. He looked back to Collin and smiled. "I think this will come in very handy for the show." Jim slid the booklet into the back pocket of his jeans before clapping again. "Alright! Positions, everyone!"

Alexandra set up the Ouija board directly on top of the stain in the wood. She grimaced at the morbid realization she was conducting a seance at the exact spot where a man had died. Shrugging it off, she exhaled slowly. Jim had insisted it would be great for views. She removed the planchette from her pocket and set it in the center of the board.

Kayla rushed around her, lighting the dozens of candles she had laid out for this shot. When she was done, she grabbed the second camera and took up position to the right of Jim.

Hannah, Alexandra, and Aubrey sat around the Ouija board. They looked at the homeowner, Collin, expectantly. When he didn't respond, Aubrey patted the spot on the ground next to her. "Sit." She flashed him a devilish smile. "We won't bite."

He followed her command, sitting cross-legged next to the girls. "Now, you won't have to say much," Aubrey assured him. "When I mention doing the Ouija board in the spot where The Butcher died, you can just say something like, 'I heard that's ideal for speaking to the dead.'" She patted Collin's arm. "Oh, and keep your fingers on the planchette at all times."

Collin nodded and stuck his fingertips out, lightly grazing the piece on the board.

Hannah giggled. "Are you nervous?" she asked Collin.

He nodded. "I've never done anything like this before. My family is Catholic, so my mom is going to lose it if she finds out."

The girls giggled at his awkwardness.

"Alright, quiet," Jim ordered. He pressed the record button on his camera and held up three fingers. He slowly dropped each finger, then pointed to Aubrey.

Jumping right into character, Aubrey leaned in close to the group and whispered, "We're about to conduct a seance directly on top of the spot where The Bayshore Butcher took his own life." She flicked her eyes to Collin.

She was grateful he took the cue and matched her body language.

"I heard this is the most effective way to communicate with the dead," he whispered.

Hannah nodded. Kayla moved around slowly with her camera, catching the gesture. "Some ground rules before we get started," Hannah said. "Once we start, we can't take our hands off until we close the portal to the other side. As everyone knows, any spirit could pretend to be The Butcher, so we have come up with a test to confirm who we're speaking to."

Alexandra leaned in with an excited expression across her face. "That's right," she said. "The Butcher's last words were, 'I regret nothing.'" Alexandra glanced over her shoulder as if making sure nobody was listening. She dropped her voice even lower, and Jim was grateful he had concealed microphones on each of them. "We will ask whoever we speak to for The Butcher's last words."

Aubrey looked around the group as Jim panned the camera to capture each face. All of them held their serious gazes except Collin, who looked absolutely petrified. "Let's begin," she said. Together, they slid the planchette around the board as Hannah spoke.

"We call upon the spirits that dwell in this house to speak to us. Is there anyone here with us?" They kept their hands on the planchette, waiting for it to move.

When nothing happened for a few seconds, Alexandra tried. "If there are any spirits in our presence, please use this board to communicate."

Jim motioned to Kayla to move in closer. Kayla followed his lead, getting a close up shot of the board in the dim lighting.

Without warning, the planchette slid a few inches to the left. Hannah screamed, and Collin yanked his hands off the board. The scared homeowner slid backward on his butt. Jim cursed under his breath as the idiot moved out of the camera's frame.

"Put your hands back on it!" Aubrey yelled at Collin. He just sat there with a terrified but dumbfounded look on his face. "Now!" she commanded. He slowly crawled forward and placed his hands back on the piece.

Aubrey took a deep breath. "Is there a spirit here with us now?"

The blanched slowly slid to the Yes on the board. They gasped in unison.

"Who's moving it?" Collin demanded. He looked at each girl as they shook their heads.

"This is real, Collin. You need to process this quickly," Hannah snapped.

Alexandra leaned in closer to the board. "Is this the spirit of The Bayshore Butcher?"

A chill ran down Kayla's back as the temperature in the attic dropped drastically.

The planchette slid to the left a few inches before darting back to Yes. They all shared an excited glance.

Jim pivoted around the group, getting a wide shot with the candles in the background. He waved his hand, encouraging the group to continue. Excitement overtook him as he looked through the screen on the back of the camera. This was going to be YouTube gold.

"If this is really the spirit of The Butcher, what were your last words?" Aubrey asked. The planchette swirled in a small circle before jerking across the board so hard it forced Hannah's hands to slip off. She scrambled to lean forward and return her hands to the planchette. When she looked down to see where the piece stopped, her heart froze. It was on the R.

The piece slowly slid over to E, then quickly to G. It followed this slow process until it spelled out REGRET.

"Can you do something to prove to our viewers this is real?" Alexandra asked. They waited a few seconds. When nothing happened, she tried to ask again. "Can you..." but she was cut off by a shriek from Hannah.

Hannah jumped to her feet and looked behind her. "Something fucking touched me!" she screamed. Jim grimaced at her use of profanity. They would have to edit that in post—YouTube didn't like cursing in their most popular videos, and TikTok would definitely age restrict anything with cursing.

"I'm serious," she shrieked.

"We believe you," Aubrey said. "Sit down so we can say goodbye to the spirit and close the connection."

Hannah slowly lowered herself back to her spot at the board. She stuck out her hands but hesitated, with her fingers a few inches from the planchette.

"Come on," Alexandra encouraged. "Let's finish this."

Hannah touched the piece, and the group slid it toward the word Goodbye. Just as it reached the G, it stopped moving. Aubrey looked up at Hannah. Her eyes were wide with fear.

"Why'd you stop it?" Aubrey asked.

"I didn't," Hannah stammered.

"What do you..." Aubrey tried to ask, but the planchette slid back toward her. "Ok, Hannah, quit messing around," Aubrey said in the sternest voice she could manage. The piece jerked to the left, forcing Aubrey's fingers off it. "Seriously, Hannah, what the fuck?" she shrieked, desperately trying to get her fingers back on it.

The piece jerked again, faster this time. Aubrey was getting ready to yell at her friend again but stopped. There were deep indents in her friend's skin, just below the elbow. It looked as if someone had hold of her arm. Hannah looked up at her with tears in her eyes. "Help me," Hannah begged. The skin around her neck was indented, just like her arm. While the group stared at their friend, the piece moved again.

Subtly, it began forming a figure eight across the board. It moved faster and faster until Alexandra realized what was happening.

"No!" she shouted at the same time as the bulbs blew out in the studio lights. She grabbed the planchette.

The candles went out.

In the darkness, someone screamed. There was the sound of glass crashing to the floor and shattering into tiny pieces.

Jim fumbled with the camera, fighting to locate the external light switch. His fingers clicked switches blindly until the light flicked on, casting its weak illumination around the room. The girls had moved away from the Ouija board and scattered across the empty attic. Collin sat alone. His hands were the only ones remaining on the board. Jim ran the light around the room, locating Aubrey and Alexandra, huddled together in the far corner of the room. Beside him, the light on Kayla's camera burst to life as she found the switch.

He scanned the room, looking for Hannah. He found her lying flat on the floor behind him. She was trembling, and a dark patch stained her jeans. Jim took a step forward but fell to his knees, struggling to hold the camera.

A burning sensation exploded up his spine, radiating from his right buttock. It rippled through his skin and seared the nerve endings. He fell forward onto his stomach, screaming in pain.

"Oh my god! Jim, what's wrong?" Kayla asked. She lowered her camera to the ground and rushed to his side.

He arched his back as the pain ripped through him, consuming every inch of his body. Gasping for air, his lips turned purple. The skin around his neck constricted, and he started convulsing. He shook violently on the ground, foam pouring from his open mouth. Kayla attempted to hold him down, desperately trying to prevent him from hurting himself. She cried for help, but nobody else moved. Aubrey and Alexandra sat curled up in the corner. Collin continued tracking the planchette in ever wider figure eights, and Hannah trembled on the ground.

Just as Kayla released him, Jim stopped shaking. He blinked slowly and pushed himself up to his knees.

"Jim, are you ok?" Kayla asked. She put a hand on his back and rubbed vigorously. "Jim, can you hear me?"

He blinked slowly and pulled the notebook from his back pocket. Flipping through the pages, Kayla saw hundreds of pages with chicken-scratch-like handwriting scribbled across them. He pressed the notebook to his lips before returning it to his pocket.

"What're you doing, Jim?" Kayla asked again.

Jim reached out and gripped his camera. Sliding it to himself, he held it in his hand for a moment, bouncing it up and down as if weighing it. Without warning, he turned and smashed it into Kayla's face. Blood spurted from the massive laceration across her forehead. She crumpled to the floor, already unconscious. He climbed on top of her, hoisting the camera far above his head. He brought it down again, crushing her skull.

Aubrey screamed at the top of her lungs but didn't move. She stayed in her corner, petrified.

Alexandra leaped to her feet and sprinted for the staircase. Jim stood up and threw the broken camera as hard as he could. It hit Alexandra square in the back, sending her tumbling forward. She yelped from the pain but continued trying to crawl toward the exit. Tears streaked her face as she muttered a prayer.

Jim strutted across the room, grabbing one of the tripods that supported his studio lighting equipment. He tore the light from atop the tripod and tossed it uselessly to the floor. Standing over Alexandra, he raised the pole up, turned it over, and drove it down with all his might. The pole pierced the back of her neck and embedded itself in the wooden floor below. Alexandra managed a few choked gurgles before the life drained from her body.

Placing his hand on his chin, Jim cracked his neck. He paused with his hand there, rubbing his thick beard as if realizing for the first time there was hair there. He shrugged and turned back toward the others. None of them had moved. He walked over to Collin, who was still in a trance-like state. The young real estate tycoon continued dragging the planchette in figure eights across the Ouija board. Placing a hand under his chin and the other on top of Collin's head, he jerked them in opposite directions. There was an ear-shattering crack as the bones in the homeowner's neck exploded. He slumped to the floor.

The crack finally brought Aubrey out of her dissociative state. She jumped to her feet and kicked as hard as she could. The top of her foot connected with Jim's head, sending him toppling to the floor. He groaned and said a curse while gripping his ear.

She tried to kick him again, but this time, Jim managed to grab her foot. He yanked hard, causing her to lose her balance. She crashed to the ground next to him. Without hesitation, he reached across her body and grabbed her nose.

Aubrey's eyes opened wide, and her heart slammed against her chest. The realization of what was about to happen set in. Jim grabbed the nose ring and pulled. The metal tore through the tender flesh of Aubrey's nose. She squealed with the explosion of pain.

Aubrey's hands instinctively went to her face. While she fidgeted with her nose, trying to stop the blood pouring down her chin, Jim felt around for something to use.

His fingers bumped into a broken shard of glass. He looked over at it and realized it was from one of the broken candles. The jagged edges of the glass bit into his skin as he grabbed it. Sucking in a deep breath, he gritted his teeth through the pain. Jim howled a barbaric roar as he swung the makeshift weapon.

Aubrey gasped when the shard of glass entered her throat. Blood bubbled from the wound and seeped onto the floor.

Jim pulled the shard out, only to stab her again. She continued her struggle against Jim, swinging her fists wildly at his face. She managed to break his glasses.

They fell from his face and cracked on the ground. The victory was short-lived, however, as Jim drove the glass home for the final time. He locked eyes with her and lowered his face until their noses were nearly touching. A cruel smile spread across his face as he watched her life fade.

Gathering up the last of his breath, Jim forced himself to crawl over to Hannah, who was still lying on the floor. When he reached her, he realized immediately why she hadn't tried to escape or help her friends.

Her neck jutted to one side at an impossible angle. It was clearly broken, and she was totally immobilized. Her eyes flicked about the room frantically. Jim sensed her panic rising as he placed his hands around her injured neck. He squeezed with all his might. The already shattered bones crunched under the pressure, giving way with little resistance. He continued squeezing until her life faded, just like her friends.

Once he was sure they were all dead, he removed the little black notebook from his back pocket. He dug a pen from one of his other pockets and flipped the notebook to a blank page near the end of the book. He began writing the details of the massacre in the same chicken-scratch handwriting as the other notes. When he was done, he stood up and admired his handy work. Once the carnage of the scene had firmly planted itself in his mind, he descended the steps and left the house.

Outside, Amanda leaned against the van, smoking a cigarette. "Everything ok in there?" she asked. "Heard a lot of screaming."

Jim nodded. "Yeah, they just got freaked out while messing with the Ouija board." Jim continued walking toward Amanda and the van. "Let's go get some food. I'm starving."

Amanda eyed him suspiciously. As he stepped closer, Amanda saw blood coating his right shirt sleeve. She reached into the van and removed a wooden baseball bat. "Why is there blood on your arm, Jim?"

Jim glanced down at his sleeve, then shook his head. He removed the shard of glass he used to kill Aubrey from his pocket. "I was hoping to do this the easy way," Jim said. A wicked smile stretched across his face. "But. . ." He held the broken glass out like a knife.

"I regret nothing."

Love Lost
LM Kaplin

J anice knew the risks involved in what she was about to do. She had read enough books on the subject to understand that even with meticulous planning and perfect execution, any attempt to make contact with the spirit world could result in disastrous consequences. Consequences that could be mitigated if she had a partner to help her with the ritual, but this was a task she had to perform alone. For her to pull off this trick, she couldn't afford to let anyone in on her little secret. It wasn't like she had any friends who would go along with something like this, anyway. So she carefully read the incantation displayed on her phone for the hundredth time, even though she already memorized the entire passage.

She spent the past three months preparing for this moment and committed every step of the ritual to memory, but she checked the words on the screen again, regardless. Trying not to think of the danger involved, her inspection of the page was more of a delay tactic to calm her nerves than anything else.

The thought of using an ancient ritual to contact her dead husband and bring him back to the physical world in a new body sounded romantic in her head. However, sitting in front of the makeshift altar with a struggling crow in her grasp, she wondered if she had the resolve to go through with it. She looked down at the unconscious man tied to her bedposts and knew she had come too far to turn back.

Janice felt a pinch in her heart at the mere thought of returning to her lonely existence—spending the days lying in bed and moping around the house with barely even enough motivation to eat. She knew it was no life for a woman in her forties, but without Andrew, she had no will to go on.

If Janice had been a little older and better prepared for the loss of her husband, maybe she wouldn't have taken it so hard. But at her age, the concept of being a widow never even crossed her mind. That changed when she received a phone call from Andrew's office letting her know he had collapsed while jogging during his lunch break. Janice raced to the hospital, but by the time she arrived, he was already gone. The doctor explained he suffered a massive heart attack, likely brought on by a lifelong love of fried foods paired with a family history of heart disease.

Needless to say, Janice took it hard, finding herself completely unprepared to continue with day-to-day life on her own. Having no children to share her grief, Jance locked herself away, staying in bed for weeks on end. She had no motivation to return to a normal semblance of life or have contact with the outside world—until the day she fell down a rabbit hole online.

An advertisement for a medium who claimed to speak with the dead caught her eye. She clicked on the banner in a desperate hope to contact Andrew and bid him one last goodbye. After looking at the website, she quickly saw through the scam offering, but the idea sparked a fire in Janice that spiraled into an obsession.

She began searching websites, forums, and libraries for claims of people who had contacted the spirit world. After only a few hours of research, she realized weeding through the fraudsters and attention seekers would be quite the task.

Determined to find a way, eventually she stumbled on a message board that caught her attention. This forum seemed different from the countless articles and websites promoting psychic abilities for sale. The posts she read described ways not only to contact the deceased, but to retrieve their soul and ferry it back to the world of the living. After reading enough posts claiming the method worked successfully, Janice was on a mission to be reunited with Andrew, no matter the risk.

She read every post on the forum, and when she finished, she read them all again, soaking up as much information about the process as possible. With a head full of knowledge on the matter, Janice had complete faith in the ritual. She would have to if she dared attempt the procedure. Although the process only required a few items, finding a new host for Andrew's spirit to inhabit could prove quite the challenge.

Janice read of one successful case where a soul was brought back into their own body, but the procedure was performed only minutes after their passing. For Andrew, returning to his body was no longer an option.

Janice knew finding someone willing to hand themselves over in order to resurrect her husband was an unlikely task. For the first few days, she blindly hoped a candidate would fall into her lap, but she quickly realized if she wanted to bring her beloved back, she would need a more proactive approach.

It would be risky, especially as a petite woman. Attempting to subdue a man and force him to take part in the ritual seemed like a tall order. Sure, there were a couple of elderly men in the neighborhood she would be able to overpower, but she didn't want Andrew to come back as a geriatric.

Her best chance for success would be to drug the unlucky man, whoever he may be. Janice had plenty of prescription sleeping pills in the cabinet. The doctor had given her a cornucopia of medications to get through the restless nights after Andrew passed. Slipping a few into someone's drink would be easy enough, but whose? And how would she get them to her house? She rarely left home and hadn't entertained in years. Her only contact with the outside world was through her computer.

That's when the obvious answer dawned on her. There was an endless supply of male suitors on the multitude of dating sites littering the web. Having been happily married and uninterested in the cesspool of online dating, she had always ignored the ads that followed her to every corner of the internet, but with her current requirement, they were the perfect answer to her problem.

So Janice created an account and browsed the available options. It felt strange choosing a new body for her husband. It was almost as if she was living in some dystopian future where people selected their mate by entering specifications into a computer and five minutes later, a fancy 3D printer extruded your perfect partner.

Although the process wasn't quite that seamless, it might as well have been.

Overwhelmed by the available options, Janice made a list of the physical qualities she wanted, ignoring any interests and personality traits which would soon be erased and written over like an old videotape. When she finished composing the features for her ideal husband, she looked it over and was surprised to see every trait listed was the polar opposite of Andrew. It wasn't that she wasn't attracted to her husband. Janice had always thought of Andrew as a handsome man, if not a little plain—but physical appearance had never been important to her. Having her pick of the litter, why not look for an upgrade? Surely a newer model with fewer miles on it would look good attached to her arm.

After narrowing down the list of potential candidates to three, she messaged them all and let fate decide the rest. The first to answer would be the lucky winner of her find-a-new-body-for-my-deceased-husband sweepstakes.

As expected, she didn't have to wait long for a reply. Within five minutes, her phone buzzed and a guy named Aiden was blowing up her inbox. He had no plans for the evening and promised to be at her house after he finished work.

From the moment his car pulled up to her house, Janice wondered if she was making a huge mistake. She took a deep breath to calm her nerves before opening the door to reveal a strikingly good-looking man holding a single red rose. He reached out for her hand and gave it a kiss, causing Janice to recoil at the romantic gesture. She stepped back into the house, clearing the entryway, and gave a motion to invite him inside.

Already mortified at the prospect of having another man in her house, Aiden's nonchalant attitude rubbed Janice the wrong way. He acted like he had done this a hundred times before, and he probably had. She would feel more comfortable with someone who was as nervous as her.

Although easy on the eyes, it became immediately apparent Aiden's personality was borderline intolerable. Between his arrogant jokes and self-centered behavior, Janice didn't know how much of him she could take. Eager to get on with the ritual and be reunited with her husband, she went to the kitchen to pour drinks, hoping to ease the tension and put her plan into action.

She retrieved a small envelope from the drawer and opened it to reveal a coarse, white powder—the remnants of four pills she crushed earlier. She dumped the contents into a beer. Just as she slipped the envelope back into the drawer, she felt something tickle her back. The unexpected touch caused her to jump and almost knock over the drink as Aiden's hands glided along the sides of her hips. She inhaled sharply and prayed he didn't see her transgression. By the time she turned and their eyes met, he moved in for a kiss.

Janice backed away and picked up the beer, putting it between them as if it was a shield. "I'm terribly sorry," she said, her voice wavering. "I'm just a little nervous. It's been a long time since I've been with anyone besides my husband, rest his soul. How about a drink first?"

"Sure thing," Aiden replied, and accepted the beer. "I didn't mean to come on too strong. You're just really pretty, and I thought that's why you invited me over."

She knew the stranger in her house was only after one thing, and it embarrassed her to think about that with anyone except for Andrew. She watched him sip the beer, willing him to drink faster. Janice didn't know how long until the drugs kicked in but hoped she could avoid his advances until then.

In the meantime, they made small talk, but every word he spoke left a worse taste in her mouth. She could never see herself dating, much less spending the rest of her life with, someone like him. Janice was ready to call the whole thing off and tell him to leave when she remembered his grating personality didn't matter. His revolting political views and tiresome social commentary would be a thing of the past when Andrew returned. It wasn't hard for Janice to convince herself she would actually be doing the world a favor by getting rid of this guy and bringing back someone like Andrew.

As soon as Aiden finished the beer and dozed off on the couch, she stood up and put her plan into action. Besides the new host, there were only two other items required to bring a soul back from the other side, both of which she had already acquired.

The soul's return journey wouldn't be possible without a crow to guide it. Known as a link between the living world and the spirit realm, crows ushered the souls of the newly deceased to their home in the heavens. Apparently, with a little guidance, they could also lead spirits back to the land of the living. The crow only needed one final item that allowed them to pick up the scent—a piece of flesh from the departed's corpse.

Luckily, Janice opted for a traditional burial instead of a cremation, mostly due to Andrew's parents' religious views and their offer to pay the additional cost. She had already performed the uninviting labor of digging up Andrew's grave the previous week.

Janice quickly learned how out of shape she was while exhuming his body. Over an hour passed before she uncovered the coffin, but she completed her task undisturbed. She prepared herself for the smell before opening his casket but had not considered Andrew's unsightly appearance. After spending three months in the earth, his brown and shriveled skin made him resemble an emaciated animal that had been cooked too long on the barbeque. Taking a deep breath in an attempt to hold down her lunch, she reached into her bag and pulled out a brand new pair of garden shears.

Janice was thankful she found the message board when she did. If she had waited much longer, there wouldn't have been any flesh left to harvest, and Andrew's soul would have been lost forever. She had read warnings about using old bones for the ceremony and knew the danger in attempting to bring back someone who had traveled too far on the other side. The more time passed since a person's death, the further their soul traveled and the harder it was to retrieve them.

Janice picked up Andrew's hand and squeezed his fingers. Although not as meaty as other parts of his body, the skin remained mostly intact and still held decomposing tissue beneath. The thin digits would be much easier to collect than opening his stomach and digging through rotting innards. Using the clippers, she took off the two largest fingers from his right hand, wincing each time at the cracking sound while she cut through the bone. She dropped the severed digits into a Ziplock baggie and sealed it.

With her prize in hand, she began the tedious job of filling in the open grave. After smoothing out the dirt as best she could, she scurried back to her car, thanking her lucky stars no one interrupted the gruesome task.

Between digging up her dead husband and drugging a strange man, finding a crow for the ceremony had been a walk in the park. The annoying creatures woke her up at the crack of dawn every morning with their squawking, without fail, even on Sundays. The trap she bought worked on its first try. Janice set it up in her backyard near the birds' favorite hangout spot, with a strip of raw meat inside. She awoke the next morning, finding her catch locked inside.

With a host for Andrew's soul, all three of the requirements were in place and the ceremony could begin. She glanced at her phone and licked her lips, taking a deep breath before reciting the incantation aloud.

Her mouth moved as if on its own. The strange sounds spewed from her lips like she had spoken the ancient tongue her entire life. Although she didn't understand the words she spoke, she said them clearly and with purpose, making sure to enunciate each syllable.

As she neared the end of the passage, Janice noticed Aiden's arm move slightly. Although he wasn't awake yet, he would be soon, and the ceremony was far from complete. Regardless of his arousal, she couldn't let herself be distracted, so she returned to the task at hand and prayed his restraints would hold.

Ready to continue to the next step, Janice opened the baggie that sat in her refrigerator for the past four nights. Gagging on the putrid smell that instantly filled the room, she removed one of the severed fingers from the bag and raised it toward the cage. The bird became instantly agitated, flapping its wings wildly inside the small enclosure.

Janice brought the rotting finger closer to the bird and it relaxed, watching her intently with its large black eyes. When the shriveled piece of flesh came within striking distance, the crow lurched forward, grabbing it with its mouth and almost taking Janice's finger along with it.

She withdrew her hand, clutching it to her chest in protection, and watched as the oversized bird opened its mouth and swallowed its treat whole. The bird's unblinking eyes remained fixed on Janice the entire time.

After inspecting her hand and counting her fingers, she approached the cage again and picked up the enclosure. Taking it outside, she set the cage down on the front lawn and unlatched the door, stepping back quickly as she did so. Although she expected the crow to fly off immediately, it remained inside the trap, staring at her.

Janice didn't know what to do. She thought back to the ritual and wondered if she missed a step, but with her extensive preparation, she found that unlikely. Just as she lurched forward to give the cage a small kick, the bird let out a loud caw and flapped its wings. A few seconds later, it was nothing more than a black dot flying off into the horizon.

Although she felt sure of the process until this point, seeing the bird fly away, Janice suddenly found it unlikely it would return at all, let alone with the soul of her husband. She wanted to kick herself for being so foolish. No. She took a deep breath and cleared her mind. Thoughts like that wouldn't help anything. She had to trust the process.

With nothing else to do but wait, she returned inside to find Aiden awake, a look of bewilderment on his face.

Upon seeing Janice enter, a flood of memories came rushing back to him, and he renewed his struggle against the restraints tying him to the bed. "What are you doing?" he asked. "Where am I?"

"You're at my house. You came over for a visit, remember?" Janice replied. "I'm really sorry about this, but if you relax, I'll untie you shortly. And if you're really lucky, you still might get what you came over here for... Although I guess you won't really be you anymore by then." The second half of the sentence she mumbled more to herself than anyone else.

"Look," he replied, "I don't know what this is or what you're doing, but just untie me and I'll forget any of this ever happened."

Janice smiled at him with a look of pity. She knew there was no point in trying to comfort the young man, so she turned toward the window instead, hoping the crow would return soon.

She had read of instances where the courier came back with the wrong spirit or failed to return at all. There were many possible reasons for a fruitless journey, some beyond the summoner's control. An unwilling soul could make the crow's return trip difficult, but she had to believe Andrew was as eager for their reunion as her.

Just as these doubts swirled through her head, she saw it. Although they all look the same to her, when she noticed the large bird perched on a branch nearby, looking back at her with a beady black eye, she knew instantly it was the one.

She opened the front door, and the bird swooped down, flying inside the house and landing on Aiden's chest. The large bird caused him to redouble his efforts, bucking and twisting his body in an attempt to make the bird flee from its spot.

Focused on the avian perched upon him, he failed to notice Janice pick up a kitchen knife from a side table until she extended her arm and the bird flew to her, landing on her palm. Aiden already felt the bruises forming on his wrists, but after noticing the blade, and with his life on the line, he had no other choice but to continue his struggle.

Holding the instrument in one hand and the bird in the other, Janice recited the next passage as if it had been etched on the back of her hand since birth. The crow tilted its head from side to side as she spoke, while Aiden watched with a mixture of horror and fascination at the foreign words.

When she finished the invocation, Janice stepped up onto the bed and straddled Aiden, positioning herself so her knees pinned his shoulders. She had to keep him as still as possible for the last part of the ritual.

Holding the bird out in front of her, she pointed the tip of the knife at the crow's neck and pushed it through the thick layer of feathers until the bird let out a squawk and went limp. With the dead bird in her hand, she dug the blade deeper into the animal until a stream of blood rolled down her wrist. Seeing the spilling fluid, Janice straightened the crow in an attempt to preserve as much blood as possible. With the bird clutched in her hand and red liquid dripping through the cracks in her fingers, she had the odd sensation of holding a melting ice cream cone—though she didn't have the urge to lick at the sticky substance slipping down her wrist.

Dropping the knife to her side, she held the dead crow in both hands and turned it upside down, squeezing the feathery carcass as she positioned it above Aiden's mouth.

He continued to fight, turning his head back and forth to avoid the stream of red juice spilling onto his face. Aiden kept his mouth sealed tight until Janice grabbed him by the jaw and squeezed his cheeks. The pressure caused his lips to open and allowed the blood to seep inside his mouth. When the first drop hit his tongue, he spat it out, but in doing so allowed even more of the fluid to find its way into his open orifice.

By the time the carcass dried up, Janice was satisfied he had ingested enough for the ritual to be complete. Dropping what remained of the dead bird onto the bed, she reached for a piece of tape to seal Aiden's mouth to prevent him from spitting out any more of the precious plasma.

With the ritual done, she rose from the bed and breathed a sigh of relief. Now, all she had to do was wait.

As the seconds ticked by in awkward silence, she felt Aiden's eyes on her, glaring with hatred. She didn't blame him. She barely recognized herself for what she was doing to this innocent man. Even if he held different morals than her, he didn't deserve this. But she was desperate. She just wanted the deed to be done and to have her husband back.

Janice watched him intently, waiting for a change in his disposition. She didn't want to remove the gag before the transition was complete, but she couldn't bear the thought of Andrew returning to this world bound in such a way.

Frozen in anticipation, finally she noticed something familiar in his expression.

Fear still glossed his eyes, but a look of confusion crossed his face as he looked rapidly from side to side, like an animal caught in a trap. Finally, his gaze found Janice. When he did, his focus remained with her.

Even in a new body and without saying a word, she recognized her husband immediately. She ran to his side and peeled back the tape covering his mouth.

Andrew gasped for air with his mouth's newfound freedom as Janice untied his arms. She didn't need to wait for further confirmation of her husband's return. When it came to Andrew, she trusted her instincts.

As soon as he caught his breath, he stammered, "Wha-what is this? Where am I?"

The man sounded no different from the stranger she met earlier, but she knew her husband anywhere, even with an unfamiliar voice and face.

"Andy, it's me, Janice. I've brought you back." By that time, she had released his bonds and wrapped her arms around him in a tight embrace.

"Back?" he replied as he pushed her away with confusion in his voice. "Back from where? What do you mean?"

It was then Janice realized Andrew didn't quite understand the situation. She hadn't thought about where he had been or what he would remember from his time on the other side. She would have to explain it to him gently. The last thing she wanted was to shock him with the news of his death and subsequent resurrection. "What's the last thing you remember?"

"I... I was out for a jog at work." He hesitated before continuing, speaking slowly as the memories came back to him. "I had chest pain, and I don't know, I think I was in an ambulance."

Not knowing how else to break it to him, she began, "I'm so sorry, Andy. That was months ago. You didn't make it." She paused, waiting for him to comprehend the news.

A flash of realization crossed his face as the details of his death came back to him.

"Then, where am I?" he asked again, looking down at his arms and chest for the first time and realizing something was different about himself. "What is this?" The panic in his tone rose as he stood, pushing Janice off him.

He stumbled his way toward the bathroom, anxious to look at himself in the mirror, while Janice grasped for his arm to prevent him from walking away.

"Please, just listen to me for a minute and I'll explain," she begged, unable to slow his advance.

When he reached the mirror and looked at himself, he didn't know what to think or say. His mind reeled, not knowing how this was possible. He looked into his reflection but saw the face of a stranger staring back.

"It was the only way," Janice said, standing in the doorway and pulling on his arm, hoping Andrew would understand.

"The only way for what?" Andrew replied. "What is going on? Who the hell am I?!"

"Just some guy I found. It doesn't matter. It's just a body. The only thing that matters is that you're back and we can be together again."

"Some guy you found? What does that even mean?" His voice wavered with a mix of anger and confusion. "I don't know you anymore. I don't even know myself," he said, motioning to the mirror. "Why couldn't you just let me rest in peace?" The questions racing through his mind overwhelmed him, and he felt his knees buckling as he tried to comprehend the situation.

"Just calm down, Andy. I needed you," Janice replied, moving closer to her husband and reaching for his hand.

"Well, I don't know what this is," he said, motioning to himself, "but it isn't me." He pulled away from her, his temper rising.

"It might be a different body, but it's still you inside. That's all that matters."

"No!" shouted Andrew, pushing Janice away.

She stumbled backward but quickly regained her balance. Andrew's reaction to his resurrection caught her completely off-guard. Regardless of his unhinged behavior, she believed he would come to terms with their new reality. He only needed time to adjust.

"Relax," she said. "Take a moment and think about it. We have another chance to be together. I realize this must be a jarring experience, but consider the possibilities. You're ten years younger and in better shape than you've ever been. Isn't that better than the alternative?"

"Maybe for you!" he cried. "I was at peace. It was the first peace I've had since... Well, since I've met you. You always think you know what's best for us, but you really only care about what's best for you. You've never once stopped to ask what I wanted."

Andrew was furious at being ripped back to this existence with no regard for his own desires. Looking at Janice, he saw an expression of deep hurt and sadness spread across her face. Although her actions came from a place of endearment, he didn't care. Any love or empathy he once had for his wife had evaporated.

Glancing back at the mirror, his mind couldn't come to terms with the alien face looking back at him. Andrew could no longer contain his anger, nor did he want to. Rearing back, he threw a haymaker at the man in the mirror. Upon impact, a shot of pain tore through his arm, and spiderwebs fractured the reflection. But instead of disappearing into the ether as Andrew had hoped, the stranger looking back at him remained, only Andrew saw an even more distorted version of the man he had become.

Troubled by Andrew's unrest, Janice stepped toward him with her arms out, hoping to ease his tortured mind. Her eagerness to help only threw fuel on the fire burning inside him, and her touch threw him into a frenzy.

He launched his closed fists at the mirror over and over until his knuckles were nothing more than scraps of tattered flesh that hung off him like an insect shedding its skin. More blood splattered the splintered surface with each impact of his fist.

Seeing Andrew's furor, Janice pulled him, hoping to stop him from inflicting any more damage to himself, but with her meager stature, her efforts did little to stop the repeated blows.

As she struggled to prevent any further injury to her husband, something unexpectedly crashed into her face, sending her flying to the ground. Stunned from the impact, she looked up to see what hit her, only to find Andrew's fist come crashing down into her jaw. Having finished with his reflection, he found a new outlet for his rage.

She gasped as one of her front teeth flew down her throat, gagging her on its way down. As she choked on the blood pooling in the back of her mouth, a hailstorm of punches pounded her into the ground, sending any thoughts of reconciliation with her husband down the garbage disposal.

Each blow felt like a million razor-sharp teeth biting at her flesh as the glass fragments embedded in Andrew's knuckles punctured and tore at her skin. Janice's vision blurred as tears filled her eyes and the muscles in her face swelled. She looked up at her attacker through her tear-filled eyes, pleading for help and struggling against his might, but only saw a hazy shadow looming over her. In the end, she was lucky not to see the hate in Andrew's eyes as he delivered repeated crippling blows to her cranium.

Just as she was ready to release her hold on this world and allow the darkness to overtake her, the brutality ceased. Janice gasped for air and strained to open her swollen eyes in time to see the hulking shape above her rise. She sighed in relief as she realized Andrew had finally come to his senses. A whisper of thanks to God escaped Janice's lips just as the heel of a shoe came crashing down into the bridge of her nose. The impact shattered the cartilage in her nasal passage and fractured a portion of her skull beneath. Within a moment, Janice left her body behind and found herself traveling into the same void from where Andrew had just returned.

With the couple's reunion at an end, Andrew stood in front of the vanity and looked at himself in the mirror again. He hadn't yet wrapped his head around the situation. Maybe Janice was right; he needed to slow down and collect himself.

Although he had no recollection of his time on the other side, he knew he had been at rest in a sea of calm. His first instinct was to find his way back to the nothingness where he had spent the past three months. It was the first peace and quiet he had in decades. For a moment, he considered killing himself in an attempt to return to the emptiness, but then he remembered that with his luck, Janice would be there waiting for him.

Eventually, another idea came to him. He was free of his wife and all the responsibilities of his past life. He had a new, younger body and could start over, be anyone he wanted to. Well, maybe not anyone. He went back to the bedroom and found a wallet and phone on the nightstand beside the bed where he had been restrained.

After taking a few minutes to look through the contents of both, he dialed 911.

"Hello, I have an emergency. My name is Aiden Goodman. I was drugged and abducted by some lady. I escaped and she attacked me. I had to kill her in self defense. The address is 65 Sunset Terrace. I'll be waiting outside. I'm unarmed."

Welcome Home

M. L. Rayner

*D*ONG.

The sound fades into the night, carried with the wind that sweeps across the country path.

Outside, the snowy garden glistens in the moonlight, its pure white covering the run-down stables and resembling a feather cushion. Just behind, a large wooden barn leans menacingly to one side. Its roof has long since collapsed, with rotting doors battered. And its brittle oak frame has grown so accustomed to the wind that I'm sure it's about to flop.

My hand grips the final post, leading me onto a red paved footpath that is sheltered by the branches of an overhanging tree. It's wet and slippery, and with each step, the loose bricks shift beneath my feet. I stop dead, my leading foot sliding to an unsteady halt.

Straight ahead, the house reaches tall out of the hillside, nestled away in the company of nearby trees and plants which, over the years, have spread wild, climbing to the base of the windows. The old house looms in shadows, its sleeping walls untouched by the light of the silvery moon, as though solitude itself is its one true companion, far from the warm, loving home I remember.

I edge closer nervously, following the path that holds back the untamed garden. With each step, the house grows taller, towering over me. Its blackened windows are soulless yet, in some unnerving way, watchful as I approach, patiently waiting to draw me in.

I'm standing on the doorstep. The doorbell's chain sways calmly to the motion of a bitter breeze. I reach out to grab it, tightening my hand around its rusty chain. My fingers are numb, dead to the bone. I pull it, but there is neither a ding nor a dong. There is simply nothing. Silence.

I try again, harder this time, giving it a good, solid tug. But as I do, the chain falls loose, striking the floor with a *clank*. *Bugger*, I think, so I rap on the door instead.

Knock, knock, knock.

Still there is nothing. So, I lean forward, pressing my ear to the door.

It's deathly quiet inside, not so much as a mutter. No footsteps, no fumbling, and no joyous voices eager to greet me home. The only sound I do hear is the faint chime of the hallway clock, signaling the lateness of the hour.

I'm about to knock again, to thump the bloody door down if that's what it takes. But as I do, the latch—it *clicks*, like someone's unlocking it from the other side. I push the door with force, half expecting the panel to push back just as hard. Only it doesn't. The door, it opens. I mean, it's actually opening, creaking on its rusted hinges and inviting me out of the cold. My head peeks around the gap, shortly followed by the rest of me as I stumble over the threshold. The clock's chime dwindles.

Inside, the hall is cloaked in gloom. A tall window looks over a steep and narrow staircase at the foot of the doorway, its banister caked in years of grime and dust. Dead leaves clutter the grey and white tiles that decorate the floor space, although the white has turned a miserable yellow over the years, matching the unpleasant sight of floral wallpaper that's clinging to the wall for dear life. Various picture frames hang crooked, each glass surface smeared with a foggy sheet of dust. And branching across the ceiling, cobwebs cling to the coving like hanging fabric.

What has happened to you? I think as my palm presses against the flowered paper, guiding my way down the hall. The wall feels wet, and the air is thick with dampness, prompting a tickle near the back of my throat. It's as if the place is dying, growing old without grace and lacking a loving soul to care for it.

I nudge a picture frame on the wall, knocking it from the hook and sending it sailing to the floor. I watch it drop, the whole scene playing out in slow motion, like a scene from a movie. The frame splinters on impact, breaking the silence and sending shards of glass scattering across the tiles in a thousand pieces.

Inside the broken frame, there's a face staring up at me—a woman. I... I know her. That long blonde hair, thick and shiny. The hazel eyes and short, perked nose. Even the faint wrinkles leading down to a heavenly smile—the smile of an angel.

I bend down, collecting the photo, somehow managing to prick my finger on the glass. I flinch, and the words "Clumsy cow," escape me.

Through the slits of my eyes, I stare at the woman, focusing as the image blurs in the dim hallway light. It's Mum. I sigh heavily, studying a face I have not seen in years. She's standing in the woodlands, just on the outskirts of the house. She's wearing her blue dungarees, a daisy-chain thingy around one wrist, while cupping both hands to her side. She looks fancy, just like one of those magazine models from the '90s.

I bring the image closer, sensing a tear which instantly clouds my sight. "Hello, Mum," I whisper. "I'm back. I'm home." I bow my head, the photo burying into my chest as I begin to squeeze. Both arms grow tighter, and the paper rustles into the groove of my breasts. And from deep within, a heartfelt gasp yearns to be let loose. The photo is cradled in my arms as the cogs of the standing clock clonk away in the corner. And from out of nowhere, a voice escapes from the darkness, prompting my eyes to bulge wide open.

"Who's there?" The tone is frail and tired, as if someone has just risen from their sleep. But it's close. Real close. So close that my imagination begins to run away with me, and I sense the breath of a stranger brush against the nape of my neck. I slap at it, striking only shadows and losing my balance as I slip on a shard of glass.

The voice begins to scream, the sound striking in every direction. "Don't go!"

My shoulders clash off wall to wall as I charge down the hall, diving forward and reaching for the doorknob. I grab it, pulling with all my might. But now the handle's stuck. It won't even budge.

"No, no, it can't. Not now!" But it does. "Turn, please turn!" I plead through knitted teeth.

"Come back!" the voice shrieks out from behind me.

I'm twisting at the doorknob. Both my hands clench around the brass handle.

Turn, twist, pull, push, twist, pull, twist.

"Come on, you piece of shit door!"

I yank back with all I've got, losing my grip, which sends me hurtling backward. My feet lift off the floor, touching the air like I'm flying in a dream. And before I know it, I'm lying flat upon the cold, yellow tiles, looking up at a dark, murky patch on the ceiling. A drop of water falls from its mold-infested center, splashing on my forehead with a gentle *tap*. I try to move, try to raise my head. But right now, I can't even breathe. It's like the wind has been knocked clean out of me. No matter how hard I try, all I can muster is a desperate gasp. My breath is trapped, lodged within my throat. I feel...faint, nauseous. And as I try to rise, the hallway starts to spin, spinning so fast I can barely think or see. I don't feel right.

Slowly, I scramble to my knees, cautious not to cut myself on the broken glass I remember scattered about my feet. When I try to find the picture, to see Mum again, it's not there. Nothing is. No photograph, no pieces of glass twinkling in the dimness. There is only the stone-cold surface of an empty floor. I stand there, dazed, my shoes sweeping the narrow space about my feet. I stop, but as I do, my attention drifts to the wall, settling on a smiling face. The picture—it's hanging back on the wall. A coldness shudders through me, a chill as bitter as the very snow that blankets the world outside. I lean in closer, eyes glued to the dirty wall, staring with disbelief at the same old frame that hangs crooked in its place, the glass perfectly intact, absent a single crack.

Through the dust, Mum stares back at me. Only, now her smile seems less innocent. Something else is there, something haunting.

A noise escapes me, a noise I have never heard before. I smother my hand to my mouth, if only to conceal it, but as I do, I pause, and what once seemed impossible now seems even worse. My finger. There is no blood. No cut. Not so much as a scratch. There is simply nothing.

The spinning of the hall has ceased for now, or at least it feels that way. Leaning against the stair rail, I drag myself back toward the front door. My hand swings clumsily from one loose spindle to the next, resembling some sort of drunken Tarzan. The pounding rhythm of my heart thuds in my ears.

Outside, the wind intensifies with each passing second. I can hear it relentlessly hammering against the door. It sounds like someone knocking, causing the door to rattle within its frame.

Suddenly, a wave of exhaustion washes over me. I feel tired. The idea of resting, of collapsing on the staircase, anything to bring an end to this dreadful night, crosses my mind. But just as my eyes begin to roll and my thoughts start to drift, another noise delicately caresses my ears—the sound of sorrow. The faint sound of someone's cries.

On the opposite side of the hall, across from the tall, old clock, the sound is coming from a closed door leading into the lounge, a large, comforting room adorned with an open stone fireplace, wooden-boarded floors, and a white rocking chair positioned by the window that I used to sit on as a child.

The sobbing goes on, seeping beneath the gap of the door, growing louder and louder as though the house itself is mourning. Mourning for what, I don't know. There are words being spoken. Well, mutterings really. What is being said, I'm not quite sure.

I creep nearer to the door, holding my breath as each finger slowly creeps around the darkened crack. And without stopping to consider what I'm about to do, I simply do what I feel I must and slowly creep inside.

At first, I can't believe what I'm seeing, or I just don't want to. Perhaps my mind is playing tricks on me, just like the picture on the wall, the cut on my finger. And what I think is in front of me, in fact, isn't. Just a trick of the dark, maybe. I rub my eyes, just to be certain. And sure enough, inside the room is a small hospital bed that's been pushed up to the corner of an alcove, stretching along the length of a long bay window. The shabby curtains hang down like grubby rags, draping over the bed's metal bars. And at the foot of the mattress, a mound of scattered blankets lies piled in a messy bundle. But that's not all. Beside the headboard, a single candle stands alight on a tall oak nightstand, flickering from the hallway's breeze and casting the faintest glow on the headboard. An old woman is lying there. At first, I'm not entirely sure she's alive. She's not moving. She's not even breathing, I don't think. But if she really is, you know, dead, where the hell were the voices coming from?

A long, nimble neck pokes out from under the covers, stretching up into a wrinkly, gaunt face. Her head is sunken back into a jumble of stained, ragged pillows, displaying grey, wiry hair which runs down the length of her cheek bones.

And...as much as I try to look away, I can't. I'm frozen stiff, wedged to the floor. I don't speak or move. I simply stand there, dazed.

The old woman's eyes peel into me. They're all iris, no pupil, wide and glassy, reflecting the weak and dreary flame of the flickering candlelight. She doesn't even blink. Not once. Not a flutter. She just lies there, still, staring at the doorway. Staring...through me.

A thought crosses my mind, and I can't help but wonder how long exactly this poor old woman has been here, waiting for someone, anyone, to find her, to stand where I am now.

Over on the nightstand, right next to the melting candle wax that's trailing onto the surface of a cabinet, I catch the glint of a small object, a piece of jewelery, I think, shining weakly in the light. It looks so familiar, like I've seen it somewhere before. A necklace? No. A bracelet? Each individual gold link is infused tightly around the other like some sort of fancy French braid.

I take one step closer, squinting long and hard but too afraid to move any farther. Just then, the penny finally drops. It's not a necklace or a bracelet, but an old gold watch. Small and dainty, it is. Its round, black face enhances the color of thin, silver hands that point to tiny mirrored markings at its edges. The light shimmers on its face. The time displays 02:00.

I begin to edge backward, my breath held, for how long I don't know, as the sound of the wind comes tunneling down the chimney, expressing an eerie howl. It sounds like a wolf howling in a horror flick. The sensation of cold air brushes over my feet as it flows into the room, forcing the candle to dance and peter.

Just then, a soft voice seeps out from the bed.

"Welcome home, love," the voice says.

I jump back, startled, colliding flat against the wall behind me with a nasty thud. My hand searches the wall in panic for the doorway. All the while, my eyes never tear away from the same spot on the bed. Not even for a split second do they drift, not if I can help it. Yet, no matter how much I try, no matter how much I'm sure the voice that spoke to me was surely hers, the old woman remains just as still, just as lifeless on her deathbed as she ever was before.

"Hello?" I muster the courage to speak. It comes out weak and trembling, pathetic. "Was that you, just now? Did you say something?"

There is no reply at first, no sounds except for the distant hoot of a bird beyond the window and the branches that tap at the pane.

"It was," the voice replies, and just like before, I find myself pinned against the wall with the same unnerving fright.

The vacant gaze of the woman's eyes suddenly stirs, accompanied by a furrowed brow that deepens with each crease. "Come, come now," she beckons, her voice luring me closer as a long, bony finger emerges from beneath the covers. "We don't have much time. I... I don't have much time."

Using the same hand, she smooths out the rumpled sheets, patting them down with a sense of purpose. Her hand remains in place until I begin to approach.

Gradually I step forward, one foot after the next.

"That's right, come closer," she encourages, her tone similar to coaxing a child. She watches intently as I make my way to the foot of the bed, where dim candle light casts a feeble glow. "Won't you sit, then?" she asks.

I offer no response.

"You will sit," she says, as if making the decision on my behalf. With a determined effort, she attempts to push herself upright on the bed. "You always do," she grumbles, her voice strained. "Eventually."

My brow cocks, caught between simple curiosity and an unwilling need to know. "Do I?" I ask cautiously. "What do you mean?"

"Sit," she replies, her body giving way as she collapses back onto her pillow with a laborious grunt. Beads of sweat glisten on her temple, matting the strands of grey, wiry hair that cling to her chalky skin.

"I'd prefer to stand, if that's alright," I assert, my voice firm yet respectful.

"Please yourself, then," the old woman huffs. She reaches amidst the jumble of filthy blankets, retrieving an oxygen mask hidden within. Placing it over her face, she presses down, inhaling deeply as if her very existence hangs in the balance. "There have been occasions when you chose not to sit. Several occasions... I believe. Those visits seemed to be much shorter."

What on earth is she talking about? I ponder silently. *Who is this woman? And what is she doing here?*

The old woman withdraws the mask from her face, leaving behind a faint imprint around the deep wrinkles that line her mouth. "You're confused," she remarks, her words more of an observation than a question, dismissing any concern I may have with a casual wave of her hand. "You usually are... Confused, that is."

"Confused?" I echo her, leaning forward and resting my weight on the bed frame. "Who are you?" I ask. "What are you doing here?"

The old woman says nothing at first, but simply stares at the nearest window that frames the moon like a painting. She begins to hum.

What the song is exactly I'm not too sure, but I know this tune. I've heard it before, a long time ago. A song my mother used to sing.

"You know this song?" the old woman asks, her stare never shifting until the melody reaches its end.

Only then do I remember it, recalling the lyrics forming on my lips. "By the light of the silvery moon," I tell her.

In that fleeting moment, the old lady's smile widens, causing the lines etched upon her face to deepen, drawing my full attention to the heavy bags beneath her weary eyes. There is an uncanny familiarity about those eyes. The more I gaze into them, the more I feel myself being drawn in, ensnared by their gaze. I become motionless, speechless. I stand there, transfixed, my own vision locked in an unbreakable connection with hers. I know this woman. I strain my mind, desperately trying to recall. I know her voice, that smile, those eyes shimmering in the soft glow of the candlelight. I know... that face.

"Mum?" I dare to ask, disbelief lacing my words. "Is that you?"

The old lady's smile remains firm. A single tear forms, tracing a path down the crease of her dry and weathered nose.

"It's good to see you, my dear," she whispers to me.

In an instant, my fear of the figure before me evaporates, vanishing as abruptly as it began. I rush to her bedside, finding myself perched on the edge of the bed, grasping her frail hands firmly within my own. A chill seeps through my fingers as I realise how cold she feels—terribly cold.

"Mum..." I manage to voice the words, my throat constricted. "What's happening to you?"

"Cancer," she states plainly, scrambling about the covers in a hurried state and retrieving a crumpled tissue hidden amidst the layers of blankets. Violent coughing overtakes her, the sound dry and sharp as she struggles to expel phlegm from her chest.

"Cancer?" I echo, my ears listening to the deathly rattle of her lungs as she labors for breath. "But, your face, Mum." My gaze sweeps across her features, once vibrant with youth, and slowly descends to the frail frame partially concealed by the sheets. Another fit of coughing wracks her body, each hack harsher and more painful than the last. "You look so... old."

Mum slumps back against the headboard, her skin pale and glistening, like that of melting snow. She lifts her free hand to her forehead, smudging the sweat with the cuff of her gown. "That," she struggles to catch her breath, "is because I am old, my dear."

I try to piece together the fragments of what she's saying, attempting to understand, to make sense of it all. Yet, I cannot. It eludes me. None of it adds up. The last time we spoke... I strain my mind, searching for the memory. It was on the phone this morning. I stood at Oxford station, Platform 6, ready to board the train. She had sounded so delighted to hear from me, expressing how long it had been since I last visited home and how eager the family was to see me. I strain harder to recall, but the memory slips away, dissolving just as fast as a fleeting dream.

"Hush now, you must listen," Mum urges, her voice frail and scratchy. "You must try to understand. I... need you to try to understand."

"Understand?" I inquire. My voice is tinged with discomfort. "Understand what?"

A weariness settles upon her face. "This will be the last time."

"The last time?"

She nods, her agreement a struggle, and for a fleeting moment, her eyes roll back, sinking into their sockets. "Yes." She moans, jolting awake once more. "The clock!" she remarks, her trembling finger pointing weakly toward the hallway. "Is it nearing the hour?"

I turn my gaze toward the hallway, and what I see astonishes me. The hall is bathed in a warm and comforting glow, devoid of cobwebs that once draped the staircase. The wallpaper blossoms with vibrant flowers, just as I remember when it was freshly hung. The scent of paste lingers in the air. And there, in the corner, stands the clock, its pendulum swinging, reflecting the light as it sways.

"It will soon strike two," I tell her.

"Good," she murmurs, easing herself deeper into the bed. "Then we still have some time left."

"Left?" I ask her, unable to hide the shakiness in my voice. "What's left? What are you saying?" I try to keep calm, to control myself, but it all came out so suddenly. "I don't understand! What has happened here, the house? What has happened to you? Why are you so old, so all alone?"

"My dear, I am old." She looks at me kindly, just like when I was a girl. "Everyone else has all gone now," she says. The coldness of her hand gently sweeps my palm.

"Gone and at peace. There is no one else left, no one but me. Soon there will be none."

Tears well up in my eyes, mingling with confusion and disbelief. "I...still don't under..."

"I know." She tries to reassure me, her touch gentle as she brushes a loose strand of hair behind my ear. "I am ninety-seven years old," she confesses, "an old woman now, yearning for the end of her life. But I couldn't depart without witnessing this night, not without saying goodbye one last time."

Images of our last phone call at the station earlier that morning flood my mind. I recall the crackling of the phone line, the passing trains on the platform, and the snowflakes falling upon the tracks. She was young, fit, and healthy, barely a woman of fifty. How can this be possible?

"No." I dismiss her, unable to comprehend what she is saying. There must be another explanation, a reason. "You're ill. You're sick. That's what has done this to you. You're not thinking clearly."

"My darling." She clears her throat, struggling to speak. "It is not I who is confused, but you. It has been so many years now since it happened. Each time you come back, your memory fades all the more. Your recollection of me, this house, it's all dwindling away."

A shiver runs down my spine as I meet her distant gaze. It's as if she is peering through me, her presence detached from this present moment.

"You're not here," she utters softly, her voice filled with a calmness. "Not really. Not in this life, at least. Not anymore. Not for a long, long time. Not since it happened."

The hairs prickle on the nape of my neck, the sound of her voice compelling me to rise from the bed.

"Do you remember the last time we spoke?" she asks, her voice catching in her throat. "That morning?"

"You mean this morning. I was at the station, traveling back home," I reply. "We spoke on the phone. You said you were in the kitchen, cooking. That you couldn't wait to see me. To hug me."

"That was forty-nine years ago." Her voice is so soft now, so soft I can barely hear her. It is but a faint whisper, a murmur. "Forty-nine years ago tonight. I know. I have counted them, every year that passes by. Every anniversary of the accident. A terrible, terrible accident." She grimaces. "One that I have never been able to let go of. Maybe that is why you are here, why you still come."

"Mum, what are you talking about?" My voice is trembling.

"That day," she began. "I waited all night for you to come home. I sat right there." Her finger points toward the windowsill as she fights to relive the memory. "The blizzard grew stronger as the night wore on. I was filled with worry, fearing that something terrible had happened to you, that you might've got trapped in the storm. I called the police, seeking their help. But they dismissed me instantly, suggesting that you had likely changed your plans or gone to visit friends. It was Christmas, after all. You were young. People often adjusted their arrangements. But I knew you better. You were my responsible and dependable girl. You would never do such a thing, not without letting me know. I pleaded with them, explaining that it was unlike you to vanish without a trace, without a word.

But they didn't take me seriously." Her eyes brimmed with a flood of tears. "Then the searches began. Your name was printed in newspapers, your face on posters throughout the town. It was then some attendant at the train station stated he had seen a lady fitting your description, encouraging the search to widen to the village. It was on the seventh day when they found you, just off the path that led to our house, half buried under the snow. They believed you had chosen to walk home, unaware of the perilous weather that awaited you. A tragic misjudgement, they said. A tremendous loss." Tears stream down her face as she displays the pain etched deep within her heart. "Even now, the thought breaks me. Knowing that while I sat there that night, yearning for your return, you were already here, just beyond my view. Alone. Dying." Her voice chokes with emotion as she pauses to collect herself, trying to find strength. "Of course, I have shared this story with you many times before, my dear. Many, many times."

I step back slightly, submerging myself into the shadows. "You have?" I do not remember. I do not remember any of it.

Mum nods, her eyes filled with sadness. "Every anniversary since it happened, every year, you come back home. You stand before me as clear as I see you now, though it never does last long." She leans herself across the bed, stretching her body to reach the bedside table. "The police," her voice strains, "they gave me this. They said they found it on your wrist."

It is the gold watch, she holds.

She opens her palm, gesturing for me to take it. But I hesitate, unable to confront the weight of the memories that taunt me. "They thought it best to return it to me. I thank them for that," she continues, her voice trembling with emotion. "Its hands stopped at two a.m. on the night you..." She pauses, her words hanging in the air. "I have never had the nerve to see it tick again. I suppose fear clouded me from doing so, the thought that it would stop you from coming back as you have. To stop me from seeing my girl again."

Her hand trembles as she holds it out farther, tears streaming from her eyes. "Please," she implores, her voice filled with desperation. "You must take it now. Take it in the hope that it will let you rest."

I don't know what to do, what to think. I look out at the view beyond the window, only to find it is not the same. The snow, it's gone. It's as if it was never there. Outside, the world is dark and still, absent of a single snowflake, a single cloud.

A loud chime rings out from the hallway as the grandfather clock begins to chime the hour, capturing my mother's attention. She glances at the clock, then swiftly turns to me, lurching forward as best she can, gripping my wrist with urgency.

"Listen to me!" she pleads desperately.

"No!" I yell, struggling to break free from her grasp. "I won't!"

Despite my resistance, she prises open my hand and places the watch firmly in my palm, closing my fingers tightly around it. "You must!" she cries. "You must listen before it is too late!"

I look into her eyes, eyes so filled with fear.

"Please, try to understand. You must!" she pleads, her attention once again drawn back to the chime. "When the last toll strikes, you will be gone. Do you understand me? The next time you come back, I won't be here. I will be gone, dead, no longer a part of this world. The house will be empty. You will be alone."

I draw back my wrist, stumbling in the process, and find myself sprawled on the floor.

"Take the watch!" her voice booms through the darkness. "Take it back with you, back to wherever it is you came from. I have seen it mended. Look!"

I glance down to the watch.

"All you have to do is press the crown. Press it and hope that it will never bring you back here again, that it will break whatever link it holds between this world and the next. That it will never see you wander this place alone again."

The room grows darker, enveloping the ceiling and walls in an abyss of blackness. All that remains visible is the bed and the window, accompanied by the incessant chime of the clock that drills into my ears. Frantically, I scramble to my feet and direct my gaze toward the bed, only to find it now empty, the mattress bare. My mother has gone, vanished. I strain to hear her voice over the chimes, urging me not to be frightened, assuring me of her love as she tearfully bids me goodbye.

I spin on my feet, leading me not to the hall but another door. The kitchen. The door swings open violently, crashing against the wall as I stumble into the room. The scent of cooked food fills my senses, permeating the air and tickling my nose. The kitchen is clean and bright, just as I remember it, bathed in sunlight that streams through the windows and dances on the surface of the table.

A young girl's laughter echoes through the room, as if she were standing right before me. The sound intertwines with my mother's voice. The child's footsteps playfully patter across the floor, encircling me, causing my neck to twist and turn. But as abruptly as it began, it all comes to a halt. The sun vanishes from the window, plunging the kitchen into profound gloom. The cupboards on the walls sag, their fixtures desperately clinging on. Plates shatter upon the floor, the once-grand wooden table collapses lifelessly onto its side, and the chairs surrounding it become smothered in filth. I pant heavily, breathing in the dust and cobwebs.

The clock's chime reaches its final notes, the sound piercing my ears and gradually dwindling into silence. Each passing second feels like an eternity as I anxiously await the concluding tolls.

With a surge of panic, I sprint out of the kitchen, a feeling pounding in my chest, propelling me toward the hallway. The door at the end stands open wide, the storm outside calling to me, howling violently and swaying the pictures on the walls. I start to run.

DONG.

The first toll strikes, thundering through the house with an intense tremor that shakes its very foundation. I stumble against the kitchen door, the impact causing my hand to rebound off the wall and the watch to slip from my grasp, skidding across the tiled floor. From somewhere above, the sound of shattering windows crashes in the chaos, while cracks crawl across the walls and floor like menacing tree roots, fracturing the plaster.

I lunge forward, pushing and grunting, my feet slapping against the floor, desperate to retrieve the watch. It crashes against the threshold, tumbling onto the doorstep. I hear it bounce and grind along the slate. I jump out after it, reaching out, yearning to seize it, my fingertips inches away. I'm close, so close. Just one more step. But before I can, everything turns black, my surroundings swallowed by darkness. It engulfs me, stealing away whatever light there is. I cannot see, not a thing.

The rumble and thunder of the house grows muffled and distant. I sense nothing, feel nothing. It's like I am no longer a part of the place I once stood, the body I thought I knew. Desperation fills me as I attempt to scream, to call out, yelling for my mother one last time. To tell her I love her. To tell her where I am. But only one sound escapes my lips now, only one haunting noise to be heard.

DONG

Searching

Ben Young

"Earlier today, Steve was onsite and spoke to the local music legend himself," says the chipper blonde woman behind the studio news desk. "Let's take a look."

The screen is overtaken by a banner saying Live Now, followed by a shot of a middle-aged man in a rain slicker, holding an umbrella and a microphone. He's standing outside in a drizzle, and behind him is a plain but aging building made of gray brick, a band of aluminum siding around its top. Beside it is an empty gravel parking lot. The building's windows are covered in plywood, and there is loud traffic noise from a busy, adjacent road.

"Yeah, Tricia," Steve says. His timbre and pacing are well-suited for regional broadcast. He sounds very much like a news reporter, emphasizing and elongating the last few words of each sentence and using strategic pauses. "Jonny Parker's has been here since 1977. But the building itself dates back to the nineteen twenties. As you can see, it's been boarded up for a few weeks, but the temporary location just had its grand opening."

Next is a brief clip of a large warehouse-type structure with a pitched tin roof. The exterior walls are composed of rigid, beige metal, giving it the appearance of an oversized shipping container and a sharp contrast from the first building seen. Then came a closeup shot of the building's front—dark glass, the door centered and bearing the words Jonny Parker's World of Music in white vinyl lettering, a cowboy hat set above the text. Next to that, in hand-scrawled blue chalk, it reads Temporary Home! with a comically-large exclamation point.

Along with these shots is Steve's voiceover. "Jonny's temporary place is in the old MacKenzie's Bar and Grill in Oakbrook. But Jonny says it's not home."

The camera then changes back to Steve, standing beside the busy road, cars whizzing past close enough as to almost drown out his voice. The overcast sky adds a gloomy quality to the scene despite the high position of the sun.

Steve is holding the microphone out to a slight, bespectacled man with wiry gray hair and the shadow of a white beard. A chyron across the bottom of the screen identifies him as Jonny Parker, owner of Jonny Parker's World of Music. An eighteen-wheeler drums past, cutting off the first words of Jonny's statement and sloshing rainwater toward the building.

"—ace has been very good to me," Jonny says. "I've been here forty-five-and-a-half years. The city of Newtown's been good to me too. But it's been on my mind for quite some time that I wanted to build a new place."

The camera again changes to a wide shot of the building, then switches through a series of close-ups that highlight its visible disrepair—rotting wood, a sagging fence, crumpled gutters, loose siding, damaged bricks. During this segment, Steve provides more voiceover.

"The land here was originally the site of a slaughterhouse, in the nineteenth century, and this current building was first used as a gambling club run by local mobsters. Jonny came here all those years later to play his particular brand of country music."

At that, the scene changes to show a younger Jonny on stage, his name on the wall behind him in a large, stylized, cursive font. His hair is dark and much longer. He's playing an acoustic guitar and singing, but the soundtrack remains Steve's voice.

"The music was first, and Jonny Parker's has hosted both local acts and household names over the years. But the stories of America's most-haunted honky-tonk have taken on a life of their own. Many would say the building is far more famous for the ghosts than for the tunes. It's a question that Jonny himself has been asked many times."

We return to the pre-recorded scene of Steve and Jonny outside the original location. "When I interviewed you a few years back, I asked if you believed this building was haunted. You said no. Is that still what you think?"

"I don't think it's haunted, no," Jonny responds, sounding bored. "I know a lot of people do, so I'm in the minority there. All those investigators have been here, you know, and I've watched the episodes they filmed. People ask me that a lot. I mean, I know the stories better than anyone. But nothing's ever happened to me in there."

Midway through his answer, the camera shows a handmade sign on curling pink poster board above the entrance that reads:

<u>Warning To Our Patrons:</u>
<u>This establishment is purported to be HAUNTED.</u>
<u>Management is NOT responsible for any actions of</u>
<u>GHOSTS/SPIRITS on this premises.</u>

There's a brief close-up on the word HAUNTED as Jonny finishes speaking.

The camera returns to Steve and Jonny.

Steve asks, "So the ghost stories have nothing to do with the decision to move?"

Jonny shakes his head with vigor. "No, nothing to do with that. If that was the reason, I'd have moved long ago and I wouldn't be coming back. It's about the music for me. This is just a temporary relocation. We'll be back here soon enough, and it's gonna be huge. You can take Jonny out of Newtown, but you can't take Newtown out of Jonny."

"Thanks, Jonny." Steve takes the microphone back and turns toward the camera. The banner reading Live Now moves across the screen again, and once it passes, Steve is alone by the building. The sun is lower, and it's raining harder.

"While a demolition date has not been set here, Jonny says he hopes to have the new bar open by early 2026."

The final shot is a wide view of the front of the original location, and as Steve continues his voiceover, he sounds less like a seasoned broadcaster. He makes a few muted chuckles, as if he's on a sketch comedy show and trying not to break character.

"As for the *shnt* ghosts of Jonny Parker's, who's to say? He told me he hasn't heard anything about it in Oakbrook. But will the spirit of Dawn Schock be in here when Jonny comes back? Still looking for her *hch* missing head? Will the demolition cover up the *kik* so-called 'hell's chimney' in the basement? What will happen to the *pfft* nameless little boy who likes to share the stage for a few seconds and then vanish? Will the ghost of the mob enforcer known as *tch* Tiny Gorga continue his assaults in the *new* women's restroom? I bet all the believers out there are curious, like me. When you move the haunted house, what happens to the ghosts? Perhaps we'll find out together. This is Steve Henderson for WLCP news."

Just before the scene changes back to the studio, Steve fails to stifle a laugh.

"A brand-new day," said Dawn Schock. Then she pondered it.

What was "day" again?

Should she know? Yes, she should. She didn't.

Time was so smeared. "Day" was a concept without point. The meaning was lost, and there was no way to know how many of them—how much "time"—had come and gone since her search began. The rising and falling of the sun? Inconsequential. Days mattered not to ghosts, and besides all the blankness, the unknown, she did have that, at least. She was a ghost. The others may not know that about themselves, but she did. So why had the thought come?

Why then?

Something was different. There was change.

A new weightlessness had arrived, permeating her, infusing her with a sensation that was both faraway and familiar. What was it? Not pain. Not fear. Not loss or longing. Those were heavy, and this was... not. What were the opposites of those? Too many non-days had passed, and she had no recollection of anything else. For her, time had been replaced with the search. It was the governing medium in which she existed. Its laws were her laws, both defining and confining her. The living had their "time," the fish had their sea, and she had her search. Her endless search.

But she had searched each room and corner and space. Above, under, within, beside. And so frequently.

I have searched everywhere, she thought.

Another one. What was this thing, "where?"

Something was certainly different.

She moved, going all the way to the world's edge, then past.

And she noticed there was nothing pulling her back.

"What?" said Thomas, aware he was shouting again. Alison didn't answer, and he worried she was annoyed. They had both been annoyed and shouting a lot this week because of the construction across the street. The heavy machinery arrived two days ago to knock down old Jonny Parker's, and it threw off the whole rhythm of their house.

They had only been living together for a month, so the tension caused by this disruption was quite a test for them. That day—day three—the crashing and roaring and grinding started before they were even awake.

Thomas went to the bathroom window, where he could see the back of the old building. It had never scared him, but Alison had taken a bit of convincing before she agreed to live so close.

From what Thomas could tell, they leveled much of the place during the first two days and were working at organizing and removing debris. Half the foundation was still intact, and there were jagged chunks of stone wall pointing up in several spots, like the remnants of a giant, shattered tooth in the ground. A massive yellow vehicle with tank treads instead of wheels was spinning its top half around and using a long, clawed arm to drop a payload of splintered boards and hunks of brick into a pile at the edge of the site.

His eyes went to the right of the machine, drawn away from the movement by a large circular shape. He saw a lip of gray concrete that jutted up two feet from the dirt.

The well in the basement of Jonny Parker's had a reputation and lore all its own. Thomas didn't know the full story, but he, like most, was aware of its name—The Devil's Chimney.

A devout skeptic, he refused to believe it was anything more than an old hole in the ground. It had been put there when the lot was used as a distillery. He knew that much. Those hokey TV shows would have you think it was a portal straight to Hell, crawling with winged nasties and smelling of brimstone. Thomas knew better, he—saw something in there, moving?

It was only a shadow, cast by the motion of the construction vehicles. That was all, just those loud monstrosities that kept roaring through the peace of his new home.

I swear, he thought, *if I'd known they were going to do this, we would have kept looking for a home somewhere else.* But he knew that wasn't true. The disruption was a temporary thing, and the proximity to both their jobs and other conveniences, coupled with the surprisingly-low cost, showed they couldn't have done any better if they spent another decade looking for housing.

This won't last, just remember that.

Still, though, he was staring at that concrete lip and wondering if it was a little less dark inside there since the machine had turned away again.

"Did you hear me?" Alison called, breaking his concentration. She stepped into the narrow bathroom behind him, reflected in the mirror, the rising sun filling her hair with light.

"No, sorry. I can't hear anything in here," he said. Thomas turned toward her and saw she was, in fact, quite annoyed.

He placed a small kiss on her forehead, and she seemed to relent. They both had been on edge this week, but there was a lifetime beyond this minor nuisance.

"I asked if you've seen my keys," she said. "I'm gonna be late for work."

Thomas shrugged. "Sorry, I haven't. We're still on for dinner tonight, right?"

"You buying?" she asked.

Thomas chuckled and said, "Hell no."

Alison punched him on the arm, and he grabbed her wrist, pulling her close for a hug.

"Maybe a ghost moved them," he said, meaning to keep it under his breath. It was a mistake either way, and a worse one if she heard.

She heard and walked out quickly.

"Not funny," she called back. "I told you I didn't want to live here, and you don't even believe that. Now they're knocking that place down. Mark my words. They're just turning them all loose."

"Can we not?" he said. "I don't want to fight about that again, okay? You'll feel better when it's gone and people stop talking about all that nonsense."

Alison didn't answer. Without meaning to, he turned back and looked at The Devil's Chimney once more.

Nonsense, he told himself, just as a bulldozer came by, pushing dirt and rocks across the lip of the well, busting the extruding concrete to bits and sealing the hole under several tons of earth. If there was anything inside that hole, it was there to stay.

Unless it already left, he thought. *Geez, now you're sounding like her.*

A few minutes later, he was dressed and walking to the kitchen, looking for his new wife. But she was gone, and so were his car keys.

These are... are... shiny. What are they? Dawn thought. Back when she was the other way, she liked shiny things. Things like these but also not like them. Shiny things she could wear. That was forgotten, along with other likes and dislikes, too, replaced by the search. Absorbed by it, consumed within the need to *find*. The rest of existence had dissolved into the search, like a sand structure succumbing to the tide.

Shiny, but not the same as my... what is the word? Jewels. She hadn't many, but those she did were treasured. Dawn clasped this shiny object in her hand and knew there was more than one because it made a clinking sound. A lesser sound, not the fine one like her jewelry would have made. She ran her ghostly finger along its edge, feeling sharp bumps on one side. The other side was smooth and straight. Its top was round, and it was joined to two others by a circle. As she held these, they made more sounds, but the sounds told her she didn't want to keep them. She dropped them on the floor, and they skidded away, beneath a piece of furniture.

She had wandered farther than ever before and was getting distracted. *Stay focused*, she told herself, scolding. *This freedom may not last, and I am still searching.* A familiar fatigue came then, and she closed her eyes. But then she pushed back against the fatigue because she knew what it meant and that if she let it come, she would only wake back in the same place as always and have to start the search over. Whenever that happened, she would try to speak, to call out for someone to help, anyone, but all that would come out was a long, sad moaning noise. She couldn't start over; she had never been this far. This new "where" and "when" meant she had a small hope again. Her long search could end if she just kept going instead of blinking away.

Again Dawn moved, and the farther she strayed, the more memory came to her. In a brutal flash of wakefulness, she saw her own long-forgotten death—a man using a dull blade to hack at her neck as the life drained from it and pooled on a wooden floor. For one eternal second, she had been alive while her head was separated. Knowing "where" and "when" once again, she tried to recall those about her death, the place and time it had occurred. And in this flood of remembrance, she even knew the people who had shown up since—whispering her name in questions, pointing strange objects covered with lights, stealing her words, and pulling on her somehow—had all been wrong about her. They knew she was searching, most of them. But they were wrong about much. He hadn't dropped her head down a well or thrown it in a hole he dug. He hadn't rolled it into the river. But where? He had... he had...

Why?

It occurred to her this was a far more important question, larger than "what?"

Why had he done that? There was a reason he beheaded her. Who was he? Had she said something to him that caused it? Or done something? What drove him to such an act?

She remembered then, what it was she was searching for. The question of "why" led her to the biggest missing piece. Energy came, banishing the fatigue, and she drifted forward.

Behind her, a deep and misshapen shadow followed.

Thomas didn't believe in ghosts. Never had. Which was probably why he pressed Alison so hard to move here, despite the stigma and her own reservations about the area. He considered himself a straightforward guy, taking much of his life's events and the larger world at face value, "What you see is what you get" as a would-be motto. He prided himself on his ability to break complexities down to their more basic components, to solve problems with expediency, and to not get worked up over trivialities.

Until the day he found a headless woman's ghost in his living room, that was.

Thomas was so rooted in typical straightforwardness that he addressed this specter before realizing it wasn't his wife.

"Hey, babe," he said as he passed within feet of it.

Perhaps he didn't notice because she was so defined, rather than appearing wraithlike or incomplete. The ghost was fully formed, leagues beyond a disembodied voice or a door creaking shut on its own, or even a floating face in the shadows. She appeared as solid and three-dimensional as Thomas. As usual, Thomas was staying on task, coming home from work at the end of a long day, headed to change clothes before diving back into his latest home-improvement project (new recessed lights in the basement). He didn't look at it, holding the ghost in his periphery as he forged ahead, taking half the flight of stairs with purpose before a distant realization chirped at him.

Not Alison, it said. *Shouldn't be there.*

He looked back and gasped, a traffic of sounds clogging his chest and locking it tight. There was an apparition of a woman, hovering across the room from him, mostly white and gray in appearance as if adding color was too much effort for whatever force had conjured her. Sections of her outline continuously swirled away then disappeared, like she was a leaky canister of smoke. Yet she never lost any of her matter or presence, somehow regenerating at the same time she was dispersing. Even with her lack of color, he could tell her clothing was outdated, a costume from another time, a faded black-and-white photo from another era.

She has no head, he thought in a bizarre tone of fact-stating acceptance, his mind backfiring and defaulting to a deep-seated pattern of seeking answers, rationalizing the impossible. Since his ability to speak failed, the voice in his head was louder than usual. *There's a headless ghost in my house,* it confirmed.

Only, she wasn't missing her head, not completely. She was beheaded, but not head-less. It was there, just not attached. She carried it in front of her at waist height, the way you would carry a tray of food. It was dripping blood that evaporated before hitting the floor. Its bright red was the only color anywhere on or around her.

"God," he said. The word slipped free, catching her attention and causing him to freeze in both stance and sense.

She pivoted, leading with her arms and extending them to hold her head toward him, its gray eyes widened and pleading. They held him in place while his trademark-rationality shattered, replaced with a primal panic and the need for flight. She floated toward him and spoke.

"Where?" she said, her detached mouth moving while the sound seemed to teleport into his ears a half-second too fast to match. Her voice was soft and firm, worming with a strained desperation he couldn't ignore. It demanded he answer her need while her phantom blood dribbled but never touched the carpet.

"Wh-where is wh-what?" he asked, unsure where to look, feeling an exaggeration of that sense of addressing someone whose eyes faced different directions.

"She. Where... she?"

"Alison?" he thought, then hated he said her name to this thing. He should be protecting her, not exposing her. "Why? Who are you?" Thomas moved his gaze from her eyes to the blood around her chin, then to the swirling emptiness between her shoulders. The stump resembled an ashtray occupied by a lit cigarette.

"No," she said. Then she turned away.

As her hold over him broke, Thomas felt a dozen alarms and realizations at once, primitive survival mechanisms tripping circuits and urging him to act. Loudest among them was the one seeking his wife. Where was Alison? She should be home. Did this ghost-woman do something to her?

"Where is she?" he called toward it, rooting himself in place with great effort, unable to leave Alison behind. "Where's my wife?"

But the ghost was already gone.

Dawn knew she couldn't waste any more time. All of this was straining. It had taken so much effort to make words, and it would be both futile and impossible to keep explaining her search to him. The man couldn't help, even if he was the only ship in an endless sea.

Her baby was out there, somewhere... alone. And so the search was all that mattered.

Since the change started and she had been free to roam, awareness had blossomed, lost information returning to her. At first it was only vagaries about her last moments, a canvas of screaming and pleading and anguish and hurt. Then blackness without borders. Then her drive to find something she desperately missed but also had never known. After that, pieces came into focus—memories, names, words, even dates.

She had been beheaded by her boyfriend, Arthur Walling, on January 31st, 1896. He was a dental student. Her current surroundings indicated it had been quite a long time since this happened, but there was no way to be sure. Dawn recognized nothing, no matter where she looked, until she moved far enough away that she saw the river. That had been there before she died, and it still looked the same.

Then, along with this blossoming awareness, the forming of memories, the clarity of her need, came the ultimate realization of why Arthur had killed her. With that, she remembered the object of her search. She told him she was pregnant, and he had gone berserk, assaulting her and then severing her head to cover his tracks.

Dawn was pregnant when she died, and no one except her killer had known. Within her dying body was an unborn daughter, whom she had named Audrey. As Dawn herself died, the baby was still alive and no one knew to save her. Somehow, Dawn had refused her own death. She stayed, vowing death would not claim her and her child before they met. As Arthur mutilated her body, she floated above it, fighting to contact her tiny Audrey, needing to see her face just once, perhaps even save her from the corpse that had become her prison. If Dawn couldn't alert someone, she would be entombed until there was an autopsy, perhaps forever.

Dawn had screamed and screamed while she fought to keep her spirit in place. But that was all she could do as the world melted away.

Before anyone arrived, the sun was up and it was hard to see anything. People had taken her body, and she could watch but not follow. Where had her baby gone then?

That was when the blackness came.

After that ended and she was back in the place where he killed her, everything was different. She had died outside, beneath the stars, but returned inside a musty building and couldn't find her way out. She searched for her remains, to find out what happened to the baby inside her, to learn if Audrey had been rescued. Only, something in that building wouldn't let Dawn leave, and she grew so tired the blackness came again. So began her cycle of reforming, searching, disappearing, and starting over in the same place.

She soon understood there was something malevolent in that building, keeping her trapped there. A shadow lived in that hole in the basement, and it fed off her ceaseless, tormented search. She had never seen it, but all the same, she knew that thing was there, in the basement, feeding off her sorrow and pinning her close by. And she wasn't the only one it trapped.

Then the building was gone, and the thing's power over her was gone with it as if whatever spell it held her under was attached to the walls themselves. That must be why she could move farther, why she was... remembering things.

Death no longer had power over her, and neither did the presence lurking in that hole.

Dawn was free. Her search continued.

"Alison!" Thomas called, racing from room to room, searching. The house wasn't large, and unless she saw what he just saw and took to hiding, she wasn't home.

Where else could she be? She always arrived home before him. They had plans to make stir fry in the wok his aunt bought from their wedding registry. It felt symbolic, even, opening the last of their wedding gifts and putting it to use. It was the beginning of a new era. They were entering a deeper phase of their relationship. When the first drop of oil hit that wok, they would be officially living the "married life," as his mom liked to say, whatever that meant. They had both been looking forward to it, and Thomas had expected her to be standing in the kitchen, tapping her foot, when he arrived.

Instead, he walked past a ghost and lobbed a greeting at it.

She must have stopped somewhere, or maybe stayed late at work. That wasn't typical, but it also wasn't impossible. He had been calling her name and searching for at least ten minutes.

He moved his search outside, scolding himself for not checking the driveway first. Both of their cars were there, which only worsened his suspicions.

Three words bulleted into his mind then, in his normal, even-keeled timbre, despite the insanity of their meaning.

Ghost. Johnny Parker's.

Alison had been right all along. They never should have moved here. He had made light of it and took stupid shots at her, telling himself it would help her warm up to the idea of living near that damn haunted bar, when really, he was feeling guilty and trying to make her look like the bad guy in all of it.

Whatever horrible fate she suffered (was suffering), it was his fault.

He ran out the front door and across the street, toward the construction site, searching. It was full dusk, but there were no streetlights nearby. The moon was wresting control from the waning sun, and the traffic was sparse.

The heavy machinery was still as he came closer, looming over him like patient yellow monsters. He stood among the debris, the ruins of fifteen decades' worth of dirty business and booze and blood, and he realized it was silent. Completely, utterly silent.

Movement a few dozen feet away caught his eye, and he looked sideways toward it. Thomas saw nothing, but his heart lumbered and the silence pushed from all sides. Again there was movement, but only in the corner of his eye. This time, he faced it and stepped closer, narrowing his eyes and urging them to work harder, to pull together whatever was hiding there. Something *was* there. His gut knew it even if his eyes said different. Suddenly, he noticed the outline of a shape, darker than the surrounding shadows. The ghost was back over here. But was it... different? And not just darker, but larger? And hunching?

"Alison," he said, whispering when he meant to yell. He scanned the ground, seeing clumps of bricks, splintered boards, ripped siding, and shattered glass, all laying in uneven piles. There was a sort of path through the debris., a short trail just a few feet wide that appeared to have been smoothed down or run over, like something heavy had been dragged across the rubble. Along it were streaks and blotches of dark liquid. This path ran from under his feet to the spot where the shadowy figure stood.

He raised his eyes to it again, a vague and misshapen form, a shadow cast by nothing in sight. He thought back to earlier, when the bulldozer covered up The Devil's Chimney.

Not the ghost, then. Something else.

The hairs on Thomas's neck stood as he realized it was looking at him. He couldn't make out eyes or any facial features at all, but all the same, he knew it saw him.

A car passed, and its headlights banished the darkened form for a few seconds. A fragment of light glinted off something lying on the ground ahead.

Thomas stepped forward and reached for it, picked it up. In the dark, it looked like a bent carrot but with something hard and shiny wrapped around its base. And it was covered in a thick, warm wetness.

Thomas pulled out his phone and held the object toward its lit screen.

It was a finger, covered in blood and wearing Alison's new wedding band.

The shadow figure was back then, closer than before. It growled, low and long.

Thomas ran, but he didn't make it far.

Searching brought Dawn to a place she couldn't fathom. She saw structures that reached the clouds, sleek vehicles that swirled by in droves., not a single plant or tree in sight.

The helplessness she felt here was no match for the helplessness she had felt in that musty old building, though. It occurred to her that the beast which had kept her there could be following. There was no sign of it, so perhaps that meant it found a replacement for her.

Regardless, Dawn couldn't afford to think about that. Searching was all that mattered. She would not slow down or give in to fear, and she pressed on, following the only possible outcome she could imagine. Surely her own remains had been taken into the city back when it first happened. The city had grown over that untold passing of time into this unrecognizable labyrinth, but the most likely place to move a body was to a morgue, and by following the river, she thought she could reach the area where the big hospital used to be. The one she had expected to give birth in.

Maybe I did give birth there, she thought. *In a way, at least.* If they took her there and did an autopsy, they would have found Audrey and removed her, like a terrible labor and delivery with grim results happening in the wrong part of the hospital. Defenseless little Audrey, who must have passed away after Dawn herself had, then been stillborn from a corpse into a darkened basement room.

But they could still be reunited. Maybe her child was still there, searching too.

As Dawn approached her destination, she heard a faint crying sound.

Publisher's Note

Thank you for reading Screams From Beyond The Veil. This anthology wouldn't exist without you, the reader. We appreciate your continued support.

If you enjoyed this book, please consider leaving a review on Amazon, GoodReads, or your favorite social media platform.

Broken Brain Books is an indie publisher dedicated to helping authors share their stories with readers around the world. Please visit our website for more information about our releases and signed copies of our books.

www.brokenbrainbooks.com

Other Anthologies by Broken Brain Books
Screams From The Ocean Floor
Books of Horror Indie Brawl Anthology

Also available
Rorschach by Aaron Lebold
Mine by LM Kaplin
Fang Fiction by LM Kaplin
Ruby's Cube by Lyla Diamond

About the Authors

Philip Fracassi
Philip Fracassi is the author of the novels Don't Let Them Get You Down, A Child Alone with Strangers, Gothic, and Boys in the Valley. His upcoming books include the novels Sarafina and The Third Rule of Time Travel.

Other work includes the story collections No One Is Safe!, Beneath a Pale Sky (named "Best Collection of the Year" by Rue Morgue Magazine and a finalist for the Bram Stoker award), and Behold the Void (named "Best Collection of the Year" by This Is Horror). He is also the author of several novellas, including Sacculina, Shiloh, and Commodore.

John Durgin
John Durgin is a proud active HWA member and lifelong horror fan. Growing up in New Hampshire, he discovered Stephen King much younger than most probably should have, reading IT before he reached high school—and knew from that moment on he wanted to write horror. He had his first story accepted in the summer of 2021 in the Beach Bodies anthology through DarkLit Press. His debut novel, The Cursed Among Us was released June 3, 2022, and went on to become

an Amazon bestseller. Next up, his sophomore novel titled Inside The Devil's Nest, released in January of 2023, followed by his debut collection, Sleeping In The Fire in June of 2023. In 2024 he is set to release two more novels, starting with Kosa, and Consumed by Evil through Crystal Lake Publishing in the fall.

Website- www.johndurginauthor.com

Twitter- @jdurgin1084 | TikTok- @johndurgin_author | Instagram- @durginpencildrawings

MJ Mars

MJ Mars is a geek, ghoul, and horror enthusiast living in Lancaster, UK. Her debut novel, The Suffering, was published by Wicked House in 2023. When she isn't writing, you'll find MJ playing pool, trying to skateboard (badly), or listening to rock music. She owes every success to her mis-spent youth.

Short story collection, We've Already Gone Too Far out now! Coming in 2025: The Fovea Experiments, a second novel to be published by Wicked House. MJ is currently working on a sequel to The Suffering.

Debra Castaneda

Debra Castaneda is an award-winning horror and dark fiction author based on the central coast of California. Her works include *The Spore Queen*, *A Dark and Rising Tide*, *The Root Witch*, and other titles in the Dark Earth Rising series of standalone novels.

Debra loves writing character-driven stories about people who experience scary things, and how they react when confronted with the unexpected. She's committed to representing Latinas and Latinos in her books. For inspiration, she draws from her experience as a TV and radio journalist, and as a third-generation Mexican American.

M. L. Rayner

Born and bred in the county of Staffordshire. Matt is a keen reader of classical, horror and fantasy literature and enjoys writing in the style of traditional ghost stories. During his working life, Matt joined the ambulance service in 2009, transporting critically ill patients all over the UK. After writing his first novel, Matt now dedicates his time on future releases. His hobbies include genealogy and hiking, and he enjoys spending time with his wife, Emma, his children, and his family.

Justin Boote

Justin Boote is an English author living in Barcelona and has been writing horrorfiction for approx. 8 years. In this time he has published around 15 novels and three short story collections. He also writes extreme horror under J.Boote which he does not necessarily recommend you read if you're squeamish!

You can find all of his books on Amazon and KU under Justin Boote and J.Boote(extreme horror pen name).

Elizabeth J. Brown

Elizabeth J. Brown was born in Kent, England. This probably explains her obsession with tea and cake. She currently writes the Brimstone Chorus series - dark fantasy horror featuring demons, witches and a whole host of things that go bump in the night.

Her debut novel, The Laughing Policeman, takes place in 1980s England and features detectives, dark supernatural forces and dry humour. When she isn't in front of her laptop or spending time with her family, Elizabeth is usually absorbed in a book, film or anything that involves the strange, fantastical or supernatural.

Get your FREE Brimstone Chorus starter story at elizabethjbrown.com

Jon Cohn

Jon Cohn is a horror novelist and professional board game designer based out of San Diego. He's written books like *The Island Mother, Slashtag, Try Not To Die on Slashtag* and *Everything Is Temporary*. Jon is very excited to finally be able to merge horror books and games together by bringing *Ghostland* to life as a board game. For other upcoming horror games, keep an eye out for *Basket Case*, and *Black Christmas* coming later this year, along with *Thanksgiving*, which Jon co-designed with Eli Roth himself!

For autographed books, head to www.joncohnauthor.com, or sign up for his newsletter for free short stories and games! You can stay caught up with him at @joncohnauthor on Facebook, Instagram and TikTok.

Leigh Kenny

Leigh was born and raised in the garden county of Wicklow, Ireland. She lives by the Irish Sea with the love of her life and their two wonderful boys. Her debut, Cursed, published in December 2023. Her most recent book, Hush, My Darling released recently. You can find out more about Leigh's work on her social media pages at Leigh Kenny Writes.

Nick Botic

Nick has been writing since 2016, and has seen his work featured in various anthologies, magazines, and podcasts. His debut novel Daughter's Drawings released in July 2023 to overwhelmingly positive reviews. He currently lives in the Milwaukee area with his fiancée, Kimmy, and their five cats.

Ben Young

Ben lives in the Cincinnati, OH area with his family and dogs, where he is currently working on more stories which may or may not ever see the light of day. He does not enjoy writing about himself, especially in the third person like this. Find him online at www.benyoungstories.com

LM Kaplin

LM Kaplin is an author from upstate New York who has been a horror enthusiast in all forms his entire life. His morbid obsession with the macabre began one night while watching Poltergeist as a young child. The next morning, he began searching for ancient burial grounds in the backyard. Dismayed at not uncovering any evil spirits, he buried his own demons for future generations to find. It's time to start digging them up. He is the author of "Mine" and "Fang Fiction."

Timothy King

Timothy King is an adult horror author who enjoys delving into the complexities of human nature. When he is not writing spine-chilling tales, he is spending time with his wife and kids in beautiful Tampa, Florida.

Heather Ann Larson

Heather Ann Larson is an up and coming editor and avid horror reader. Although Christopher Pike was a favorite, Stephen King's The Dark Tower is what pulled her in and kept her on the journey. She has several edits under her belt, including The Children and The Gods series by Angel Vn Atta, They are all Monsters by Justin Boote, and their collaboration They End of Things as He/She Knew Them. She continues to grow her journey by taking Aces editing courses and delving deep into the Chicago Manual of Style. In her spare time, she... Who are we kidding? There is no spare time!!!